C000056823

In the Roots

– BOB CHAPMAN –

To JULIE
THANK YOU SO MUCH
FOR LOOKING AFTER
PAT.

Bob Chapman

An environmentally friendly book printed and bound in England by
www.printondemand-worldwide.com

http://www.fast-print.net/bookshop

IN THE ROOTS
Copyright © Bob Chapman 2016

A catalogue record for this book is available from the British Library

ISBN 978-178456-300-4

First published 2016 by
FASTPRINT PUBLISHING
Peterborough, England.

In memory of Harold

My grandfather who was

A villain thankfully......

CHAPTER ONE

Very carefully, with the index finger and thumb of his left hand, he plucked the intrusive, imaginary piece of fluff from the shoulder of his battle dress tunic. He placed it on its hanger and opened the wardrobe door; the sudden pungent aroma of ancient mothballs immediately assaulted his senses. His nose twitched, he rubbed it and smiled quietly to himself as he remembered the old joke, why do moths fly with their legs open? He suspended the wooden coat hanger from its rickety old, dull brass rail, closed the squeaking door and with a last lingering look at the now redundant tunic turned towards his old, worn single bed. Laid out precisely on the ancient candlewick bedspread was his brand new demob suit, six years three months and four days in the Royal Artillery had taught him all there was to know about precision. He could see his breath funnelling through the cold damp air of the bedroom, it's even colder than my old barrack room, he thought.

Shivering, he dressed quickly, then inspected himself top to bottom in the full length wardrobe mirror; he drew the comb through his already black, wavy, immaculate Brylcreemed hair and jauntily trotted off down the stairs. 'I'm off now Auntie Cath,' he called through the doorway into the living room.

'Don't you go rushing off like that young Jimmy, come in here son and let me take a good look at you.'

He walked into the living room and stood stiffly and smartly to attention in front of his aunt; she peered at him approvingly over the top of her reading glasses and cooed 'If only your mum and dad could see you now they'd be so proud.'

'Yes Auntie,' was the only reply he could muster up, his face falling, his voice faltering.

'Come here son and give your old aunt a cuddle. So where are you off then Jimmy,' she said chirpily, 'to find yourself a nice young lady perhaps?'

'You never know, Auntie, you never know,' he said and he tapped the side of his nose, smiled and winked.

Jim dutifully cuddled his aunt, they said their goodbyes and he walked out into the crisp cold evening air.

Jim made his way through the familiar streets he had played in as a boy before the war, here and there were piles of rubble, old Mister and Missus Jones lived right there, he thought as he walked past a crater in the ground, the two houses either side of it dangerous looking, shorn up precariously by some criss cross timbers and some oddments of tubular metal scaffolding. He walked around the corner but just couldn't bring himself to look across the road; he knew there was nothing left to see of his old house. The unheard explosion intense and vivid in his brain. His pace quickened and he hurried on, hands thrust deep into his trouser pockets, memories of his now dead parents coursing through his mind. He turned the corner and crossed over the road into Mansion Street and saw the familiar brightly illuminated pub sign at the end of the road; he remembered well the last time he saw it was when he was home on leave; it was totally in darkness then, as was the whole pub, owing to the blackout. And as he remembered it he was only in the pub half an hour before they ran out of beer, yes, Hitler had a lot to answer for, he thought.

'Hello young Jimmy, look like you're home to stay, looking at your whistle.' Bert Tompkins the landlord of the Sceptre leant on the bar all smiles, beaming at Jim.

'Yes I'm home to stay now Mister Tompkins,' Jim replied.

'I think you're old enough to call me Bert now Jimmy,' he said with a broad grin. 'Come on son you can have the first one on me, now that you've done your bit for King and country.'

'Thank you Mister...I mean Bert,' Jim answered, he realised that he was really a man now Bert Tompkins had shown his approval. He could remember two days before his eighteenth birthday being kicked out the pub, with all the regulars howling with laughter, much to his eternal embarrassment.

'What d'you intend doing with yourself now you're back home then Jimmy? Are you going to work in the boot factory like your dad?'

'Well I'd like to do something a bit different really, I am on the lookout for a job Bert, but at the moment I feel just like a fish out of water, I really just don't know what I'm going to do with myself, if I'm honest.'

'Yes I know the feeling son; I was just like that at the end of the last lot, just excuse me a minute son,' and Bert turned away to serve another customer in the snug.

Jim looked around; He was the only young man in the

bar, all still away or dead, he thought.

A couple of young girls were sitting in the corner, talking furtively behind their hands, glancing in Jim's direction and giggling. He looked over and smiled at them.

'Like what you see?' Bert Tompkins was back, and looking disapprovingly at the girls, 'Don't seem right somehow, women coming into the pub on their own, I don't know what the world is coming to, it wouldn't have happened before the war, I can tell you.'

'They're not bad looking, though are they?' Jim replied.

'Well you can forget all about that, you've got an interview for a job.'

'A job for me, when, where?'

'Right this minute, go through to the snug, Harry James is looking for a new man.'

'I seem to know that name from somewhere.'

'You're probably thinking of Harry James the band leader; you know the one that married Betty Grable.'

'No, I've heard his name somewhere else, what does he do Bert?'

'Everything and nothing, that's what Harry does,' Bert said with a grin, tapping the side of his purple bulbous nose with his index finger. 'Go on then son, don't keep the man waiting, he won't take too kindly to that.' Jim hurried down his drink, quickly pulled his comb through his already flawless hair, straightened his tie and cut through into the snug.

Harry James was standing at the bar, his hair was wavy and very similar in style and colour to Jim's but slightly receding and quite a lot longer, with tinges of grey. He sported thick sideboards that were almost white and came down almost to his chin. A small white scar ran high across his left cheekbone to his ear, which he constantly touched and worried. His upper lip sported an immaculately trimmed pencil thin moustache and his suit, with its hand stitching was far removed from the Fifty Shilling Tailors. He was slimmer and shorter than Jim, and a large cigar was sticking out of the corner of his mouth, on which he constantly chewed.

'Come here son,' he boomed and held out his hand; Jim took it and was quite shocked; for although Harry James was lean his grip was powerful.

'I'm pleased to meet you Mister James,' Jim murmured.

'Likewise, I'm sure, pull up a stool, what can I get you?'

Jim had been brought up to be polite, 'Just a half of bitter, please Mister James.'

'Give the boy a pint Bert, now Bert tells me you boxed for your regiment, heavyweight no doubt, looking at the size of you?'

'Yes, Mister James,' I never won anything though, Jim thought.

'Can you drive?'

'Yes sir, I was a driver in the army, they taught me.'

'Right you'll do, here,' Harry James reached into his inside pocket, produced a roll of white five pound notes and thrust one into Jim's hand, 'Get yourself down to Isaacs' tailor shop in the morning, get yourself a decent whistle and meet me in here wearing it at nine tomorrow night, understand?'

'Yes Mister James.'

'One other thing, you're working for Harry James now, you'll wear a trilby. Enjoy the rest of your evening.'

Jim knew he had been dismissed, he climbed off the bar stool and clicked his heels, and before he could stop himself saluted. Bert Tompkins and Harry James roared with laughter, turning red faced Jim grabbed his pint and scuttled back into the bar. He noticed the two girls had gone and felt quite relieved, he felt that had had quite enough excitement for one night. Jim had a thousand questions for Bert Tompkins but the pub was filling up, so the opportunity didn't present itself.

Smack on ten Bert Tompkins hauled his half hunter gold watch from his waistcoat pocket, opened the case, studied it and shouted, 'Time ladies and gents please, time please.'

By five past ten Jim was strolling home, oblivious to the heavy rain bouncing back off the pavement, as he neared the site of his old house, he looked across the road and whispered to himself, 'Mum, Dad, I've got a job.'

He let himself into his Auntie Cath's; he knew she would be in bed and fast asleep by now, so his news would have to wait until the next morning.

Morning came and Jim couldn't get down over the stairs quick enough. 'God you're up early Jimmy, have you peed the bed?' Auntie Cath remarked, 'you quite startled me.'

'Sorry Auntie,' Jim said excitedly, 'I've got a job.'

7

'Where have you been at this time of the morning to get a job? It isn't even light yet.'

Jim laughed, 'I'd hardly be out job hunting in my dressing gown now, would I? No I got it last night in the pub.'

'Yes well, your dad always used to say that all the best business is done in the pub. This job, what is it doing?' Auntie Cath asked.

'Well,' Jim hesitated, 'I don't really know, to be honest.'

'You don't really know, well I never did. Where are you going to be working then?'

'I don't know that either,' Jim replied rather sheepishly.

'You'll be telling me next you don't know the name of the firm you're going to work for.'

'I don't know that either Auntie, but I do know the name of the boss,' Jim blurted out.

'Well come on then, who is it?'

'His name's Harry James.'

'Oh! My good Lord,' Auntie Cath raised her hands in horror. 'No, Jimmy no, not that bloody man. Please God no.'

Jim was quite taken aback he had never heard his aunt swear before, 'Why what's wrong Auntie?'

'What's wrong, what's wrong,' Auntie Cath's voice began to rise. 'I'll tell you what's wrong my lad. That *man* is nothing more than a black marketeer, a crook, he's a spiv, he's a gangster, some even say a murderer, you'll be in trouble with the police before you can say knife, forget it Jimmy.'

8

'But Auntie look at what he gave me,' Jim quickly produced the five pound note from his dressing gown pocket, 'he told me to go and buy a proper suit.'

Cath shook her head and said softly and firmly, 'Be a good boy Jimmy and take that five pound note back to him. Tell him where he can put it and tell him to keep his job, please.'

'Look Auntie Cath, you know that I would never do anything I shouldn't, and if I don't like the job, well I can just pack it in, and I can always get one in the boot factory.'

'Jimmy please, listen to me, please,' but she knew she was wasting her breath.

It was with a lively step that Jim left the house at a little after nine, he made his way along Regent Street and pushed open the faded brown and cream door of Mr Isaacs' shop. The old brass bell suspended from its curled spring startled Jim with its tinny jangling noise, he walked over to the counter and after a few moments an elderly man appeared in a doorway behind the counter, he obviously had a mouthful of food. 'I'm not open, go away, I'm having breakfast.' He said angrily in a thick Jewish accent.

'But the front door is open.' Jim said.

'So the front door is open, what does the sign on the door say?'

Jim turned around, 'It says open,' Jim pointed towards the sign.

'Idiot, what does the sign tell you if you were standing in the street?'

'Closed,' Jim felt foolish.

9

'Now go away let me finish my breakfast in piece.'

'Mister James sent me for a suit.' Jim blurted out.

'Harry sent you,' Jim nodded his head. 'Why didn't you say so in the first place? Did he give you any money?'

Jim produced the five pound note and Mr Isaacs' eyes lit up. 'Come in, come in, don't just stand there, now let me see you are a big lad it will take extra material, more sewing, more work,' he stroked his chin and looked thoughtful. 'A lot more work, four guineas, yes four guineas, here give me the money, I will get change.'

The old man disappeared into the back of the shop mumbling softly away to himself all the while, Jim looked around him, the bare walls hadn't seen a lick of paint for years, in places the plaster was peeling off, and an old black out curtain hung precariously from one nail in the grimy front window.

'Here you are,' Mr Isaacs slapped the change down on the counter.

'Mister James said I had to have the suit for tonight.'

'Tonight,' he repeated, 'tonight, a miracle worker, the man thinks I am a miracle worker, no man alive could do it,' Mr Isaacs picked up the money from the counter. 'Let me see,' and he stroked his chin again and paced up and down, 'yes another half a guinea. I think that will just about cover it.' He greedily snatched up the money.

Jim picked up the remaining change and put it in his pocket.

'Well, don't just stand there, come through, come through, all day long I haven't got.' Jim did as he was told; he followed the old man through the door at the back of the shop, looking around him, he couldn't believe the suit

10

that Harry James wore had come from this pig sty, how the old man could find anything he couldn't understand. The old man produced an ancient looking tape measure, the numbers barely discernible and hung it around his neck. 'Stand still boy,' he commanded.

Jim stood stiffly to attention as the old man deftly measured, muttering away all the time. When he had finished Jim said, 'Excuse me sir, but you haven't written down my measurements.'

The old man flashed him a withering look, 'Be here at eleven for first fitting and don't be late.'

'Don't I get to pick the cloth sir?' Jim asked.

'No. Harry's has got his own roll for the likes of you, now go.' Jim stood there. 'Well go on then, are you completely stupid?' Jim was thankful to leave the shop.

The time dragged into an eternity as Jim kicked his heels around town; he did go to The Labour Exchange where there were plenty of jobs advertised, the boot factory, building site work, driving jobs, shops, but nothing seemed to capture his imagination. Eleven o'clock on the dot he was startled yet again by the brass door bell.

'You're late,' came a voice from the back of the shop, then, 'well come through, come through, hurry, all day I haven't got.'

Skilfully and quickly Mr Isaacs wielded a piece of chalk, mumbling all the time. 'Which side do you dress?' he enquired.

'What do you mean sir?'

'Idiot,' Mr Isaacs' hand reached down.

'Ouch!' Jim exclaimed.

11

'Be back at three and don't be late next time.'

'Will the suit be ready at three then sir?'

Mr Isaacs sighed impatiently. 'Second fitting, now go.'

Jim turned quickly and made to move away, 'Well hurry up, hurry I say.' Jim closed the shop door and breathed a sigh of relief.

Jim went back at three but couldn't really understand why, the suit seemed to fit him like a glove, the old man pulled roughly and tweaked at the suit, talking to himself all the while, and then he was told to be back at six sharp and not to be late.

'I'm going to get my suit in a minute Auntie,' Jim said.

'I've already told you what I think, it's all going to end up in trouble, you just see.' Jim wished he hadn't spoken.

The old brass bell startled Jim for the fourth time that day. Jim had checked and he was smack on time.

'Ah it's you, too early, much too early, come back in ten minutes.'

At last, twenty minutes later Jim left the shop proudly carrying his new suit wrapped in a thick brown paper parcel and tied with thick twine, glad to have seen the last of the old man. Perhaps Hitler had bombed the wrong shops, he thought chuckling to himself. He decided to smuggle the suit into Auntie Cath's house, no point in waving the red rag in front of the bull, he reasoned.

He checked the clock a thousand times and then at

12

eight thirty, far too early really to see Harry James at the pub, he said cheerio to a very subdued Auntie Cath and made his way to the Sceptre.

'Hello young Jimmy, what's it to be?'

'Pint of bitter, please Mister Tompkins.'

'Bert.'

'Oh yes, of course Bert,'

'No bitter I'm afraid, only mild until next week, still can't get a proper delivery, that's one thing that even Harry James can't fix.'

'What is it that Mister James actually does Bert?'

'It's like I said to you last night son, everything and nothing. Buying, selling, he's got property, fingers in all sorts of pies, all sorts of things.'

'What do you suppose I'll be doing then Bert?'

'God knows, whatever Lefty used to do I suppose.'

'Who's Lefty? Did he go for another job?'

Bert chuckled, 'Well no, not exactly son. Look son don't ask me questions I can't answer, Harry will tell you what's what and that's that.'

Jim kept glancing at the clock on the pub wall, 'Harry's always on time Jimmy, but do yourself a favour; don't wait here in the snug, wait in the bar till you're called.'

'Why's that Bert?' Jim asked.

'Well it's just that being very important is all that Harry understands, young man.'

Jim did as he was advised and a little after nine he was summoned to the snug. Harry was accompanied by two companions, one was enormous but not fat, broad shouldered with a trim waist, he stood at least a good six inches taller than Jim, and Jim came in at a little over six feet. The other was completely the opposite; he was round shouldered, skinny and just over five feet tall, he sported an identical moustache to Harry James and his hair was remarkably similar.

'Here's the new boy, boys meet Jimmy, Jimmy this is Ron,' Harry said pointing at the biggest, 'and this is Weasel.' Jim stepped forward to shake hands; his outstretched hand was shaken briefly. 'Jim's joining the firm; he's just come out of the army.'

'Which regiment?' Ron spoke for the first time.

'I was in the Royal Artillery,' Jim replied.

'They were founded in 1716,' said Ron.

'Well it was 1722 really, but yes in 1716-.'

'Yes I remember now,' said Ron, 'it was George 1st he formed a couple of companies in 1716.'

'Yes that's right Ron, were you in the artillery then?'

Harry answered on Ron's behalf, 'Royal Artillery, Ron,' he started laughing; 'More like the Royal Stand Backs, and Weasel here, well he was in the Skin Back Fusiliers. Don't take any notice of Ron, Jimmy, he's full of crap, he's always coming out with some old load of baloney.'

'I read it somewhere Harry, honest.'

'Ron you don't know the meaning of the word honest. Right Jimmy, Weasel here will pick you up at ten in the morning from outside here, OK?'

'Yes sir, here's your change Mister James,' Jim extended his open palm.

'Put it away,' Harry James beckoned, 'how much did he charge you Jimmy? No don't tell me. You went in the shop you were either too early or too late, then he told

14

you the suit would be more money because you're a big lad, then he wanted more because it had to be done in a hurry, am I right, Jimmy?' Harry glanced around at his companions for their approval.

'Mister James, that's spot on.' Harry's companions guffawed with laughter; Harry James looked well pleased with himself. 'Mister James can I say something?'

'Course you can son.'

'Do you mind calling me Jim, please Mister James?'

'Jim it is then, here you are son,' Harry James took a half crown from his pocket, 'get yourself a drink.'

'Thank you Mister James,' and Jim made to approach the counter.

'No, not in here son,' Harry pointed, 'in the bar son, in the bar.'

'Sorry Mister James, goodnight, goodnight all.'

But Harry James had by now turned away and Jim was already forgotten.

CHAPTER TWO

What was it that my dad used to say? Another day another dollar, ah yes, thought Jim, it is another day and I'm earning my first dollar in civvy street. He decided to say nothing to Auntie Cath about the fact that Harry James had told him to keep the change from the tailor, and the half crown he was given to get a drink; it seemed that even mentioning his name to her was like mentioning the devil.

At ten to ten Jim was standing outside the Sceptre waiting for Weasel, he was still standing there at ten thirty. Eventually at a quarter to eleven a black Humber pulled up by the side of him.

'Get in,' it was Weasel, 'bit of a heavy night last night.' But there was no sign of any form of an apology.

'What do I call you?' Jim asked.

'Weasel,' came the answer.

'Where are we going?' Jim asked to try to make conversation.

'You'll find out,' was all that he got as a reply.

They drove out into the countryside for about twenty minutes, in total silence and Jim realised that Weasel had nothing to say, well at least not to him anyway.

Jim spotted the road sign "Hambrook" and Weasel turned the Humber off the road and onto a narrow rough dirt track. After about a quarter of a mile, a wooden five bar gate in front of them stood blocking their way. The Humber came to a halt. 'Well don't just sit there,' Weasel stared at Jim, 'open it!'

Jim dutifully jumped out of the car and opened the gate, he expected the car to wait for him on the other side but the Humber sped off.

What do I do? Jim thought. Do I wait here? Or do I follow the car? Jim decided to follow.

He made his way up the muddy track cursing quietly to himself at the state of his shoes. As he walked into the farmyard proper he was greeted by a lanky pimply youth holding a vicious looking dog by a long chain. 'It's alright,' said Jim, 'I'm with Weasel,' and he pointed in his direction. Gingerly he passed by the dog and strolled over to the car.

Weasel was leaning against the car, puffing away at a cigarette, 'Took your time didn't you?' Weasel grunted and pointed towards a pen. 'Get in there and grab a cockerel.'

Being a city lad Jim didn't know the first thing about farms or animals. He let himself into the pen and tried to grab a cockerel, Weasel looked on, laughing helplessly at Jim's futile efforts, there were feathers flying and loud squawks as Jim went round and around the pen chasing first one, then any cockerels that came anywhere near him..

Attracted by the commotion the farmer put in an appearance, 'What's that clown playing at? Here you come out of there.'

'I'm sorry sir,' Jim said.

'Who have we got here then Weasel?'

'He's Lefty's replacement.'

'He's gone then?'

'Oh yes he's fucking gone all right.'

'Okay lad,' the farmer said, 'I'll show you how to

17

catch 'em.' The farmer went into the pen quietly and put his hand flat over the back of the nearest cockerel, about two feet above it, the bird immediately crouched down, and the farmer scooped it up. 'There you are son, that's all there is to it,' and he handed the cockerel to Jim.

'What now?' Jim asked.

Weasel smiled and produced an evil looking flick knife with a blade about eight inches long from inside his jacket, and handed it to Jim. 'See that post over there,' Weasel pointed at a stout post about four feet tall, by the side of the post leaning against it was a thick rounded piece of wood about a foot long, and strung from the top of the post to the pen was a taut piece of galvanised wire. 'Put the bird's head on the post, give him some anaesthetic,' he pointed at the piece of wood, 'then slit his throat and hang him out to bleed.' Weasel started to chuckle.

Jim's thoughts strayed to when he was a small boy, he could remember how when the family cat had kittens, eight or nine at a time. His father would, eight days after they were born before their eyes were open, take them out into the garden in an old shoe box, stand Jim on the dust bin so that he could see into the water butt, then Jim would smooth the kittens and kiss each one before handing them to his father. His father would then plunge them one by one into the water butt. He would lift Jim up and Jim had to drown the last kitten. "Now don't forget son get a good grip and keep its head under the water until it stops struggling," he would say. The kittens would be then unceremoniously dumped one by one into the dust bin. "He's got to learn how to do it," he would tell his mother. For days after, the mother cat would go round and round the house plaintively mewing, searching for her dead offspring. Jim would cuddle the cat, but the mewing didn't stop.

'Well go on then,' Weasel interrupted Jim's thoughts, 'what are you some sort of fairy?'

Jim swung around, grabbed Weasel by the throat, easily lifted him right off the ground and hissed, 'You little bastard, you never call me a fairy, understand?' Jim effortlessly dumped Weasel down into the mud. Placing one foot on his head he said. 'Ever say that again, and I'll squash you like an ant.'

Weasel screamed out. 'Please please, don't hurt me I didn't mean anything, let me up, I'll do the killing.' Jim took his foot off Weasel's head and walked back to the car, Weasel ashen and visibly shaken, leant against the killing post and hastily with shaking hands lit a cigarette.

After a few minutes Weasel called over, 'Jim could you get two blankets out the boot of the car and spread them on the back seat and floor please?'

In total silence Jim performed his task.

Between them they loaded the dead fowl into the boot and back seat of the car; Weasel looking down at his filthy suit, spread another blanket on the front passenger seat and sat on it. 'Here Jim you can drive, if you like.'

Jim took the driving seat and when they got to the gate, before Jim could move Weasel was out of the car, opened the gate and waved Jim through. Jim drove through and just for a moment Jim thought to leave him behind, but besides it being childish he had no idea where he was going. Weasel climbed back in and in silence they made their way back down the track and out onto the main road,

I don't know if I'm going to like this job, thought Jim, he liked it even less when he spotted a police car coming up behind.

Jim heard the sound of the police car bell and immediately pulled over; the police car overtook and pulled up in front of them.

'Christ,' Jim whispered. Weasel appeared quite nonplussed by the whole thing.

Jim watched as an arm with three stripes on the sleeve of a police tunic emerged from the police car, followed by the figure of a burly looking policeman of at least six feet six tall, he ambled around to Jim's side of the car, 'What have we got here then?' he asked. Another policeman appeared at Weasel's side of the car. Weasel leant across Jim, 'Oh! I didn't see you there Weasel, who is this then?' he asked looking at Jim.

'It's the new boy Sergeant.'

'Yes I've got a new boy with me as well,' he glanced towards the other policeman, 'Jesus, look at the state of you Weasel, been dragged through a hedge?' Weasel ignored the question. 'Where's Lefty Wright today then Weasel?' Weasel put his index finger to his throat and drew it theatrically across his neck.

'So what had Lefty been up to, then Weasel?'

'Fingers in the till, well hand more like it Sergeant.'

'Mad Ron took care of things, did he?'

'Yes as the Yanks would say he's at the bottom of the

Severn wearing concrete galoshes.'

'Good job too, I would have felt his collar more than once if it wasn't for Harry, evil little toe rag, I couldn't stand the sight of him, good riddance I say.

'I hear you've fallen out with the Newman brothers again?'

'No Sergeant we've buried the hatchet with them.' Weasel said.

The sergeant started to laugh, 'Buried the hatchet in one of the Newman's heads if I remember it rightly, Ron as usual, wasn't it?' Weasel nodded. Jim couldn't believe he was being privy to such a conversation.

'Anyway Weasel, what you got in the back today?'

'Nothing,' said Jim, simultaneously with Weasel as he said, 'Cockerels.'

The younger policeman came forward and undoing his tunic breast pocket he reached inside for his notebook, 'You won't need that son,' said the sergeant and smiled at Weasel.

'Best ones in the boot are they Weasel?'

'Yes Sergeant, yours are right on the top,'

'Right son,' the sergeant said to the constable, 'get two and put them in the boot of the police car, and we had better give you an escort Weasel, we don't want you being stopped, do we?' he chuckled. 'Usual place is it?'

'You got it Sergeant, oh and Harry sent this for you.' Weasel handed the sergeant a long white envelope which immediately disappeared inside the sergeant's tunic.

Jim sat there with a glazed look on his face he was both shocked and frightened.

'Well go on then, start driving,' Weasel was sounding

more like his old self, 'keep up with the police car.'

Jim realised he was still just sitting there, he found first gear with a crunch and lurched forwards, both his legs still shaking uncontrollably with fright. He could see Weasel was enjoying the situation. 'Why didn't we get arrested back there?' he eventually managed to blurt out.

Weasel sensing Jim's uneasiness, relished the moment and answered, 'Well back in forty two or three when the Yanks came over here first, Harry got friendly with a Yank, Hank his name was, Hank the Yank, he ran the quartermaster's store at the army camp. He and the Yank had a right good fiddle going on, then one night in the blackout Harry was coming back from the Yank's camp, and the sergeant there, well he was a constable at the time flagged him down.

'He sees that Harry's got silk stockings, jam, cheese and all sorts of stuff and nicks him. So Harry says to him, "Look, you can take me in, and no doubt it'll be a feather in your cap, but let me off the hook and we can have a nice little arrangement, you and me, no more ration books for you, you won't need them. You'd like some silk stockings for your girl, wouldn't you?" He was taking quite a chance trying to bribe a rozzer. Harry said the copper hardly hesitated and they've had an arrangement ever since. Them stockings cost the rozzer dear, Harry had him right in his fucking pocket, and us lot became untouchable on the manor. They do say, but Harry has never let on who it is, that he's got an inspector on the pay roll as well.'

The police car in front was coming to a halt, 'Pull over here Jim, and make to get out,' the police sergeant tooted his car horn and drove away. Weasel walked round

22

to the boot, opened it, and as soon as the police car was out of sight slammed it shut again.

'What's going on Weasel?' Jim asked.

'We don't let him know too much, he only thinks he does, drive on Jim and take the first turning on the left.'

Jim drove along the road until Weasel told him to slow right down, and turn into narrow road, about a hundred yards along it suddenly the road widened and there was a pub on the right hand side, 'Well I've lived around here all my life and I didn't know there was a pub here,' Jim sounded quite surprised, 'The Charnbury Arms, well I never.'

'Yes well-kept secret this one, suits us just fine, see those tall wooden gates at the side, go through them, and drive right around the back.'

Jim drove around the building, a middle age man was standing in the middle of the pub yard smoothing a black Labrador dog, he was bespectacled, bald headed and a cork tipped cigarette hung from his lips, he was wearing a dark waistcoat and Jim noticed a chunky gold Albert draped across his chest. Although not very tall or big built, the impassive cold expression on his face told Jim he wasn't the sort to take any messing. As he spotted the Humber he slipped a chain around the dog's neck and led it to its kennel.

'Stay here a minute Jim, that dog's a vicious bastard, wait until we get the go ahead. '

The man beckoned and Weasel walked over to him, they shook hands and there was a brief conversation. Jim watched from by the car as the man produced a fat light brown hide wallet from his hip pocket, took a brown rubber band from around it and started to count money into Weasel's eager upturned hand.

Weasel beckoned. 'Start getting the fowl inside Jim,' and he pointed to a door that was slightly ajar.

Jim grabbed two cockerels from the boot and walked through the door, inside was the pub kitchen, there, three middle aged overweight females were sat around chatting and smoking, and as soon as they saw Jim they started wolf whistling and making ribald comments, 'He could do me a bit of good,' and, 'a bit of talent at last.'

Jim felt his colours rising; he dumped the cockerels down on the wooden kitchen table and beat a hasty retreat to the shrieks of laughter by the women. Jim hung around by the boot of the car red faced.

'Come on Jim we haven't got all day,' Jim didn't move, 'what's up?'

'It's that lot in there,' Jim said.

'Take no notice, they're always the same, randy lot, come on I'll introduce you.'

Jim followed Weasel cautiously through the door, this time only one looked up, the other two had almost finished plucking the first two cockerels. 'This is Jim, girls,' said Weasel.

'Hello Jim,' they chorused and that was that. Jim and Weasel walked back outside and started to unload the rest of the cockerels.

'Make sure you leave two nice ones in the car Jim.' Weasel said.

Back and forth to the car they went, Jim noticed that

Weasel was doing less and less, suddenly he reached in his jacket pocket for his cigarettes, lit one up, and leant against the wall, Jim was on his own from now on.

Jim was glad when the last cockerel was inside the kitchen as he now realised why Weasel had stopped unloading; the stench in the kitchen from the birds being drawn was unbearable, the women totally oblivious of it carried on chatting and smoking away. Jim placed one hand against the wall outside, leant over and began to heave, Weasel was chuckling away, pleased and amused and unconcerned at Jim's discomfort.

After Jim had stashed the blankets away they got back in the car and drove off. 'Right next stop middle of town,' said Weasel, 'you know Frogmore Street?'

'Can't say as I do, 'Jim replied.

'D'you know where the Hatchet pub is?'

'Yes.'

'That's Frogmore Street, there's a pub just along the way from the Hatchet, it's called the Horse and Jockey, that's where we're going.'

'What are we going there for Weasel?' Jim asked.

'We've got to collect from Red Ruth.'

'Red Ruth?'

'Yeah Ruth's in charge of Harry's girls, they work from the Hatchet, but she always sees us in the Jockey.'

'How d'you mean work?'

Weasel looked at Jim shook his head from side to side and laughed. Jim pulled up outside the Horse and Jockey, and got out of the car, by the time Jim had locked the car Weasel was already in the pub, 'I've called them in,' he said, 'you pay.'

Jim paid for the drinks as instructed and took them to where Weasel was already sitting. 'What now Weasel?' he asked.

'Just sit and wait, she'll be here in a minute, she's in and out of here all day long.'

Sure enough after a few short minutes Red Ruth appeared at the front door, a tall woman. Big, not fat and not unattractive, but muscular in a masculine way, her flaming wavy red hair hung three quarters of the way down her long back. Her make-up was overdone and heavy and her lips were the colour of a pillar box. She spotted Weasel and came straight over to where Jim and Weasel were sitting, 'Hello Weasel,' she said, 'look at the state of you; Harry got you working on a building site has he?' Ruth squawked with laughter, Weasel chose to ignore her, his lower lip quivering. Jim noticed her voice was very high pitched, totally at odds with her manly appearance. 'Weasel,' she continued, 'I hope this isn't a punter, you know what that miserable old sod is like behind the bar if he thinks I'm working.' She glanced over to the bar; the Landlord was scowling at her disapprovingly. 'Keep your hair on,' she called over, 'I'm in here for reasonable refreshment, straight gin please, large one.'

'What's up with him?' said Jim to Weasel as Ruth was being served at the bar.

'Licensing laws and prostitutes that's all.'

'Prostitute, is that what she is?'

'No she's a fucking fighter pilot, what d'you think she is?'

'So who's this then, Weasel?' Ruth asked, returning

26

from the bar.

'He's Lefty's replacement.'

'So he's gone then? Have you told him the score Weasel?'

'What d'you mean?' Jim asked.

'Oh it can talk,' Jim felt his cheeks reddening, 'you collect the money, and you can have one of the girls, same as Lefty did, but no more than twenty minutes and none of that dirty stuff. Here you are Weasel,' she handed Weasel an envelope. 'Tell Harry, Joan is still playing up and give him my love,' she downed her drink in one and looked at the landlord. 'Alright, alright, I'm going,' she said, and walked out of the pub door.

Weasel smiled, 'If I were you Jim I wouldn't take her up on her offer of one her girls, I think that between them they're to blame, for all the syphilis and gonorrhoea in the British navy, and every other fucking navy as well I expect. Lefty managed to get himself a runny nose from one of them, twice.' Weasel started to laugh. 'Come on then Jim, drink up let's go.'

They climbed back into the car and started to drive back out of town, 'You can take the car home Jim,' Weasel said when they got near the Sceptre. 'Drop me off here but don't pull away until I've got my cockerel out the boot.'

'What's the other one for?' Jim looked puzzled.

'The other one's for you,' Weasel shook his head and got out of the car.

'Where do I pick you up again, Weasel?'

'The Sceptre.'

'What time this afternoon?'

'Not this afternoon, tomorrow morning at ten,'

Weasel shook his head again.

'What do I do this afternoon then?'

'Oh, do what you want,' he pointed at the dirty bottom half of the car. 'Clean the fucking car,' he turned away and was gone.

Jim drove home and got there a little after one; he let himself in and called out, 'I'm here Auntie.'

Auntie Cath was seated at the dining table puffing away on a cigarette; she barely glanced up as Jim entered, 'What have you been up to? No good I wouldn't be surprised my lad, well there's no dinner you didn't say that you were coming home.'

'It's alright Auntie I've already had something to eat,' Jim lied. 'I've got something for you out in the car,' he continued tentatively.

'What car?'

'Harry's car.'

'So, it's *Harry* now is it?' she said testily, 'it didn't take you long to get your feet under the table, did it?'

'I don't actually call him Harry,' Jim stammered, 'I call him Mister James.'

'I can think of quite a lot of things to call him and it's not Mister, anyway so what's this present?'

Jim hurried out to the car and came back in proudly carrying the cockerel by its feet. He held it up high for his auntie to see; she glanced at it and then looked away. 'I'll have none of Harry James black market goods in my house, take it away.'

'It's not what you think Auntie,' Jim lied for the

28

second time,   'It's my wages I thought it would be a nice idea to get you it on the way home.'

'Wages, you've only been there for half a day.'

'He insisted I had a sub.'

'Mmm,' Auntie Cath was not convinced.

Thirty minutes later Jim was heaving for the second time as the smell of bird's innards filled the kitchen so car cleaning seemed the more favourable option. Steadfastly he cleaned the Humber from top to bottom, and when he had finished he went back into the house, 'Come and see the car Auntie now it's all clean and shiny.'

'Harry James car doesn't interest me in the least,' she said sharply.

By the time tea time came around Jim was ravenous, the smell of the now cooking cockerel only added to his hunger, but he knew there would be none today.

'Bread and dripping for tea Jimmy, I don't know, things are worse than during the war, I heard the Ministry of Food is planning on rationing bread now, I've never heard anything like it.' it was the first time Auntie Cath had spoken all afternoon.

'Bread and dripping's fine, thank you.' Jim couldn't stand bread and dripping, he knew he was being punished. Jim tucked into the bread and dripping sandwiches, and because he was so famished he demolished the plateful in no time.

'I didn't think you were all that keen on bread and dripping Jimmy,' said Auntie Cath.

'It's a bit of an acquired taste, now that I'm older I quite like it,' Jim found he was lying again, but it seemed to be coming easily.

Afternoon wore into evening and Auntie Cath sat knitting away, the click of the needles just audible above the noise from the wireless. She doesn't even want to talk to me, thought Jim. He had no intention of going out, but the atmosphere became quite unbearable, so at eight o'clock he quietly slipped out of the front door pulling it gently together after him. He glanced at the car but decided to walk to the pub. I think I'm going to have to find somewhere else to live, he thought, I can't live in that atmosphere.

'You're the early bird, Jim,' said Bert, 'how did you get on, on your first day?'

'Yes it was alright Bert, thank you,' Jim decided not to mention the trouble he had with Weasel. Jim positioned himself at the bar nursing his pint. Looking in the mirror behind the back fitting of the bar he could see the same two girls that he had seen in the bar previously. Far away with his thoughts, he suddenly became aware of his surroundings when he realised there was one girl standing at each side of him.

'You're Jimmy Britton, aren't you?' the taller one of the two spoke first.

'Yes,' Jim found that making conversation with girls was difficult.

'Hello,' the shorter girl spoke.

'Hello,' Jim replied.

'Well aren't you going to buy a pair of nice girls like

us a drink?' the taller one asked.

Jim fumbled about in his pockets and produced a ten shilling note.

'Coo, look at him a ten shilling note the day before pay day,' the taller one spoke again. Jim decided he didn't like her, much too pushy, the shorter one seemed to be reserved and more his cup of tea.

'Two shandies please,' the shorter one said.

'Come on sit over here with us, come on don't be shy, we won't bite you,' it was the taller one again.

Jim sat himself down, immediately the taller one plonked herself down beside him, and pressed her body up close against him, her cheap perfume oozed into Jim's nostrils, Jim started to feel decidedly uncomfortable. A stony silence descended on the trio; Jim was beginning to wish he had stayed home with Auntie Cath. 'Cheerio,' he blurted out and raised his glass.

'Cheers,' the girls chorused and silence reigned again.

'It's no good,' the taller girl said standing up, 'I've got to go and wet my lettuce.'

Jim was left with the other girl, 'You don't like my friend, do you?' she asked.

'I'm not struck, to be honest, she seems a bit well, coarse, and pushy to be truthful,' Jim replied.

'I could tell, actually she's not really a friend, she's my cousin, you can choose your friends but not your relatives.'

'How very true,' Jim said, thinking of Auntie Cath. 'Listen I like you, can I get to see you on your own?'

'There's a film on at the Odeon, it's called Blithe Spirit, it's supposed to be very good, so I've heard,' said

31

the girl.

'Seven thirty Saturday night outside then, if that's okay?' the girl nodded enthusiastically, Jim had himself a date. Jim picked up his glass and went back to the bar. Looking in the mirror he could see the other girl had returned and the two were whispering away to each other.

'Harry's in the snug, could you go through Jim?'

'On my way Bert.'

Harry James was in his customary position at the end of the counter sucking on his Havana and Ron was dutifully positioned at his side, of Weasel there was no sign.

'Evening Mister James, evening Ron.'

Ron nodded, 'Drink son?' Harry enquired.

'Yes please Mister James.'

'Harry, call me Harry.' Jim couldn't believe it, first Mr Tompkins and now Harry James. 'Give the boy a large scotch, Bert.'

'I'm afraid I don't drink spirits Harry.'

Harry James gripped Jim's arm in a vice like grip, 'When you work for Harry James son, you drink what Harry James tells you.'

Reluctantly Jim took the glass and raised it to his lips, 'Cheerio,' he said, the potent liquor stung his inexperienced sensitive mouth and he spluttered scotch all over the wooden floor.

The others hooted with laughter, 'Mind the carpet,' Bert Tompkins said sharply.

Jim looked down, 'What carpet?' he asked, and they all hooted with laughter again.

Harry, still laughing looked at Jim, 'Where's my car?' he asked

'It's back at the house.'

'What's it doing there?'

'I didn't like to drive it Harry, there's a petrol shortage on.'

Ron immediately rocked with laughter, Harry rounded on him with an icy stare, 'Quiet you.' Ron instantly fell silent. 'Take no notice, son,' he said kindly, and patted Jim on the shoulder, 'there's no petrol shortage around here, but it is very praiseworthy of you to be so considerate. Tell me Ron my son, any idea at all where Weasel is tonight?'

'I think he's at the dry cleaners boss.'

They both began to chuckle, 'So what do you suppose we ought to do with this young scallywag Ron?' Harry asked fingering the scar on his cheek.

Ron stroked his chin and shook his head, 'Don't know boss.'

'I do. Bert, another large scotch over here.'

By the time Jim left the pub at closing time, he was feeling quite tipsy, he looked in the bar on the way out, but the two girls were gone, I don't even know her name, he thought. By the time that he had ambled back to his auntie's, the fresh air had sobered him up, he could see that the house was in total darkness. Jim knowing that his auntie would be in bed felt quite relieved, he glanced at the shiny car, and rubbed his sleeve affectionately over the bonnet. Jim Britton was feeling rather pleased with himself, he settled himself into his bed, and with the

33

thought, another day another dollar, running around inside his head he drifted off to sleep.

CHAPTER THREE

Bright winter sunlight flooded in like fresh air through the bedroom window, Jim lay there for a good few moments wondering how he could get back into his aunt's good books, he really didn't want to fall out with her, and he knew she would be mortified if he moved out.

The answer came to him as he came down the stairs, 'Morning Auntie,' he said chirpily.

Auntie Cath grunted back, 'there's a trilby hat hanging in the hall, we're working class Jimmy. A cap was good enough for your father and his father'.

Jim sat himself at the table, 'I've got a date tomorrow night Auntie.' He blurted out.

Jim watched as her face gradually lit up, 'Oh, Jimmy,' she said her voice softening, 'I'm so pleased, what's her name? Where does she live? What does she do?'

Jim looked at her shamefaced, 'I don't know her name, Auntie, and in fact I don't know anything about her at all.'

'Well surely you can tell me what she looks like.'

'She's got short brown hair.'

'Well go on then.'

'That's about it really.'

'Are you sure you're telling me the truth Jimmy?'

'Yes honestly Auntie, there's a picture on at the Odeon, and I'm taking her tomorrow night.'

'Yes that's right, it's got Rex Harrison and Constance Cummings in it, mind you I don't know if it's your sort of film, still I expect you'll have other things on your mind,' and she winked and nudged Jim. Jim declined to answer.

Jim told his auntie all that had happened between him and the girls, and why he didn't get to find out her name, but he was careful to leave out the fact that he had been drinking with Harry James.

At ten o'clock Jim was outside the pub, Weasel turned up at ten to eleven.

'I'm driving,' was Weasel's idea of good morning.

'Are we going to the farm today?' Jim asked.

'Today's pay day,' came the answer. They drove for some time and into the district of Montpellier, a part of town that Jim was totally unfamiliar with, and eventually they pulled up outside of a row of three storey scruffy looking houses.

'Here catch,' Weasel threw something to Jim, Jim caught it and looked in his hand, it was a thick heavy brass knuckle-duster, 'It belonged to Lefty but he doesn't need it now,' Weasel said with a smile.

Jim didn't like the thought of the knuckle-duster and wondered what was going on and why he would need one.

'Right Jim number two first, get in there and collect the rent, nine shillings and sixpence, any messing and you know what to do,' he said, pointing at the knuckle-duster.

Jim got out of the car and walked slowly to the front door, he decided he had to imagine he was a gangster and look tough. He drew himself up to his full height, puffed out his already barrel like chest and gave the ornate brass front door knocker a good banging; the knocker looked to be the best part of the house.

A voice from inside called out, 'All right, all right, keep your hair on, I'm coming.'

The door opened and a small, grey haired elderly man stood in front of him. Surely I'm not expected to hit a man his age, Jim thought. Jim decided to sound tough for Weasel's benefit, 'Rent,' he said sharply and held out his hand, the man placed some coins of different denominations in his hand and quickly shut the door.

Jim sat back in the car and handed the money to Weasel, 'How much did he give you?'

'I don't know Weasel, I didn't count it.'

Weasel quickly scanned the money in his hand, 'He's a shilling short, get back in there; he's trying it on because you're new, and remember anything you don't collect will come out of *your* pocket.' Jim felt like letting it go, but with Weasel breathing down his neck he knew he would have to go back in. To impress Weasel he took the knuckle-duster out of his pocket and slipped it over his knuckles. 'That's it, get in there, and rearrange his face.' Weasel was in his element, Jim could see that the very thought of impending violence was exciting him.

Jim strode up to the front door more quickly this time and banged on the door even harder, a voice from inside called out, 'Who is it?'

Jim could see that Weasel had the car window down so he bellowed at the top of his voice, 'You know damn well who it is; open up now or I'll take the door off the hinges.' Jim already knew what he was going to do; as the door opened he grabbed the man by the throat and pushed him back in the house pulling the door to behind him.

'Please, please don't..... .' the man's voice petered out. Jim released his grip the man slumped to the ground, and then he looked up at Jim and said pitifully, 'You'll just have to kill me, there is no more money.'

'Look tell you what,' Jim said, 'give me the shilling you owe next time and we'll say no more about it.'

Tears welled up in the man's already watery eyes, 'Thank you son, oh thank you,' he whispered.

'Now stay where you are on the floor,' Jim ordered, 'I want him outside to think I've beaten you up. You could groan a bit as well if you like.'

Jim opened the front door wide and with a show put the knuckle-duster back in his pocket. Weasel jumped out the car and came running over, the man lay on the ground moaning and groaning for all he was worth.

'Got the money?' Weasel asked.

Jim opened his hand a shiny new shilling nestled in his palm, 'See, told you what they're like, they're all the bloody same,'

Weasel stepped inside the narrow passage way and kicked the man straight in the side of the head, the man winced, Weasel grinned and aimed another kick, Jim pushed him away, 'He's half dead now, I don't want Harry getting upset because I've killed a tenant.'

Weasel laughed, reached up and clapped his hand around Jim's shoulder, 'You know something Jim, you're beginning to grow on me.'

The rest of the morning turned out to be uneventful to Jim's relief, until Weasel said, 'I've kept the best till last, go in there, number thirty two and see Mister Passmore, and Jim put that knuckle-duster on you'll need it,' Jim hesitated, 'I mean it,' Weasel said seriously.

Jim did as he was told and walked up to the front door, bang bang bang; Jim called out, 'Rent,' in his most fierce some sounding voice.

The door opened and Mr Passmore stood in front of him, about six or seven years older than Jim, just as tall and broad and looking very fit and powerful, 'Well, well, well,' he said, 'what have we got here then?'

'Rent,' Jim repeated.

'Piss off!' Passmore started to push the door together, Jim pushed it back.

'Looking for a fight?' Jim didn't answer.

Passmore raised his fists; Weasel was out the car like a long dog, to watch.

Passmore lurched forward clumsily, Jim used the old left hander's ploy of feigning with his right hand, Passmore took the bait, Jim's blow caught Passmore just above his right eye with a sickening thud, and Passmore staggered back, the blood already pumping from the gash that Jim had inflicted. With a roar Passmore came awkwardly lurching forward again, Jim nimbly side stepped and hit him again, this time Jim heard the crunch of Passmore's nose caving in and Passmore dropped to his knees a beaten man. Weasel hurried over excitedly, 'I would have been there if he got the better of you Jim,'

'Yeah, course you would, Weasel,' Jim replied.

'Where's the fucking money Passmore?' Weasel cried excitedly.

Unable to answer Passmore, clutching his nose with one hand, he pointed to his waistcoat pocket, Weasel reached inside, pulled out two ten shilling notes, a handful of change and counted out the rent, ' Oh look, there's an extra quid in this pocket, all right if we have a drink?'

Passmore nodded, 'Watch Jim,' Weasel said, 'watch while I stripe him.'

Jim looked on in horror as Weasel produced a mother of pearl handled cut throat razor from inside his jacket, opened it, and drew it slowly first down one side of Passmore's face then down the other.

Passmore stayed quiet for a couple of seconds then as the blood seeped and then oozed from his wounds he screamed out with pain and clutched at his face, just for good measure Weasel aimed a kick at his head, and said, 'Come on Jim time for the pub, you can drop me at the Sceptre and make sure you come to the pub tonight at nine.' Passmore was already forgotten.

They returned to the car in silence, and drove away, after a while Jim said, 'Can I ask you a question Weasel?'

'You can ask,' he replied.

'All these houses, well they seem to pay a lot of rent for them and they are falling down, I mean they are in a terrible condition, don't you think Harry should spend some money doing them up?'

'Do that and we wouldn't get paid so well.'

'I've been meaning to bring that up, exactly how much are my wages?'

'See Harry tonight,' Weasel replied. Arriving at the Sceptre, Weasel jumped out of the car. 'You be in the pub tonight then Jim.'

'Haven't you forgotten something Weasel?'
'Like what.'
'Like the half a quid you owe me.'

'Fuck me, didn't take long for you to catch on, did it? I thought I'd got away with it.' He replied.

Jim made his way back home, opening the front door he was greeted by the smell of Auntie Cath's cooked dinner,' Come on Jimmy, I'm just dishing up.'

'I'll just freshen up a minute Auntie,' Jim went into the scullery where over the sink there hung a decrepit cracked old mirror, as Jim swilled his hands he stared at his distorted reflection, 'Look at me.' he said aloud, 'what am I turning into?'

To Jim's relief, Auntie Cath was back to normal. They sat eating their dinner, and towards the end of the meal Jim said, 'Look Auntie I'm free all the afternoon, would you like to go across town and visit Auntie Ivy, I've got the car outside.'

Auntie Cath dropped her knife and fork with a clatter, 'I'd love to go and see our Ivy but it will be on the bus, I'm not going in that,' and she pointed towards the front of the house. 'I wouldn't ride in that if it was the last car on earth, I wouldn't go to my own funeral in it.'

Reluctantly at a little after two Jim walked straight past the car, just touching the bonnet as he did so, Auntie Cath strode past without giving even a glance. The journey across town was dire and took the best part of an hour and a half; Jim was left thinking that perhaps his idea wasn't such a good idea after all.   Staring blankly out of the bus window his mind wandered back to long before the war, when his mother would take him every Sunday

41

after chapel to visit, first his Auntie Ivy and then his grandparents.

He always liked his Auntie Ivy because he could do more or less what he wanted and his Uncle Reg was always ready to play games with him. A different kettle of fish when they got to his grandparents. He could always remember the exact layout of the house although; he hadn't been there since he was a small boy. In through the front door there was a door immediately to the right, no one was allowed to go through it, the front parlour was beyond that door, and it was out of bounds to all. The only time he ever saw inside the room was when his grandfather was laid out in his coffin and he was made to go in and touch his grandfather's corpse, to stop him dreaming about him, he was told.

Opposite was another door, the living room, inside, a battered old dark leather Victorian chaise longue was set along the dark cream painted wall by the window, an aged oak oblong table covered with a dark green cloth stood in front of the chaise longue and three wooden kitchen chairs in line on the other side. Immediately at the end of the chaise longue was a well-used, wooden captain's chair, almost touching the hearth of the fireplace and a row of elderly, well-loved briar pipes were sitting in a wooden rack on the mantle.

He would be ushered into the room which was, either summer or winter usually either full of smoke from the chimney, or his grandfather's pipe, or both. His grandfather, a big man, with wispy silver hair and a close clipped moustache would always be sat in the captain's chair when Jim arrived, he would be pushed forward by his mother and would stand in front of his grandfather, Jim would say hello and his grandfather would acknowledge him with a grunt, and a puff on his pipe, Jim could never forget the smell of the black shag tobacco that would take his breath right away, and then Jim would have to be silent for however long his mother chose to stay.

He would sit on the chaise longue and would be offered a biscuit and either Tizer or limeade, it didn't matter which he chose, both would be lifeless and flat because the same bottles came out week after week. At a very early age Jim was introduced to total, mind numbing boredom.

The adults would talk for what seemed to be hours on end about things that Jim didn't understand and had little or no interest in. Sometimes they would whisper in subdued tones behind their hands, sometimes silently gesticulating adult matters. In the winter the light would gradually fade, only the flickering glow of the coal fire would light the room and then eventually, when the room was almost completely enveloped in the pitch blackness of the night, his grandmother would turn on the solitary overhead light. A dumb pallid yellow light would attempt unconvincingly to flood the room. Jim never really worked out which he disliked the most, the darkness of the night or the feeble light from that lamp.

The ding ding of Jim's aunt ringing the bus's bell shocked him back to reality, 'I said Jimmy, for the second time, we're here.'

'Sorry Auntie I was far away.'

Auntie Ivy was overjoyed to see Jim, 'Hello stranger,' she said, 'here, stand here let me look at you. Just look at him Cath, just the same as when he was a boy, he could look clean and tidy in a coal sack, very smart, and that's no demob suit you're wearing that's for sure and a trilby hat no less; got yourself a good job, have you Jimmy? '

'I'm working for Harry James.'

'Oh, my good God!' Ivy exclaimed, she clutched her clenched fists up to her mouth in horror. 'Your dear mother would turn in her grave if she was alive now. What have you done Jimmy?'

Jim started to laugh, 'She'd hardly turn in her grave if she was alive now would she?'

Ivy was becoming quite irritated; her voice sharpened, 'You know very well what I mean, that's nothing to laugh about Jimmy,'

Auntie Cath chipped in, 'I've already told him Ivy, that Harry James is a bad lot, but he just won't listen.'

'Well he should especially as....' Cath gave Ivy a withering look and her voice tailed away.

'Especially as what?' Jim asked.

'Especially the way he treated our family when things were tight during the war,' Auntie Cath said quickly.

'Why what did he do?'

'He wouldn't give us any credit,' Auntie Cath replied.

You wouldn't want credit if you saw the way he treats non payers, Jim thought, instead he said, 'Well business is business, you know.'

The conversation changed to small talk which bored

Jim as much as when he was a child, but he tried to pretend to be interested and tried to say yes and no in all the right places.

'Jimmy's got himself a girlfriend,' Auntie Cath remarked, out of the blue.

'Really, come on then Jimmy tell us all about her, what's her name? Where does she live?'

Auntie Cath spared Jim's embarrassment, 'God is that the time? Come on Jimmy we've got to get our skates on or we'll miss the bus.'

The journey back across town was even more time consuming and by the time they got back home Jim had decided that Auntie Cath or no Auntie Cath, he would take the car next time.

Conversation with his aunt was quite a light hearted affair until Jim mentioned that tonight was pay night and he was off to the pub.

'Don't make any noise when you come in and don't be late.' Jim's aunt turned on the wireless and picked up her knitting bag.

'Yes Auntie Cath,' Jim said.

Jim got to the Sceptre at a quarter to nine, he deliberated whether to go straight into the snug or to wait to be summoned and prudently he decided to choose the latter.

At five past nine Bert Tompkins came through from the snug. 'They're waiting for you,' he said.

Jim made his way through, and as per usual Harry James was settled in his usual position at the end of the

45

bar, Ron was there as well, but again no sign of Weasel. This time a new face to Jim stood beside Harry, a broad shouldered man in his mid- fifties, with a watering can for a nose and huge banana like fingers stuck on the ends of the enormous palms of his hands. His high colour betrayed the fact that he was partial to a drink or three, 'Come on Jim,' Harry said, 'come over here and meet Anal Harris.' Jim stepped forward and extended his right hand.

Anal Harris grasped it and pumped it up and down, surprisingly gently, 'I bet you're wondering why I'm called Anal?' he said with a smile.

'To be honest,' said Jim, 'not wishing to be rude, it's the size of your hands I can't get over.'

'Well before I met Harry I was an iron fighter for twenty odd years and the reason I'm called Anal is-'

Harry James interrupted with, 'You'll find out soon enough. Anyway Jim, I'm getting good reports of you, seems you sorted that prick Passmore out. When Lefty went round there he took a right good hiding, I had to send Ron around to explain to him where he was going wrong, didn't I Ron?' He started chuckling and nudged Ron in the ribs. 'Bert get the boy a large scotch would you? And have one yourself, Jim pull up a stool and sit here next to me.'

Jim was beside himself, sitting next to the boss being bought a drink, Auntie Cath and Auntie Ivy have got it all wrong, he thought.

Harry James reached into his pocket and produced the now familiar roll of notes, 'Here you are Bert that's for the drinks, and here's your wages Jim. No week in hand

46

here,' he said with a smile.

Jim stared as Harry James placed four white fivers in his hand; his face gave the game away. 'What's up son,' Harry said, 'not enough for you?'

'No, I mean, no well I mean, it's too much, in the army I was on twenty one shillings a week, and I've already had money from you in the week.'

'See what I mean Anal, what did I say to you? I told you I've discovered a gem, here you are son,' Harry James produced another fiver and thrust it into Jim's hand, 'call it a little bit of a bonus, if you like.'

Jim sipped his whisky; it was all like a dream that was happening to somebody else.

'What about tax and insurance Harry?' Jim asked.

'Hear that Ron, the boy's worried about tax and insurance; tell him what he needs to know.'

'Well, tax is something that keeps the carpet down in the corners, and as for insurance,' Ron produced a revolver from inside his jacket and placed it on the counter, 'that's all the insurance you'll ever need, never mind William Beveridge, and the rest of the government's insurance scheme.'

Bert looked across the bar, 'You can just put that away Ron,' he said sharply, 'you know I'll have none of that in here, pull that stunt again and you'll be barred.'

'Sorry Bert,' Ron murmured, sheepishly pocketing his weapon.

'Have you remembered to bring the car with you tonight Jim?' Harry James asked.

'Yes it's outside Harry,' Jim replied.

'Good lad, I'll get Anal to drop you home when the

47

pub shuts and then he'll pick you up tomorrow night at seven,'

'Well, actually I was supposed to be going on a date tomorrow night Harry, it is Saturday,' Jim said.

'Bit of fluff eh! Well, she has to wait my boy, when you work for Harry James you're available all the time, *understand*?'

Jim didn't like the intimidating way he said understand, but muttered, 'Understood.'

'Good boy, now then get the drinks in.'

At closing time Jim and Anal staggered to the car and after three or four attempts managed to start the engine and meander slowly along the road. Jim liked Anal, he seemed much more affable and approachable than Weasel, and he felt totally relaxed and comfortable in his company.

'Jim,' Anal said, 'while I think of it, don't wear that posh suit tomorrow night, wear something, well something that you don't mind spoiling.'

'Why's that then Anal?'

For a reply, Anal chuckled drunkenly away.

Jim looked across at the alarm clock, a quarter past eleven; he knew he was going to be sick; making it to the outside toilet wasn't an option. Before he was three steps down the stairs it had started to come up, by the seventh stair it was up, into his cupped hands and all down his pyjamas. He rushed through the kitchen where his auntie was sitting reading the morning paper and out into the outside toilet. She'll kill me, he thought. He grasped the down pipe of the toilet cistern, leant over, and heaved; the stench of stale whisky filled the lavatory. Christ I feel rough, he thought. Suddenly he realised it was going to come out of the other end as well, he struggled with his pyjama bottoms and sat on the lavatory with sick still dribbling out of the corner of his mouth.

'Are you alright, Jimmy?' Auntie Cath called from outside the toilet.

'Yes fine,' Jim tried to sound cheerful, 'I had a pork pie in the pub last night and I think it must have been gone off.'

'Pork pies indeed where ever did the landlord get pork pies from? Harry James I shouldn't wonder, I'll go and make you a nice cup of tea.'

'Thanks Auntie,' Jim said, Jim didn't know how long he sat there, but the stench of the toilet and the now cold sick spurred him into action. He wandered back into the kitchen.

'Oh my word, look at you Jimmy, you poor thing, take those things off and I'll get the tin bath in.'

Looks like she's gone for the pork pie story, Jim thought.

'That man in the Sceptre should have his licence taken away, selling rubbish that Harry James got him, you could have food poisoning you poor thing, I'm going round to see him and give him a piece of my mind, just you wait and see and I'll call the doctor.'

Oh no, thought Jim, 'Don't make a fuss Auntie, I can tell him myself, I'll be all right after I've had a cuppa.' But he wasn't, and he was back to the toilet and back in bed until five in the afternoon.

49

'Feeling better now Jimmy?'

'Yes Auntie,' Jim lied.

'Big night tonight then eh, Jimmy? I'll run the iron over your suit.'

'How do you mean Auntie big night?'

'Well your date of course.'

'I have to work tonight, I'm afraid.'

'What d'you mean work? It's Saturday night. Tell Harry James you're busy.'

'I'm afraid it doesn't work like that Auntie, look I know I'm letting the girl down and I feel really badly about it, but there nothing I can do, nothing.'

'Um,' Auntie Cath replied.

Unlike Weasel, Anal arrived on the dot of seven; Jim was ready waiting and looking out from behind the net curtains for him. 'Perhaps you'd sit in the back if you don't mind Jim; we've got to pick up Ron and you know how much space he takes up.'

'Where exactly are we going Anal?' Jim asked.

'South of the river,' Anal replied.

'And what are we going to be doing?'

'We're paying that toe rag Peter Newman a little visit,'

For the second time Jim had now heard of the Newmans, 'Is he anything to do with Matthew Newman?' he asked.

'You don't seem to know much, do you Jim? There are six of them, five brothers, and a cousin, Jack, well no, there are four now. Used to be Matthew, Mark, Luke, John,

Peter, that's the brothers and Jack he's the cousin. The boss took care of Matthew and the Ron took care of John, so there's just the four of them left. After John Newman bumped off Harry's brother things got real bad, and when Ron bumped off John, well things went right downhill, we couldn't walk the streets, but it all settled down until the week before last. Then when Weasel went round the spic restaurant in Colston Street to collect and found they were paying out the Newmans instead of us, well, hands in our till Harry says. Here we are, that's Ron's house.'

What a dive, thought Jim. The brown paint, what little paint there was, looked dirty and was peeling off the rank rotting woodwork, an old broken mangle stood at one side of the front door, an old rusty chainless bicycle at the other and one of the downstairs windows was boarded up. Ron slammed the front door three times before he eventually got it to close then he ambled over to the car; Jim could see that in his right hand he was carrying what appeared to be an axe, about the same size as a fireman's. Jim could feel his mouth drying out.

Ron wedged his huge frame into the front seat of the car, moaning and groaning about the lack of leg room. 'Hello young Jim, hello Anal,' he said. 'All set for it, then Jim?'

'Well I don't actually know what I've got to do,' Jim could hardly speak, his mouth had dried right out and his tongue felt like it was twice as big as normal and stuck firmly inside his mouth.

'Weasel will tell you when we pick him up,' Ron said.

51

They drove to Weasel's house and after Anal had spent several minutes blowing the horn and making comments about Weasel and his lack of punctuality the front door finally opened and Weasel came out. Anal left the wheel and slide in besides Jim, while Weasel climbed in the driver's seat.

'You were just starting to annoy me Weasel, you little prick,' Ron said. Sensibly, Weasel chose not to answer.

The journey commenced in silence. In towards the centre of town and then on towards Bedminster. As they came to Bedminster Bridge, Anal leaned over to Jim and said, 'Just open your window Jim, there's a good lad.' Jim was about to find out why he was called Anal Harris. A dire stench rose up and filled the car. 'Sorry about that Jim, these occasions always brings the worse out in me, I think it must be nerves.'

Jim could hardly breathe; in fact he felt he didn't want to at all.

Ron turned round in his seat, 'Foul assed git,' he said. The journey continued in silence.

As they approached East Street, Weasel pulled into a side street and switched off the car's lights. 'Right then Jim,' he said looking at Jim in the rear view mirror, 'this is what you do, but first are you tooled up?'

'I don't know what you mean.'

'Christ Almighty, where have you been? I mean have you got any weapons?'

'No.'

'That's good because in the club you'll be frisked.'

'What club? frisked?'

'Bugger me, don't you know anything? You'll be

searched. Just listen, in the boot there are three cases of scotch, we know that Peter Newman likes a bargain, he knows all of us, and so you'll have to go in. So you go in the club, with one bottle and ask to see him. Tell him you've got scotch for sale at a rock bottom price, then you coax him out to the car to see the other stuff, and then open the boot and stand right back out of the way, and I mean right out of the way, that's all you've got to do okay?'

'Yes I think so.'

'Never mind I fucking think so, listen, get this wrong and you'll be mincemeat, if Newman doesn't have you, Harry will.'

If Jim thought he was dry in the mouth before it was nothing to how he felt now.

Weasel started the car engine and they set off once again, the smells issuing from Anal Harris got worse, if they could, and despite that, all too soon for Jim the car came smoothly to a halt. Weasel climbed out of the driving seat and gave Jim the car keys, and then he, Anal and Ron disappeared into the darkness.

Jim could see Weasel had parked about ten yards from a doorway, there was a dull flickering amber light above it, and that was it, this must be the place, he thought. He walked up to the door, his heart pounding, it appeared to be firmly shut, they must be closed, he hoped upon hope. Tentatively he put a hand on the door and gently pushed. Noiselessly it swung open to reveal a narrow corridor, crudely painted in cream gloss paint, a shabby old stained carpet covered the floor and there was a smell of damp, old tobacco smoke and cheap perfume hanging in the air. At the end of the corridor there were a couple of beer crates and a small barrel stacked against the wall and adjacent to them stood a battered old oak desk. Behind it a large fat man sat, lounging back in his seat with his feet on the desk, smoking and looking bored to tears with his head in a newspaper. He barely looked up at Jim as he approached, 'You a member?' he grunted.

'Um no,' replied Jim.

'Then sling your hook,' the man lowered his newspaper, puffed on his cigarette and stared past Jim into space.

'I want to see Mister Newman, I've got something he might be interested in,' at that point Jim realised he had forgotten the whisky.

'What you got?'

'Three crates of whisky.'

'Where is it then, this whisky?'

'Well I wasn't going to carry them in here if he doesn't want them.'

'What brand is it?'

'Jim was stumped, 'If you care to tell Mister Newman I'm here, I'll go and get a sample.'

The man lethargically climbed up from behind his desk and slowly wandered off into the club, Jim beat a hasty retreat back out to the car. As he approached it he heard a voice come from out of the darkness, it was Weasel. 'You prat,' he hissed quietly, 'you forgot the scotch, over here, come over here.' Jim walked into the darkness towards the voice, 'Here,' the whisky bottle was thrust into his hand and feeling a fool Jim quickly went back inside the club.

As he approached the desk, he could see the man now had someone else with him, broad shouldered, short, square and balding, but with the customary pencil thin moustache, 'Mister Newman?' Jim enquired.

'Who's wants to know?'

'I'm Jim Britton,' too late, Jim wondered if he should have used a false name, 'I've got some whisky for sale.'

'Pat him down Fred.'

Fred searched Jim and then he said, 'Pull your trouser legs up to your knees.' Jim did as he was asked. 'It's alright boss no weapons, he's clean.'

'This whisky, how much do you want for it?' Peter Newman asked.

Jim realised he wasn't very good at this sort of thing, and was out of his depth, 'The going rate,' he replied.

'Let's see it.'

Jim handed him the bottle. 'Bells, alright I'll take it, go and fetch it and I'll get you the money.'

Things were going wrong, 'No,' said Jim, 'if I bring the whisky in here, I might not get paid, you come out to the car.'

'You're not stupid are you? Go out to the car with him Fred.'

'I'm only dealing with the organ grinder,' Jim said.

'You cheeky little bugger,' Fred lunged forward.

Jim had his fists up in an instant.

'All right calm down Fred, I like his spirit, come on let's go, you can carry it in Fred.' The trio walked outside.

At the entrance of the club, Peter Newman stopped dead in his tracks. 'That your car?' he asked, pointing at the Humber, 'hang on a minute... I know that car.'

'Well it's my car now,' Jim said hurriedly, 'if you want to know I pinched it.'

'Look Fred, look whose car he's nicked, I don't believe it, if they catch you my son it'll be curtains for you.'

'Whose car is it?' asked Jim innocently.

'Never mind, come on let's get on with it.'

They walked to the back of the car, Jim threw the boot open and smartly stepped to one side, Peter Newman and Fred peered into the boot, a single shot rang out and Fred slumped to the ground. Out of the darkness bounded Anal and Ron, almost effortlessly between them they bundled Peter Newman into the back seat of the car, Weasel jumped into the driving seat and with Jim in the front, in an instant they were gone.

Jim looked around at Peter Newman; even in the half-light he could see his face had turned ashen. Peter Newman fixed Jim with an icy stare, 'You're fucking dead,' he spat.

'Do you hear that Jim?' said Anal laughing adopting a posh voice, 'I think you might be in a spot of bother, d'you think he's in trouble Ron?'

Ron replied, in an equally refined tone, 'It jolly well looks like it, old chap.' They all laughed except Jim and Peter Newman.

'Stop the car Weasel,' Ron said, 'I can't sit back here with that fucking stink anymore and I can't stretch my legs.' Weasel stopped the car, Ron got out and slipped a gun into Jim's hand, 'Here take this and keep it, and don't be afraid to use it if you've got to,' he whispered.

Jim slipped into the back seat, and by way of an apology Anal said, 'Sorry Jim, I think I've had a little bit of an accident.'

Their journey continued out into the country and north along the A38 until Weasel turned off to the left, Jim spotted the sign post as they passed, "Aust 4". They drove down the winding lane until another sign appeared, "New Passage Ferry," and an arrow. As they approached the ferry Jim could already feel the icy cold wind blowing off the river and quickly wound up the window. The ferry was there standing at the end of the slipway, dimly lit with a mediocre lantern; Jim could see the words "Severn King" emblazoned on the side.

'Harry's already here,' said Ron glancing at the black Rolls Royce standing on the slipway. Between them they bundled Peter Newman out of the car, Peter Newman looked skywards at the night sky. 'Yes, take a good look my son,' said Ron. Jim shivered. Together they walked him onto the ferry and into what appeared to Jim to be the engine room, the whole place stunk of diesel, oil and fried food and impending death, Anal quickly disappeared into the lavatory.

Harry was sitting in the middle of the room in a captain's chair beaming all over his face, puffing on his customarily overly large cigar. 'Mission accomplished then boys,' he said. 'Come in, come in Peter my son, long time no see, nice to see you, here you sit here, take my chair

57

please, make yourself comfy.'

'Why don't you just get on with it?' Peter Newman asked grimly.

'All in good time, all in good time my son. Jim run out to the car and bring in a couple of bottles of scotch, and if you go to the roller you'll find some glasses. I don't fancy drinking out of this crap,' he held up a grey, grimy looking chipped enamel mug and set it back down distastefully.

By the time Jim got back inside, a grim faced Peter Newman was tied to the captain's chair, his legs were still free but his upper body was securely bound and his arms were tied and outstretched along the length of the chair's arms, both fists were tightly clenched.

'Right now you're here Jim, we'll begin. Right then Mr Newman,' Harry said, 'you've been on our territory, that's bad enough in itself, but not only that, you've been in the Italian restaurant and it wasn't for a spaghetti fucking bolognaise and that's just not cricket, just not cricket at all.' Peter Newman didn't reply. 'The way I see it, is that you've been thieving, you've had your hand in the till,' his voice rose, 'my fucking till.' He paused, 'Ron.' Ron stepped forward,

'Jesus Christ no!' Peter Newman screamed out. Ron brought the axe down and in one movement it cut completely through both Peter Newman's wrist and the arm of the chair. Peter Newman screamed out in pain and terror, his head fell forward blood pumping and squirting in all directions from his wrist, his severed clenched fist dropped to the filthy oily floor.

'You won't put your hand in my till again, well not

that one anyway,' Harry laughed, 'Anal put your belt round his arm, nice and tight we don't want him to bleed to death, now do we?' Harry was all smiles, 'and Jim pick his hand up and stick it in that shoe box I've brought with me, his brothers can have it back, we'll think of something clever to write on the box later.'

Jim stooped to pick up the hand, he'd seen a lot worse during the war, but it was still a gruesome and unpleasant task. He looked down at the sleeve of his suit, it was now bloodied, he realised why he had been told not to wear his best.

'Pour the drinks Jim and an extra-large one for our guest when he comes round.' Harry was in his evil element; Jim dutifully filled the glasses and filled Peter Newman's right to the brim. 'That's it fill it right up after all he's bought it,' Harry said. 'Have a look and see if he's conscious son.'

Jim gently lifted up Peter Newman's head, his eyes were wide open, staring and filled with dread, 'Here drink this,' he said quietly.

Jim carefully lifted the glass to his mouth and he drained the glass all in one go, 'Thank you,' he whispered.

'Another one?' Jim asked, Peter Newman nodded.

'Steady on there young Jim don't spoil him,' said Harry.

'You did say he's bought it Harry,' Jim replied.

'Fair comment, pour away Jim.'

Weasel piped up, 'Can I stripe him yet boss?'

'Stripe him, stripe him, that's all I ever get from you,' Harry said, 'you're like a fucking gramophone record.'

Jim poured another generous helping and this time

59

Peter Newman sipped at the drink.

'Jim go just outside, you'll find a fire bucket hanging up, we need some water.' Harry said.

Completely mystified, Jim went out and found the fire bucket, filled it and brought it back in and set it down in front of Harry.

'Alright Weasel, go ahead,' said Harry. Weasel jumped forward, put both his hands in his waistcoat pockets and produced two mother of pearl handled cut throat razors. With both hands he set to work, screaming out with pleasure at every slash, he managed to remove the end of Peter Newman's nose almost completely before Harry shouted, 'That's enough!' Peter Newman sat whimpering, the blood oozing from his wounds and his face now almost unrecognisable

Harry looked at Jim, 'You can have the pleasure my son,' said Harry,' then you'll truly be one of us.'

'What do I have to do, Harry?'

They all roared with laughter, 'Well drown the bastard of course.'

Ron stepped forward, 'I'll hold the bucket; make sure you get a good grip.'

Jim tried to stall for time, 'His head will never fit in there.'

'His fucking brother's did,' replied Ron. Harry screamed out with laughter.

Jim's mind flashed back to his childhood, kittens were one thing, but they were asking him to kill a man in cold blood, no not asking, telling him. He knew if he refused he would end up the same as Peter Newman,

60

reluctantly he grabbed the back of Peter Newman's head, 'Hold the bucket Ron,' he said. Gripping the doomed head, he thrust it into the freezing water, Peter Newman hardly struggled to begin with and it was as if he was already resigned to his fate. But quite suddenly he began to jerk up and down violently.

'Keep a good grip Jim my son,' said Ron, 'he's nearly a goner.' Jim held on and as suddenly as it started the jerking stopped. 'Keep him under a bit longer Jim we don't want him waking up.' Jim held on until Ron signalled for him to relax.

Jim went straight to the whisky bottle, panting heavily and with a shaking hand attempted to pour out a drink. 'Here let me son,' said Anal kindly, 'first time was it? Never mind Jim you'll soon get used it.' Jim stood alone in the corner of the engine room trying to come to terms with the enormity of what he had just done. Murdering...soon get used to it, he thought, my God...soon get used to it...murdering, screamed inside his brain.

'Jim,' Harry said interrupting Jim's thoughts, 'come and give a hand here.'

'Yes sorry Harry, I was far away.' Anal walked outside and beckoned for Jim to follow him. 'What have we got to do now Anal?' Jim asked.

'It's time we mixed up a banker of concrete; give us a hand to get the gear from Harry's car. Take your time son, Anal said thoughtfully, ' you'll be alright.'

Jim and Anal carried bag after bag from the boot of Harry's car into the engine room.

61

Jim could see that Ron was busy constructing a wooden box around Peter Newman's feet.

'Four two one Jim,' Anal said, 'and not too much water I don't want to be here all bleeding night.'

'I don't understand you Anal,' Jim replied.

'Four of chippings, two sand, one cement, not too much water I don't want to be all night,' he repeated. Jim finished carrying the bags in from the car and Anal showed him how to go about mixing the concrete and although the night was chill Jim soon had his coat off and was sweating profusely.

'Shovel it in then Jim,' Ron said. Jim shovelled away until the concrete was just above Peter Newman's ankles.

'That's not quite enough,' said Anal who sounded well versed in that sort of thing, 'is there any more left in the car, Jim?'

'No that's it, that's the lot,' Jim replied.

'Fuck it we were short last time, we need something to bring the level up, a bit more,' Anal said.

'No problem,' said Ron, he raised the axe and proceeded to hack at Peter Newman's neck. Raising his head off his shoulders he pushed it down into the concrete between his feet.

'Here look at this Harry,' said Anal with a grin, 'he can see right up his own fucking arse now.' Harry roared with laughter.

Jim was feeling increasingly unsteady on his feet and decidedly queasy.

'Right then Jim have a look through his pockets, see what he's got,' said Harry. Jim searched and came up with a wallet and some loose change.

'Give it over here,' said Harry. Harry stood at the table and counted it out. 'Right then Jim if I take out the cost of the scotch, there's two hundred and sixty two pounds one and eleven pence left, here you are my son, take it, it's yours.'

'But,' said Jim.

'No buts, that's the way we operate, you do the business, you get the money, now take it,' and he thrust the money into Jim's hand.

Jim put the money in his pocket he was completely dumbstruck; he had never seen or had so much in his whole life.

'Okay then boys all done?' Harry asked. 'Right then Anal, see you when I see you, keep your head down, they will come looking, especially when they get this, he lifted the shoe box off the table and tucked it under his arm. 'Ever driven a roller before, Jim?' he asked.

'Can't say as I have Harry,' Jim replied.

Harry tossed the keys to Jim, 'Now's your chance, come on you lot let's go.'

Jim climbed in the Rolls Royce and turned the key and repeatedly pushed the starter button, much to the amusement of Harry, 'Why are you laughing Harry?' Jim asked.

'This is a roller, it started first time you just can't hear the engine.'

'Well I never,' Jim was impressed.

They headed back up to the A38 and Harry said, 'When you come to it take the turning for Tytherington

Jim, then head for Rangeworthy.' Jim peered into the gloom until the sign for Rangeworthy appeared. 'Pull over here Jim.' Jim stopped the car and without a word Weasel and Ron got out of the car. 'Drive on Jim,' Harry said.

'Why have they got out Harry?' Jim asked.

'Can't let the Newmans know where I live, now can I? They don't know you, but they do know those two, you can pick them up after you drop me off, you've done well tonight son, I'm proud of you. Now tell me all about what happened when you went into the club.' Jim told Harry everything with his discourse being punctuated by Harry, saying, 'Good boy,' and, 'well done my son,' and, 'quick thinking.'

Jim followed Harry's directions around the winding lanes until they came to a turning on the right, where a sign read, "Bird Sanctuary," 'Turn down here Jim,' Harry ordered.

Jim pulled up in front of two huge ornate wrought iron gates, 'How is it the authorities haven't taken the gates for the war effort Harry?' Jim asked.

'Connections my son, connections,' Harry smiled. 'Toot the horn Jim,' Jim blew the horn and after a short wait an elderly man emerged from the darkness carrying a double barrel shot gun in the crook of his arm, Jim could see a pair of pyjama bottoms and carpet slippers showing beneath a long dark overcoat. Harry wound down the car window, 'Open up Tom,' he said, 'young Jim here will be going back out in about five minutes.'

Jim drove along a long gravel drive which swept around in a semi-circle until he came to an imposing mock

Tudor mansion, he looked at Harry, 'Some bird sanctuary this Harry,' he said.

Harry smiled, 'Not bad is it Jim, play your cards right and you'll be looking at something like this one day. Now Jim as soon as you see Ron I want you to tell him to get rid of the Humber, from what you've said the Newmans know the car and it's too dangerous to drive about in, tell him to pick up another motor and tell him to phone the club and warn Darky Dillon what the score is. Under no circumstances are any of the boys to go to the Sceptre, we'll all meet up in the Charnbury tomorrow night, after me and you have been to see Eddie Sims. Pick me up here at seven tomorrow night, understood.'

'Yes Harry.'

'Oh and Jim see that the Newmans get this back,' Harry handed Jim the shoe box, 'and try to think of something witty to write on the box.' Then just as Jim thought he would be driving the Rolls Royce for the weekend Harry pointed across the drive. 'Take the Flying Standard and I'll see you tomorrow, and Jim, you've done well tonight, good night son.'

'Goodnight Harry.'

CHAPTER FOUR

One look at Auntie Cath's face on Sunday morning told Jim he was in deep trouble, Poor barren Auntie Cath, Jimmy was the son she'd never had; the golden child; how she'd yearned for a baby and grew to resent and then in the end despise her husband; too late now, and now the golden child was tarnished, 'All right Auntie?' He ventured cautiously.

By way of a reply she threw the brass knuckle-duster across the kitchen table, 'What's this all about Jimmy?' Auntie Cath glared.

'Oh, thank God you've found it, where was it?' Jim responded.

'I decided to press your best suit, if you remember and,' Jim suddenly remembered the blood all over the sleeve of his demob suit, 'I found it in the pocket.'

'You're a life saver Auntie, come here and give us a kiss, Mister Harris told me to be careful with it,' Jim thought Auntie Cath wouldn't appreciate Anal.

'You mean it's not yours?'

'Of course it's not Auntie,' Jim replied, 'why would I want a horrible looking thing like that?'

'Then why is it in your pocket?'

Good question, thought Jim, 'Well the thing is, I know you think that I'm hanging around with some unsavoury characters, but Mister Harris is actually a plain clothes policeman, and he asked me to look after that as evidence.'

'Evidence of what?'

'Well I don't know Auntie, they don't tell you anything, the police, now do they?'

'What d'you mean, you're helping the police?'

'I'm helping Mister Harris, if that's what you mean Auntie?'

'Is it to put Harry James where he belongs?'

'I told you Auntie the police don't tell you anything, but it could be.'

'Sit down here Jimmy I'll make you a nice cup of tea.' Jim was in the clear.

'Have a guess where I went last night Jimmy,' she said.

'Go on Auntie tell me.'

'I went to the pictures with Audrey, we sat in the one and nines, it was ever such a good film; mind I don't think you'd have liked it.'

'Audrey, I don't know an Audrey, who's Audrey?'

Auntie Cath began to laugh, 'She's your new girlfriend that's who she is, you see I went on your date for you, and explained to her that you had to work. She's only a slip of a thing, poor girl, a straight up and downer, never mind you bring her round for tea and we'll soon put some meat on her. Anyway here's her address,' Auntie Cath handed Jim a slip of paper, 'and I told her you would definitely see her tonight.'

'I'm working again tonight Auntie,' but before Auntie Cath could say anything Jim added, 'but I will go around there and see her this afternoon.'

'I think you should consider this one you know Jimmy, she seems like a nice girl.'

'Oh Auntie, for goodness sake,' Jim sounded

exasperated, 'I don't even know her.'

'Yes, but Jimmy it's time you settled down and thought about starting a family.'

'Give me a chance Auntie Cath this time last week I was still in the army.' Jim looked at the piece of paper he had been given. 'Well look at that she only lives a couple of streets away, and I've never ever bumped into her, isn't that strange.'

'That's because she used to live in the middle of town, but she got bombed out, she's working at G.B. Britton's factory now.'

'You seem to know all there is to know about her Auntie,' Jim said with a smile.

'Oh yes, we had a right good chat, in fact we got told off in the pictures for talking, by some man in front, he had a trilby hat on and Audrey said to him, "We're only talking because we can't see through your hat, most rude take it off."'

'What did he say?'

'He didn't say anything; he took his hat off and slumped down in his seat. The trouble was that meant that we had to sit quietly then.' Auntie Cath started to giggle and Jim joined in. When they had collected themselves Cath continued, 'What time do you intend going around there then Jimmy?'

'I don't really know, I don't want to be too near to dinner and I don't want to be too close to tea time. I'll have to think about it.' Jim reached into his pocket. 'Here you are Auntie,' and he produced two fivers, 'housekeeping.'

'I'm not taking any of his money,' Cath said quite

firmly, emphasising the *his*.

'Listen Auntie Cath it's wages, all I do is chauffeur Harry and his colleagues around.'

'And you get ten pounds a week, huh! Harry indeed, I get twenty six shillings a week pension to live on and you come in with ten pounds, there's something badly amiss somewhere Jimmy, something badly amiss.'

'Here you are Auntie, please take it, please,' Jim pushed the money into her hand.

'I don't want all of your wages, let me get my purse you need pocket money.'

If only she knew, thought Jim. 'Auntie, when Mister Harris and me were coming home last night, we saw an old man slip and fall in the street, he hit his head on the curb, anyway we put him in the car and took him to Cossham hospital and I'm afraid I got some blood on my suit.'

'I'll see what I can do with it Jimmy, what a good boy you are to look after that old man, was he alright?'

'We waited while they stitched him up, he was a bit shook up, so then we took him home and made him a cup of tea.'

'That was very thoughtful of you Jimmy; you are such a good boy.'

In the clear again, thought Jim. Just after dinner Jim went up to his bedroom, and took all of his money out of his pockets and laid all the notes and the change out neatly on the blue bedspread of his bed. Jim stood back against the wall of the tiny bedroom and took in the view, he could hardly believe that he had all that money, suddenly he remembered how he came by it, I'm a murderer, he thought, he caught a glimpse of himself in the dressing table mirror, 'I don't think I like you very much,' he said aloud and turned away.   He quickly gathered all the money up and, except for the change and a pound note put it on top of the wardrobe, together with the gun Ron had given him the previous night. He knew he would have to find a better hiding place but Auntie Cath wouldn't do any cleaning, not on the day of rest anyway.

Jim glanced at the clock, ten to three, and ran down over the stairs, 'Right then Auntie I'm away,' he said.

'Come here Jimmy and let me have a look at you,' Cath cooed and clucked around him like an old mother hen. 'Very smart, very smart indeed, now off you go and don't forget to invite her back here for tea.'

'Oh Auntie, give me a chance,' Jim said. 'Right then, I'm off.'

Jim sauntered out to the car, in daylight he could see it wasn't as posh as the Humber, but it was quite tidy. Jim had a quick look at the address on the piece of paper in his hand; he was vaguely familiar with the street but not the number. Within five minutes he was slowly cruising past the rows of houses looking at their numbers, he spotted the one he wanted and was glad to see it stood out from the rest, freshly painted with the net curtains neat and tidy, he walked up to the front door, the brass door knocker shone. Jim straightened his tie and ran his hands through his hair; he took a deep breath and nervously tapped the door, the door swung open to reveal a middle aged man, 'Can I help you?' he asked.

'I was wondering if Audrey is at home,' Jim said.

'Hang on,' then Jim heard the man say, 'Audrey, someone for you at the front door.'

Audrey came to the door, 'Jimmy, oh no, look at the state of me I haven't even done my hair, you were supposed to come tonight.'

'You look just fine to me Audrey, listen I've got to work tonight, so what if we take a spin in the car now?' Jim pointed towards the Standard.

'I can't go anywhere looking like this Jimmy, come on in and I'll get ready.' Jim hesitated. 'Come on silly, it's only my mum and dad, they don't bite.'

'I don't know,' Jim felt his colours starting to rise. Audrey grabbed his arm and frog marched him into the house, 'Mum, Dad, meet Jimmy.'

Both parents extended their hands; Jim shook each one and said, 'pleased to meet you Mister and Missus ….' Jim's voice tailed away as he realised he didn't know their surnames.

The man saved the day, 'Mister and Missus Amos,' he said.

Jim shook their hands again and repeated Mr and Mrs Amos.

'Entertain Jimmy for me would you Mum and Dad? I need to change and do my hair.'

'Come and sit down here Jimmy,' Mrs Amos said, 'and tell us all about yourself.'

Looks like I'm going to be vetted, Jim thought.

'There's a fresh pot made, how do you like your tea Jimmy?' Mr Amos asked.

'No thank you, I had one just before I came out.'

'Nonsense, now mother you go and pour Jimmy a nice cuppa.' Mr Amos glanced towards the kitchen door.

Mrs Amos went off into the kitchen pulling the door behind her, barely waiting for her to leave the room Mr Amos looked at Jim and said, 'Right then lad, what are your intentions with our Audrey?'

God I hardly know her, thought Jim, 'Strictly honourable Mister Amos,' he replied.

'I hope they are young man, now tell me what you do for a living?'

'I'm a chauffeur Mister Amos.'

'Chauffeur,' Jim could hear the distain in his voice, 'no trade then lad?'

'No but I earn twenty pounds a week.'

'Twenty pounds a week,' Jim could tell by his voice that he didn't believe him, he shook his head, 'I don't earn twenty pounds in a fortnight.'

'You see I work for a group of business men and I drive all of them around, I'm on call twenty four hours a day, seven days a week, that's why the money is so good.'

'What's the farthest you've been chauffeuring then Jimmy?' he asked.

Jim decided that Aust didn't sound quite right, so he replied, 'Birmingham.'

'I used to work in Birmingham, what part?'

'Sort of south or east,' Jim said lamely.

'Yardley by any chance?'

'Yes that's it Yardley.'

'I used to work in Yardley, I used to have a drink in the Ring of Bells, do you know of the Ring of Bells?'

Before Jim had time to answer, Mrs Amos opened the kitchen door carrying a tray which Jim could see sported the best bone china, 'How do you like your tea Jimmy?' Mrs Amos asked.

'Milk and sugar, please Missus Amos, if you've got any.' Jim replied.

'I expect we can spare a sugar for a guest, here,' she said and handed Jim a couple of photographs, 'that's our Audrey when she was a little girl, proper little tomboy she was, always climbing trees, wouldn't look at a dolly.'

'Very nice,' Jim said, looking at the photos.

'I was just telling Jimmy, I used to work in Yardley, where about is it you say you used to go up there Jimmy?'

'Leave the boy alone George,' Mrs Amos put in, 'work, work, work, that's all I get out of you, that or football.'

'I take it you're a Bristol Rovers fan then Jimmy?' Mr Amos asked.

Jimmy knew that which side of the river you were born determined which football club you supported, 'Of course I am Mister Amos,' he replied.

'Good lad, we don't want any city fans in here, do we?' Mr Amos pulled his cigarettes out of his waistcoat pocket and offered one to Jim, 'No thank you Mister Amos,' he said, 'I don't smoke.'

'You don't smoke,' he looked incredulous, 'you're not a man till you smoke you know,' he said popping a cigarette into his own mouth and lighting it. Jim glanced at the clock on the wall. 'Not a bit of good you looking at that Jimmy,' Mr Amos said, 'she'll be hours yet.'

But with that the door opened and in rushed Audrey,

73

'Sorry I've taken so long Jimmy.'

'That's alright.' Jim replied.

'If you've finished your tea, we'll be off then.' Jim gulped down the last of the tea and politely thanked Mr and Mrs Amos.

'Where are you two going, then Jimmy?' asked Mrs Amos.

'Only for a spin, Missus Amos, I can't be long I have to go to work tonight.'

'Work on the Sabbath, whatever next?' said Mr Amos, he shook his head and grunted disapprovingly.

Once outside Jim remarked, 'I don't think your dad approves of me, is he like that with all your boy friends?'

Audrey went bright red, 'I haven't ever had a boyfriend Jimmy,' she said.

'Well that makes two of us.'

'What you mean you've never had a boyfriend as well?' Audrey started to laugh.

Jim blushed and stammered, 'I mean I've never had a girlfriend.'

'I'm only teasing you Jimmy.'

Jim ushered Audrey to the passenger's side of the car and opened the door for her, Audrey climbed in, and they drove away, 'What's this Jimmy?' Audrey asked, reaching down to pick up the shoe box.

'I wouldn't go too near those Audrey if I were you, it's my old shoes going for repair and they are just a bit smelly.' Jim paused and said. 'Audrey; can I ask you a favour?'

'What is it Jimmy?'

'Well I'd rather you called me Jim, if you don't mind; you sound just like my Auntie Cath.'

'Alright Jimmy, from now on it's Jim,' she said laughing.

Half an hour later and they were parked on Clifton Downs, 'Do you know Jim, I've lived in Bristol all my life and I've never actually seen the suspension bridge before, only pictures of it.'

'Me neither, it's a bit rusty looking isn't it? You know, I've been thinking, it seems that we've got a lot in common you and me, tell me do you like football?'

'Can't stand it, I think it's because my dad is always going on about the Rovers.'

'See Audrey we do have a lot in common, I hate football as well, but I told your dad I was a fan, I thought it was for the best. You know something Audrey, I feel comfortable with you and I feel like I have known you all my life.'

'And me you Jim.'

They carried on chatting away; the time flying by. Both oblivious to the fading light, it was quickly getting darker and the car growing colder.

'God, it must be getting late,' said Jim, 'have you got a watch?'

'No, I haven't.'

'When's your birthday, I'll buy you one.'

'My birthday isn't until October, and anyway watches cost a lot of money Jim.'

'If you want a watch you shall have a watch, and we won't wait right until October.' Jim started the car's engine

75

and he drove Audrey back to her house.

'I've had a lovely afternoon Jim, thank you so much.'

'I have as well Audrey, you know I work strange hours, but I promise I'll see you whenever I can.'

Audrey leant over and kissed Jim on the cheek, got out of the car, turned, waved and walked to her front door. Jim still having no idea of the time quickly drove away.

Arriving at Auntie Cath's, Jim dived through the front door and ran to look at the clock, twenty past six, Auntie Cath done up in her Sunday best, said disappointedly, 'Where's Audrey, Jimmy? I thought she was coming to tea.'

'Sorry Auntie, we went for a spin and we got so engrossed with each other's company that time went right out of the window.'

'Oh that's lovely, how romantic, I'm so pleased, so this is the one then Jimmy?'

'Auntie please, I hardly know the girl.'

'So come on tell me all about it, where did you take her, what did she have to say?'

'Tell you all about it tomorrow, I must dash.' Jim gave his Auntie Cath a peck on the cheek and rushed back to the car.

When Jim arrived to pick Harry up he could see he was none too pleased, 'What fucking time do you call this?' he asked sharply.

'Sorry Harry, I was with this girl and I haven't got a watch.'

'Buy one, now let's go.'

As the journey into town progressed Harry became

more of his usual affable self, 'Come on then son, tell me all about this girl, is she hot?'

Jim thought he should tell Harry what Harry wanted to hear, 'Harry,' he said, 'she'll do anything, and I mean absolutely anything, anything at all, she does things you haven't even thought of.'

Harry patted Jim's leg, 'That's my boy,' he said all smiles.

'Harry I have a confession to make, because I was with that girl I haven't delivered Peter Newman's hand yet.'

'Not to worry Jim,' Harry said chuckling, 'I'm just glad to see you had your priorities right. Tell me Jim are you church or chapel?'

'I'm chapel Harry.'

'Good boy, that's what I like to hear, I'm chapel myself, there's a nice little chapel in Rangeworthy, I go every Sunday afternoon, when I can that is, after dinner, or lunch as Missus James likes to call it, we've been today,' Harry started to hum Onward Christian Soldiers much to Jim's amazement, and then a medley of hymns, Harry stopped humming suddenly and asked. 'Did you go to chapel when you were in the mob Jim?'

'When I told them that I was chapel they just put down C of E, so I had to go to church.'

'Terrible, that's fucking terrible, what a load of fucking heathens making you do that, still never mind, you can come to chapel next Sunday with us, that'll be nice.'

'Well I was rather hoping I could take my girl to chapel near us next Sunday, Harry,' Jim lied.

'You'll bring her to *our chapel* Jim,' Harry had spoken.

Just as they reached the top of Muller Road, Harry pointed to the side, 'Pull over there somewhere Jim, and park up. See this road Jim, Ron recons it's the longest road in Bristol without a pub, Christ knows where he got that from.'

Jim pulled into the side of the road; Harry looked across and said, 'Jim are you carrying anything?'

'Yes a knuckle-duster.'

'Leave it in the car. There's a nice little pub just around the corner in Gloucester road, we'll have a quiet drink in there before we see Eddie, don't want to seem too keen.'

'Too keen for what, Harry?'

'I don't want him to think I'm coming cap in hand to sort out the Newmans, I want him to think I am giving him a business opportunity.'

'I don't understand you Harry.'

'Well, look if there are no Newmans we can split their territory with Eddie Simms, straight down the middle, then just when Eddie thinks everything is going honky dory, we nail him and take the lot,' Harry chuckled.

Yes, thought Jim, Auntie Cath has got the measure of Harry James.

Harry looked at the pub clock, 'Right ten past nine, one more and we'll make a move.' Jim was beginning to wonder why Harry had been so keen to leave his house at seven.

Eddie Simms' club entrance turned out to be to Jim, very much like the Newmans', a dingy corridor leading to a desk with a bespoke suited gorilla sat behind it.

'Evening gents,' said the gorilla, are you members?'

'I'm here to see Eddie, I'm Harry James.'

'Ah yes, Mr James, he's expecting you, go on through and get yourself a drink, it's on the house and I'll tell Mr Simms you're here.'

Harry and Jim went through into the club, Jim cast his eyes around, down one side the length of the surprisingly small, dimly lit room was a long bar. Along the length of the other wall were a line of small wooden booths with a table and built in seats. Standing in the corner was an almost new Seeburg juke box, playing quietly away to itself. Four or five girls with small silver chains around their ankles were sitting at tall bar stools, smoking and chatting and a couple of unsavoury looking individuals were sitting in one of the booths playing cards, there didn't appear to be any actual customers. Harry had read Jim's thoughts.

'Bit of a dive, isn't it? Best part's the fucking jukebox. the Charlton beats this into a cocked hat.'

Jim nodded in agreement, although he had never set foot inside the Charlton, 'There are no customers Harry,' he said.

'It's early yet Jim, by eleven they'll be turning them away, you get all the screws from Horfield nick in here, Eddie's got it well sorted out. He sends the screws in to the prisoners with booze, snout and dirty pictures; he gives the screws a drink or a favour with the girls. The cons settle up with Eddie when they come out, the screws get a nice quiet life in the nick, the world keeps on turning and everybody's happy.'

Another gorilla appeared before they could get a drink, 'This way please gents,' he said.

Harry and Jim followed the man through a door, along another dimly lit corridor and up some rickety wooden creaking stairs. Along the end of the corridor a door stood open leading to a room. Jim could see an enormous fat man standing just inside. As Harry and Jim approached, he turned and Jim realised just how big he was, not tall though, about five foot six or seven, Jim thought he looked like Sidney Greenstreet, although bigger, much bigger. Wiping his sweating brow with a handkerchief in one hand he extended the other to Harry James, 'Long time no see Harry, you old bugger,' he said completely ignoring Jim.

Harry pumped Eddie's hand up and down, 'It's good to see you, you old sod.'

'Likewise, I'm sure,' Eddie said. 'Don't mind if Sid here checks your boy over?'

Sid ran expert hands over Jim, 'He's clean boss,' he said.

Jim stepped forward, 'Don't mind if I check yours, Mister Simms?' he said.

Jim patted Sid down.

'Satisfied?' Eddie Simms said.

'No,' said Jim, 'pull your trouser legs up.' Sid pulled up his trouser legs to reveal a holster strapped to one calf, from inside it protruded the silvery handle of a small calibre revolver, Jim just pointed.

Eddie moved his huge bulk surprisingly quickly until he was standing directly in front of Sid, 'I'm disappointed in you Sid,' he said, 'very fucking disappointed indeed,

80

here give me that.' Sid shamefaced, reached down, removed the weapon from its holster, and handed it over. 'What did I tell you before Harry got here, no guns, didn't I? Have some fucking respect. Sorry about this Harry, well spotted lad, you can come and work for me anytime.' Eddie Simms reached up, took Sid's ear between his finger and thumb, and stretched it away from his body. 'Next time when I speak use this for listening,' calmly he raised the gun to Sid's ear and pulled the trigger. 'Now get out my sight,' he said. Sid shuffled out of the room clutching the side of his head, the blood oozing through his fingers. 'Right now that's sorted out,' said Eddie, 'we'll get down to some business, your boy here can go down to the bar, the drinks are free son, and if you ask for Gloria she'll get you sorted out.'

Harry chuckled, 'And I'd put two french letters on if I were you Jim.'

Jim went down to the bar, he was relieved to see that of Sid there was no sign, he ordered a beer and stood at the bar slowly sipping it, but declined to ask for Gloria. Feeling a tap on his shoulder Jim turned around; standing in front of him was a short plump female, brassy looking, with bright red lips, bleached blond almost white hair, and a low cut top which exposed most of her more than ample breasts. She chewed frantically away at a lump of spearmint chewing gum like her life depended on it, 'I'm Gloria,' she announced in a broad Bristolian accent, 'Eddie says I'm to look after you, want to come upstairs now?'

'Can I have a drink first?' Jim asked, pointing at his glass.

81

'Suit yourself big boy, I'll have a gin and orange.'

Gloria ushered Jim into one of the cramped booths, 'You're certainly a cut above the average,' she said, eying him up and down, 'you'd be amazed at some of the ones I've had to entertain.' Jim suddenly realised why she was chewing gum, her breath was disgusting despite the powerful spearmint aroma. 'Come on then big boy,' she said, hurrying her drink down in one, 'I need some cock, I'm nearly coming off sitting here.'

'One more drink first,' said Jim.

'I'll have a gin and orange,' Gloria said.

Jim sat trying to hold his breath while Gloria wittered on, 'Come on then big boy,' she said pointing at Jim's glass and moving even closer, 'drink up, your boss will be back if we don't hurry,' and then as if to emphasise the point she reached down to Jim's crotch, 'Mmm.... I'll soon put some life into that.'

Gloria caught hold of Jim's hand and started to drag him from the booth, Jim was never so pleased to see Harry as he appeared in the doorway at the end of the bar, ' Sorry Gloria, there's the boss,' said Jim, 'got to go.'

Once back in the car Harry said to Jim, 'So what did you think of our Gloria then Jim?'

'Apart from her breath, all right Harry.'

'Only alright, she's a dirty little cow, I've been there a couple of times myself, in my opinion I'd describe her as very enthusiastic, not just alright.'

'But Harry, her breath.'

'Didn't you turn her over? You should have turned her over; bad breath or no bad breath, when you get to my age,' Harry laughed, 'it's any port in a storm.'

Jim didn't know if he should ask, but after a while he said, 'Can I ask how you got on with Mister Simms, Harry?'

'Course you can Jim, I was beginning to think you weren't interested.'

'I didn't want to pry, Harry.'

'You're one of us now Jim, I'm an open book, he's gone for it alright, so the agreement is, we each take care of one of the three brothers and we'll have a monkey on who gets the last one first.'

'So which one are we taking care of Harry?'

'The brown hatter.'

'I don't understand you, Harry.'

'The queer boy.'

'Which one's that, Harry?'

'Mark fucking Newman, that's who, if there's one thing that makes my blood boil it's queers like him, God slipped up there Jim, he slipped up badly,' Jim glanced at Harry he could see his face was full of hatred; Jim had touched a raw nerve.

'Have you got a plan Harry?' he asked.

'No not at the moment, but I'm working on it.' They travelled on in silence, when Harry broke it by saying, 'Missus James likes to go shopping on Mondays Jim, she always says she likes to go around ten in the morning, but I know her only too well, so if you turn up at half past she still won't be ready. I've never known anybody like it.'

'I expect Missus James is just like any other woman Harry.'

'Oh no, you're wrong there son, she's unique, you tell me another woman who can spend two and a half

83

hours in the sodding bath, and her shouting down the stairs for more kettles of boiling water, I've been up and down those bloody stairs more times than we both have had hot dinners.'

'Where will she want to go tomorrow, Harry?'

'Could be Bath, Bristol, or anywhere, just humour her, all right?'

'Anything you say Harry.'

CHAPTER FIVE

Jim turned up at Harry's the next morning just before ten, he found his way barred by Tom brandishing his double barrel shotgun, 'Clear off, or you'll get both barrels,' he said.

'I'm Jim, remember me from last night?'

'Can't say I do, now sling your hook.'

'Look, just tell Harry I'm here, will you?'

'He ain't here, now clear off,' Tom raised the gun in a threatening manner.

'I'm here to take Missus James shopping.'

'I won't tell you again, now bugger off.'

Jim got back in the car, turned it around and drove back along the main road, parking up he pondered what to do. He didn't have long to ponder as Harry's Rolls Royce came sliding into view in the rear view mirror. 'What's up Jim broken down?' he asked.

'Tom won't let me in.'

Harry started to chuckle, 'Silly old sod, I'll have to think about putting him out to grass, he's getting that he won't let anybody in. Come on Jim follow me, who knows Missus James might even be ready to go out by now.'

But she wasn't, there wasn't any sign of her, and by a quarter to eleven Harry said to Jim, 'Five more minutes Jim and you can go home, I won't have her messing my staff about like this.'

Four and a half minutes later Mrs James swept down the curved oak staircase into the hallway where Jim was waiting. Jim didn't know what to anticipate, but he certainly didn't expect to see a very attractive, slim blond haired woman at least twenty years younger than Harry, sporting a clearly very expensive fur coat. She clipped clopped in her overly high, high heels across the ornate patterned marble floor of the hallway, 'You must be Jim,' she said extending her hand, 'sorry, I'm running a tad late.'

'That's alright Missus James I've only just got here,' Jim ushered her out to the Standard.

'I'm not going anywhere in that thing,' she said pointing disdainfully and walked over to the Rolls Royce.

Jim opened the back door and she slid into the back seat, as she slipped closely past him he caught the delicate aroma of her expensive perfume. Slowly Jim drove up the winding gravel drive and noticed that by the time they got to the gate Tom was already opening it, as they passed by Tom raised his hand in a salute. Jim started to chuckle to himself.

'Come along then Jim, share the joke,' Jim noticed she had quite a cultured and clipped slightly North Country accent.

'It's just that five minutes ago he was going to shoot me.'

'Yes,' she said, 'that's Tom for you.' A little way up the road Mrs James said, 'Jim, just pull over for a minute will you?'

Jim brought the car to a halt and Mrs. James opened the car door, got out and sat in the front beside Jim. She turned facing him and parted her red lips, 'Now let me have a good look at you Jim,' she purred, 'Very smart, I see Harry has got me someone decent at last.'

Jim was somewhat at a loss, and they continued

their journey in silence.

'What's up Jim, a wee bit shy are we?'

'Look Missus James.'

'Call me June.... June James, yes it's a bit unfortunate isn't it? There's a turning coming up on the left Jim,' she pointed, 'take it please.'

Jim took the left turn and after a couple of hundred yards he could see a gap between the hedges, again on the left, 'Just pull in there Jim,' she pointed.

Jim pulled up; Mrs James reached over and turned the engine off. 'There that's better Jim. You see Jim, candidly, Harry is a lot older than me, twenty six years older to be precise, and he likes to have me on his arm, he likes to show me off, but that's about all, nothing else. Since poor Lefty has been gone I have got very lonely, very lonely indeed, do you understand what I mean?' she paused and stared at Jim intently. 'Do you like me Jim?'

'I... I... think you're very nice Missus James,' Jim stammered.

'June I told you, call me June, tell me Jim, do you think I have a nice figure?' she said running her hands down her sides. Jim nodded in agreement.

'Do you know the old saying Jim, fur coat and no knickers?' Jim nodded again. Slowly and sensually Mrs James unbuttoned her fur coat, she opened it and pulled her skirt up to reveal a pair of shapely legs covered in black silk stockings; she pulled her skirt up further to reveal a suspender belt and Jim could see that she was wearing nothing else. 'Well?' she asked.

Jim just sat there with his mouth wide open completely stunned. Mrs James undid her blouse and pulled both breasts from her bra, 'Not bad, eh Jim? Here feel,' she panted. Taking Jim's hand she placed it on her heaving breast, Jim could see her nipples were pink and hard. Suddenly she reached down, her breasts almost right in Jim's face and grabbed at his groin, her face fell, 'Jesus Christ,' she said frustration in her voice, 'I don't believe it, it's that bloody man, it's Harry's fault, you're frightened of Harry, that's what it is isn't it? You're frightened of bloody Harry James, aren't you?'

'Petrified, I'm absolutely petrified, I'm sorry Missus James, I just can't do it.'

Mrs James got out of the car adjusting her dress and buttoning her coat as she went, she slammed the door as hard as she could and flopped back in the back seat of the car, 'Take me to Brights store in Clifton, I'll spend some of the bastard's money instead, in fact I'll spend as much of it as I can.'

By the time they got back to Harry's it was twenty past six, Jim was tired and hungry and fed up. Mrs James had left him strict instructions not to leave the car on any account while she was in the shops. So apart from quickly using the public toilet and getting a drink of water from the wash basin he had had nothing.

Harry was standing in the middle of the drive, puffing on the inevitable cigar as they arrived. 'Just beginning to wonder about you two then,' he said.

Mrs James swept past him and said, 'Don't just stand there Jim, get the parcels into the house, now.'

Jim noticed that she didn't even acknowledge Harry, she clipped clopped hurriedly across the hallway and disappeared up the stairs.

Eventually, when the last parcel was deposited inside the house Harry said, 'Come through to the study Jim, we need to have a little chat, you and me.' Harry clapped his hand on Jim's shoulder and guided him through the study door. 'Get me a large whisky Jim and have one yourself, and then sit yourself down, you look bushed.'

'To be honest Harry, I'm tired, hungry, and thirsty,' Jim said.

'Haven't you had anything all day Jim?'

Jim explained about him having to stay by the car. 'Sit there and relax son,' he said gently, 'I'll soon sort you out.' Harry went over to the telephone. 'Hello Tom, ask your Missus to bring something to eat up to the big house please, it's for Jim, oh and Tom, ask her to be as quick as she can, Jim hasn't eaten all day.' Harry came back across the room and sat opposite Jim. 'Don't think you and Missus James quite hit it off, did you Jim?'

'Not exactly no Harry.'

Harry James leant forward in his seat until his face was inches from Jim's. He caught hold of Jim's arm firmly and squeezed, 'I want you to tell me exactly what happened today, exactly and no bull shit, do I make myself *understood*?'

Jim took a large gulp on his drink, 'Well we drove out of the drive, and then Missus James came and sat in the front of the car with me...we drove along the road and then...'

Harry interrupted, 'Then she told you to turn into a lane on the left hand side just the other side of Iron Acton.'

'That's right, but how do you know that then Harry?'

'Never mind, just go on with the story.'

'She told me to pull up in between these tall hedges,' Jim hesitated.

'Go on Jim.' Harry said reassuringly.

'Well she,' Jim paused, '....she showed me...what was on offer.' Jim blushed, 'if you understand me Harry?'

'Go on son, tell me exactly,' Harry said gently.

'She pulled up her clothes, she wasn't wearing any,' Jim hesitated, ' wasn't wearing any... any... undergarment, and then she showed me her breasts, she made me touch them and then she grabbed me, you know, down there,' Jim pointed. 'Then when I told her I wasn't interested, she got really nasty, well I've got a girlfriend anyway Harry, and you're my boss, and I respect you.'

'Good boy, good boy, anything else?'

'Then she got even shirtier and she said she was going to spend some of your money.'

'Yes she did that alright, judging by the parcels. I'm very pleased with you Jim, very pleased indeed, now drink your drink, I've got something I'd like you to see before you eat.'

Harry led the way out of the back of the house, across a cobbled yard and over to an old barn which had seen better days. Harry produced an overlarge key from his pocket and placed it into the lock of the dilapidated door.

'Have a job to mislay that,' Jim quipped.

Harry smiled, turned the key, and swung open the creaking old door, 'Hang on there Jim while I find the light switch.'

Suddenly the barn was lit up and Jim blinked against the sudden bright light, in front of him was a battered old pre-war Ford van, 'It's as rusty as an anchor Harry,' he said.

'Maybe but it's just the job if you don't want to be noticed,' said Harry, he reached inside, bent forward, and emerged wearing a tatty old chequered flat cap. 'Who would think that Harry James would be wearing this and driving around in that?'

'I don't understand you Harry.'

'Come back in the house and I'll explain.' Harry locked the old barn and they returned to the house just in time to see that the food had arrived, a tray of bread, cheese, onion, beetroot and pickles. On the side of the tray was a large slice of cake. Harry pointed at the cake, 'You'll never taste better Jim, I guarantee it. You sit yourself down and I'll pour us another couple of drinks, you eat and I'll talk.'

Jim settled himself down into one of Harry's comfortable leather chairs and started ravenously devouring the food. Harry pulled his chair up closer and sat opposite Jim, 'You are hungry Jim. That bitch,' he added. 'Right where was I, oh yes, the van, no I'll get to the van in a minute.

' Going back about six months ago June asked me if she could go shopping, so I told Lefty to pick her up, much the same as I told you. The first time she went she was gone all day and came back laden, like she did today, then after a couple of weeks she would come home earlier, moaning and groaning that they had nothing in the shops that she wanted. That's not like June, I can tell you, and the one thing she's good at is spending money, my money. Then it got that she wanted to go shopping a couple or maybe three times a week. Anyway, about a month ago I decided to get an old van, follow them and see where they went, I followed on behind one morning and they were so wrapped up in each other, I followed them all the way to that lane and they never twigged.

'I parked up the lane a little way and walked back down trying to look through the hedge, in the end I almost went right up to the car. Now there's a very soft suspension on my roller, it gave the game away; it was rocking like a ship in a fucking storm. I thought about killing the both of them there and then, but I had second thoughts, I wanted to make them suffer first.

'You see Jim, I knew that Lefty had had his hand in the till. He was going around collecting the money from the businesses in town for me; the money was always put in white envelopes. The arrangement was that he would collect the money, and give it to Weasel; Weasel would count it and enter it up in the book. Then one day Lefty got the bright idea that if he brought his own envelopes he could charge more and swap envelopes before Weasel got hold of them. It all went all right, and I don't know for just how long, until one day Lefty took sick suddenly and Weasel, working alone, found he had more money than he should have had. Now if Weasel had been clever he would have put the screws on Lefty and made himself a few bob, but he came running to me. I was doing all right, and I had a mind to let it go, thinking ten out of ten for Lefty coming up with the fiddle, but then when I found out where else his hand had been, he had to go.'

'So why is Missus James still with us Harry?'

'Good question, it's not that I wouldn't kill a woman, no it's that she looks good on my arm. I don't know really, perhaps one day I will kill her,' Harry paused and worried the scar on his cheek. 'Yes perhaps I will. Weasel can't stand the sight of her; I can just hear him saying can I stripe her boss? It's like this Jim, I'm getting no younger, I always wanted a son to carry on the business, I thought June would oblige. Perhaps it's me I don't know. Anyway enough of that, drink up Jim, one for the road eh?' Harry glanced over, Jim was fast asleep.

When Jim woke up he was freezing cold, his head was pounding and daylight filled the room. For a moment he was totally disorientated and couldn't recognise the unfamiliar surroundings. Where am I? Jim thought and then suddenly he remembered he had not made it home. Auntie Cath will be sick with worry, I have to get out of here, he thought. Screwing his half asleep eyes together, he squinted at the large grandfather clock, ten past ten, oh no, he thought.

As Jim rushed out to the car Harry called, 'Where are you off in such a hurry Jim?' Harry was standing in the doorway, beaming from ear to ear. 'Come on into the kitchen there's a fresh pot going, and I need to talk to you.'

'I was worried about my Auntie Cath Harry; she'll wonder where I am.'

'You didn't worry about her last night lad, did you?'

Jim followed Harry to the kitchen, 'I need the toilet Harry,' he said.

93

'Through there to the karhzi,' Harry pointed, 'I'll be mother.'

When Jim came back in he could see that Harry was eager to talk, 'Right, now this is what I want you to do, we know the Newmans took an interest in the spic restaurant so we need to know if they're trying to muscle in anywhere else. I want you to go to all the addresses on this list and collect their dues, except the top one and I want you to start at the bottom of the list and work your way up. Normally Weasel and Lefty used to start at about eleven, I want you to start at least an hour later, I don't think the Newmans know which businesses we control but there's no sense in taking chances, I want you to go looking like a commercial traveller, and without Weasel, that way if there is anybody from the Newmans around they won't have any suspicions. The address at the very top is the spic restaurant so don't go there until early evening, you might like to take your girl for a meal, that way if the Newmans are watching they won't suspect anything, then after the meal I want you to pick me and the wife up at about eight thirty, I think I might like to take her for a meal myself.'

'What's that some sort of a reconciliation then, is it Harry?'

'No son, let's say, more like the last supper.' Harry flashed a twisted grin.

It seemed to Jim that Harry had made up his mind.

It was eleven thirty when Jim finally got back to Auntie Cath's, 'Jimmy where have you been? I've been frantic with worry.' Jim could see she had been crying.

'I'm so sorry Auntie, I had to drive the boss to London,' Jim lied glibly, 'and I didn't know I was going, but listen I'm going to have the phone put in for you.'

'And where do you think that you've got phone money?'

'It's all right Auntie, Harry is paying for the phone,' Jim lied, 'he said it would be better if he needed me urgently.'

'And what was he doing up the smoke Jimmy? Up to no good I'll bet.'

'I don't know what he was up there for Auntie; I just drive the car, don't I?'

Jim managed to get to the first on the list by one o'clock after stopping off to buy himself a rather stylish brown leather attaché case. The employees in the first establishment were all smiles at Jim until he mentioned Harry James, then their attitude immediately changed to sullen compliance coupled with an obvious fear. Jim worked his way through the list and by five thirty he had a pile of white envelopes inside his attaché case, he didn't open any to save time, and he took the chance that the money was right in each, but he was careful to mark all the envelopes to know from where they came. On the way back to Auntie Cath's he popped into see Audrey and she agreed to meet him at seven o'clock.

At home Auntie Cath was waiting behind the net curtains looking out for him, 'You're late Jimmy,' she said, 'I'll go and put your tea on the table.'

'But Auntie,' Jim hesitated.

'Yes Jimmy.'

Jim didn't have the heart to tell her he was going for a meal, 'I was just going to say that I could do with a bit of a wash first Auntie.'

'To think that when you were a boy we couldn't get you to go anywhere near water, go on then, but be quick.'

When Jim came back from the scullery Auntie Cath was holding his attaché case. 'This must have cost a pretty penny Jimmy,' she said.

'It's a firm's one Auntie.'

'What's a chauffeur doing with a brief case?'

'It's Ron's he forgot it when he got out of the car,' lying was coming easily to Jim these days, 'I thought I'd bring it into the house, you never know, do you?' he added.

'Who's Ron? You've never mentioned a Ron before.'

'He's just one of Harry's business associates Auntie, that's all.'

Jim was obliged to undergo the usual inspection before he was allowed to leave Auntie Cath's and being careful to put the shoe box well out of sight in the boot Jim drove to Audrey's house. When he arrived he was glad to see she was ready smack on time, unpunctuality being the one thing Jim couldn't stand.

'How are things with you then Audrey?'

'I'm fed up with Mum keeping on because I wear trousers all day in the factory and I wear trousers at night. I look all right to you though, don't I Jim?'

'I know I haven't seen you in a dress but I prefer you in trousers, I know that sounds silly, but well I mean I don't think a dress would suit you somehow.'

'That's good, I'm glad you've said that, I never ever feel comfortable in a dress.'

'Listen Audrey I know I've only just picked you up, but I've got to go to work later, I'm sorry.'

'That's all right Jim we'll just have to make the best of it that's all, where is it we're going Jim?'

'Well Harry told me about this nice little Italian restaurant in town, apparently the owner was a prisoner of war here and he stayed on after the war finished and opened the restaurant, I thought you might like to go there for a meal.'

'That would be nice Jim, thank you,' she answered.

Arriving at the restaurant they were ushered into a window seat, the rest of the restaurant was quite empty. 'That's an old trick,' Audrey said.

'What d'you mean? I don't understand.'

'They sit you in the window so when people walk past, they think that the restaurant is busy and then they will come in.'

'Well I never knew that.' When the waiter came for their order Jim said to Audrey, 'I don't want any soup, but you feel free.'

'No I don't want any either thank you Jim.'

'Audrey, look I've got something for you,' Jim slide his hand into his pocket and produced from it a small silver coloured box, he placed it on the table and slid it across to Audrey,

'What's this?' she asked.

'Open it, and see,' Jim replied.

Audrey opened the box, 'Oh Jim, you shouldn't have, it's lovely, it must have cost a fortune.'

'Put it on.'

Audrey slid the watch onto her wrist, 'Oh but Jim, it's smashing, thank you, thank you.'

'Look,' said Jim and he held his arm up to show his watch, 'his and hers,' Audrey's watch was a smaller version of Jim's.

'They must have cost you a fortune Jim.' Audrey said, admiring her watch.

'Peanuts, they were having a sale in Kemps the jewellers.'

Their food duly arrived and Jim started to make a half-hearted stab at it, when two spiv like characters came through the front door. They quickly glanced warily around and walked briskly to the back of the restaurant near the kitchen door.

'I don't like the look of those two,' Audrey said.

Jim felt the hairs on his neck start to prickle, 'Audrey,' he started.

'Shush Jim!' Audrey put her fingers to her lips.

Afraid to look around, Jim sat motionless with his knife and fork extended in front of him, the hairs on the back of his neck prickling, his palms damp. After what seemed an eternity, Jim still not daring to look round, heard the front door of the restaurant shut and he saw the two men pass by the window, 'Why did you shush me just now?' he asked.

'Well, working in all the noise of the boot factory I've learnt to lip read, so I was ear wigging.'

'What did they have to say?' Jim asked, trying to sound as casual as he could.

'Nothing much, just asked if anybody's been in and

to phone that number if they did and they gave over a piece of paper, nothing interesting.'

'You don't seem to be getting on with your meal very well Audrey, is it all right?'

Audrey giggled, 'To tell the truth Jim this is the second tea I've had, you see I didn't think we were going out to eat.'

'I'm not very hungry myself. Tell you what, I'll go and pay the bill and we'll go to the Sceptre for a drink before I go to work.'

Audrey nodded and Jim got up and made his way to the back of the restaurant, the waiter approached him and said, 'Can I help you sir? Everything all right, is it? Is your meal satisfactory?'

'I'll see the manager if you don't mind?'

'Certainly sir,' the waiter replied and disappeared through a swing door.

When he reappeared he was accompanied by a short, swarthy white haired man. In a thick Italian accent he said to Jim,   'What-tas the problem sir, how can-na I help-a you?'

'I'm from Harry James; I'll take the envelope and the phone number and pay the bill.'

The man's face fell, he reached into his inside pocket and produced a white envelope, then he reached into his jacket pocket and gave Jim a scrap of paper, 'Here you are, sir, ' he said, 'I don't a want no trouble.'

'Right how much do I owe you?'

'Izz-a free,' the man replied, 'no charge.'

Jim wasn't having any of it, 'How much do I owe you?' he repeated.

'No, nothing, now you go please-a .'

Jim turned away, and went back to his table; Audrey looked crestfallen, 'What's up Audrey?' Jim asked.

'I can lip read, remember?'

'I might as well come clean then Audrey, Harry told me to come to this particular restaurant and collect some money that he was owed, that's all.'

'And what about the telephone number, what's that all about?'

'I don't know what that's all about; Harry said to tell him if anything odd happened, and that was pretty odd wasn't it?'

Audrey seemed satisfied with Jim's explanation and taking Jim's arm said quite cheerily, 'Come on then Jim let's go.'

Jim pulled a pound note from his pocket and left it on the table.

Jim leant on the counter of the Sceptre patiently waiting for Bert Tompkins to put in an appearance, 'Pop into the snug Jim,' Audrey said, 'perhaps he didn't hear us come in.'

Jim went through into the snug; the two men who were in the restaurant were there, one had Bert Tompkins by the throat and was pulling him across the counter, the other man was standing with a frightening looking flick knife in his hand, 'Come on tell us where we can find Harry James, or else,' he said menacingly.

'I've told you I've never heard of him,' Bert looked terrified.

Jim stepped forward slipping his knuckle-duster on.

He caught the man with the knife just, behind the left ear, with a grunt the man let go of the knife and dropped to the floor. The one holding Bert Tompkins turned to look at Jim and for his trouble was hit full in the face, he let go of Bert Tompkins and staggered back, Jim hit him again and this time he caught him in his right eye, meanwhile the other man, had pulled himself up the counter, Jim speedily moved forward and hit the man again, this time full on the nose and as quickly as it started it was over. 'Now get out,' Jim said, 'and you leave my dad alone.' Jim picked the flick knife up from the floor and pointed it at the two men threateningly; without a word the pair slowly staggered out of the pub.

'Thank you son,' said Bert, Jim could see he was visibly shaken, 'I'm getting too bloody old for all this malarkey,' he took a wine glass from the shelf and helped himself to a generous measure from the brandy optic; taking a gulp he said. 'Why did you call me Dad just now Jim?'

'Couldn't say, here you two don't come in here looking for Harry James, because we've never heard of him, could I?'

'Come on Jim, in here gassing, where's my gin and orange?'

'Bert this is Audrey, Audrey meet Bert.'

'Bert extended his hand over the counter and said, 'Right this one's on me, you know young lady you've got one in a million there, you want to hang on to him.'

'I intend to, Bert,' she replied.

At ten to eight Jim suddenly remembered the dismembered hand in the boot of the car, 'Audrey, I'm sorry but I've got to go to work now.'

'I thought you said that you had to start at eight thirty?'

'Yes I have but I've got to get there by half past and I've got to do a delivery first.'

'A delivery, that's all right I'll come with you.'

'I'd love for you to come with me Audrey, you know that, but the delivery is on the way to Rangeworthy, so I would have to double back to drop you off.' Jim could see that Audrey was a little disappointed, so he said. 'Maybe next time Audrey.'

He took her home and they parted with Audrey giving Jim a peck on the cheek and thanking him again for the watch.

Jim glanced down at his own watch, he didn't really have the time to deliver the hand, or think of anything to write on the box so he decided to come clean and tell Harry the truth. Jim timed it just right and pulled up at Harry's gate right on time, this time he noticed the gate was open and Tom was standing deep in the shadows with his shot gun nestling in the crook of his arm.

Harry was standing in the doorway of the house dressed in a tuxedo with his overcoat draped over his shoulders and he was puffing away on the customary huge cigar, 'Come in Jim, come in let's have a drink and you can tell me all about your day, any problems?

'A few Harry,' Jim went on to tell him all about the two men, and the goings on with Bert in the Sceptre.

'And you say Bert never said a word.'

'Not a word Harry.'

'He's a good man; I'll square him up when I see him.'

'Harry, I've still got the hand.'

'Christ, it'll stink the car out Jim, listen when you drop us off deliver it and then you can pick us back up at about eleven. Jim glanced at his watch, 'I see you've taken my advice and bought yourself a watch then Jim.'

More of an order than advice, thought Jim, 'Yes Harry,' he replied, Jim glanced at his watch again.

'No good you looking at that, she won't be ready yet, she'd be late for her own bloody funeral.' Harry started to giggle an infectious giggle, Jim couldn't help but join in and in a matter of seconds they were both laughing uncontrollably.

'Come on then Harry, share the joke,' Mrs James said haughtily, entering the room, completely ignoring Jim as if he didn't exist.

'Go and start the car Jim,' Harry said suppressing his laughter, 'we'll be there now, keys are in it.'

The journey into town passed in silence and because of the frosty atmosphere Jim was glad when he was on his way to deliver the hand. He stopped a few streets away from the club and sat pondering what to write on the box, and then it came to him. He wrote. "*We heard you were shorthanded so here's one for you.*" Chuckling away to himself Jim drove past the front of the club and along the road a short distance, he pulled the car over and chewed over his next move. Just across the road was a pub, he noticed a small boy in a pair of ragged shorts, sitting outside on the pub step. Jim got out of the car and steadily walked over to the boy, 'Hello, what are you doing sitting there?' he asked, crouching down beside him.

'I'm waiting for my mum and dad mister, they're in

the pub,' Jim could see by the lack of teeth that the boy was about seven years old.

'How would you like to earn a tanner?' Jim said, producing a sixpence from his pocket.

The boy's eyes lit up, but he said, 'A tanner, I'm not supposed to talk to strange men mister.'

'I'll tell you what,' said Jim, 'if I tell you my name, and you tell me yours then we won't be strangers will we?'

'I'm Jimmy,' the little boy said.

'What a coincidence,' said Jim, 'my name's Jimmy too.'

Jim extended his hand; the little boy pumped it up and down enthusiastically. Jim instructed the boy to take the box into the club, gave him the sixpence and sent him on his way. Jim sat back in the car, started the engine, and intently watched the rear view mirror. He saw the boy disappear into the club and about thirty seconds later reappear accompanied by a man, he watched as the boy pointed towards the Rolls Royce, Jim put the car in gear and quietly drove away.

Jim was back outside the restaurant well before eleven and between dozing and daydreaming he reflected on the events surrounding him since leaving the army. Jim's mind was in turmoil, he didn't like what he was doing or for that matter what he was turning into by what he was doing, but somehow there was some sort of a morbid fascination there, and of course he had never had so much money in his life, and most of what he did wasn't so bad, a few chickens, collecting rent that was due anyway. Then there was Audrey, he really liked Audrey and she was keen he could tell that, but somehow there was no spark and

Jim knew that there could never be, all a bit of a dilemma really. Jim's thoughts were interrupted by the car door opening, 'Evening Harry, evening Missus James, sorry Harry I was miles away.'

'Sit there Jim,' Harry said, 'don't get out, we can manage to shut the doors ourselves.' Jim noticed that once again Mrs James had totally ignored him; Harry reached over and held Jim firmly by the shoulder. 'Take the A38 son,' he said pointedly.

Jim felt the hair on the back of his neck bristle and a cold shiver go across his shoulders and down his back, he knew in an instant where he was going, his palms grew clammy. Could he be a party to watching a woman being murdered? Would he be expected to murder her? 'Nice meal Harry?' Jim felt he had to say something.

'Not bad son, not bad at all, the wine was rather, shall I say palatable, as was the brandy. Tell me have you made that delivery?'

'Yes I have, Harry.' Jim went on to tell Harry all about the small boy and the message he had wrote on the box. At this point Harry howled with laughter, Jim could tell by the way Harry was slurring, and laughing too long and too loud, that he had had far too much to drink, was the thought of the impending events getting to him as well?

The journey continued along the A38 until Mrs James looked out of the window and for the first time spoke to Jim, 'Where the hell do you think you're going dopey? This isn't the way home.'

Harry answered on Jim's behalf, 'Just a little surprise for you my dear, that's all.'

When they came to the turning for Aust, Jim took it

and waited to see if Harry had anything to say, he glanced in the mirror at Harry, Harry looked back at him, nodded and gave Jim a slow wink.

There was a car already parked on the slipway, and Jim could see lights shining within the ferryboat; looks like the reception committee is already here, Jim thought.

Harry was out of the car before Jim could move, he caught of Mrs James arm, 'Come on June,' he said and pulled her roughly from the car.

'What's going on Harry?' she asked angrily, 'what are we doing here? What are you playing at?'

'I told you dear, it's just a little surprise,' he said bundling her onto the ferry.

Jim followed the couple into the engine room; there was no chair in the middle of the room this time, only an old stained double mattress lying in the centre of the floor. Weasel, Ron and Anal Harris were standing along the far wall and Anal beckoned to Jim to join them.

'Right then June,' Harry said harshly, 'let's get straight on with it, you're going to give the boys a treat, undress yourself.'

'I'm not undressing in front of these morons, what d'you think I am? Have you gone completely mad Harry?' she said raising her voice.

'Probably,' Harry replied, 'now just get on with it.' June took one look at Harry's grim face and proceeded to strip down to her lacy underwear and faced Harry.

'Don't face me, face them,' she turned around as she was told. Weasel started to wolf whistle, but one look from Harry silenced him. 'Look Jim,' Harry pointed, 'she's managed to remember her drawers tonight. June take it all off.'

June sullenly took off the remainder of her undergarments, stood with her hands by her sides and then turned and defiantly stared at Harry.

'Ron,' Harry said, Ron stepped up to June, grabbed her by the hair, and forced her face down onto the mattress.

'Now Jim you're about to find out the other reason we call Anal, Anal.'

Anal produced a jar of Vaseline from his jacket pocket and proceeded to take off his belt.

Jim watched as Anal dropped his trousers and produced his already erect member, if Harry was waiting for screams of pain from June as Anal entered her, he was to be disappointed, she thrust her pelvis back hard against Anal and looking up she said, ' Look Harry, watch, this is how a real man does it.'

'Cunt' Harry hissed through his teeth. When Anal was sated, Harry looked at Weasel. 'Your turn.'

'Turn her over Ron,' Weasel said.

'No need,' June said, 'I can turn over myself,' she turned herself over and said. 'Come on then Weasel,' she spread her legs wide apart, 'I know you've always wanted to fuck me by all the dirty talk when Harry hasn't been around, let's see what you can do for me, more than that useless bastard, I'll bet. Did you know boys? He can't get it up.'

Jim was watching Harry, his arms were down by his sides and his fists were clenched tight; Jim could see that from the look on Harry's face things weren't going exactly to plan. When Weasel had finished Ron, not waiting for an invitation took his turn, 'Come on Ron give it to me, give it to me,' June cried out, Jim looked again at Harry, his expression hadn't changed.

Harry saw that Jim was looking at him, 'You're next Jim,' he said.

'I didn't want her yesterday Harry, and I certainly don't want her today.'

'Good boy Jim, I've seen enough of this crap, take me home.' Harry turned and walked quickly from the engine room, Jim followed on, quite relieved, he realised he didn't have the stomach for what was going on. As they walked away they could hear Mrs James calling, 'Come back Harry, don't you want to shag me as well?'

Harry climbed into the back of the Rolls Royce, Jim started the engine, put the car into gear and pulled away, looking into the rear view mirror he could see in the half-light the tears were streaming down Harry's face, ' Are you all right Harry?' Jim asked.

'Just drive the fucking car,' Harry replied.

CHAPTER SIX

Next morning Jim knew he had a lazy day coming and he was quite looking forward to it, but marring the day were the events of the night before. Desperately, unsuccessfully, he tried to block out the memories. The hand, the ferry, June, what had happened after?

'Everything alright, Jimmy?' Auntie Cath said.

'Yes, I'm a bit tired that's all, but I've got an easy day today, Auntie I've only got to take one of Harry's business associates into town so I'll see about the telephone later.'

'I hope you didn't keep Audrey out too late Jimmy.'

'No not too late Auntie.' Jim decided against telling his auntie about the watches he had bought, in case she asked awkward questions about from where the money had come.

'Well tell me then Jimmy when are the wedding bells going to ring?'

'Auntie I've only been out with her twice.'

'Your uncle proposed on our very first date,'

'Well I'm not Uncle Stan.'

'But do you think this is the one Jimmy?'

'Auntie please don't keep on to me, please.'

'But she's a nice girl isn't she Jimmy?'

'Yes she's a smashing girl, and I really like her Auntie, there, now are you satisfied?'

'I'll only be satisfied when you are walking up the aisle Jimmy.'

Jim left the house at ten; he was all on his own today,

Harry's boys were keeping their heads down. He drove out to the farm at Hambrook where he was waved through the farm gate; he didn't even have to open it himself. He pulled up in the farm yard and was surprised to see that the farmer and his men already waiting for him. The farmer came straight to the car, 'Stay in the car and we'll load you, then get out of here as quick as you can.' Jim was bemused as there didn't seem to be any rush the last time he had been here. Within two minutes he was heading back down the farm track, he pulled onto the main road and headed for the Charnbury. Just as Jim was thinking that there was no sign of the police he glanced in his mirror to see a police car emerging from a side turning, Jim didn't wait for the blue light and ringing bells he pulled straight over and turned off the engine.

The police car pulled in front and a lone policeman stepped out, Jim was relieved to see it was the young policeman he had met the last time. 'Hello mate,' he said with a broad cockney accent, and looking in the car he added. 'Let you out on your Jack Jones today then.'

'I could say the same about you.'

'Yes it's my first solo patrol today.'

'Mine too,' Jim said.

'What you got today then,' he hesitated, 'sorry I can't remember your name.'

'It's Jim, Jim Britton.'

The policeman put his hand out, 'I'm John Crewe.'

'Pleased to meet you John Crewe.'

'Me too, and plain John will do,' they shook hands and then the policeman, continued, 'Right then Jim what have we got today?'

110

'You know I haven't got a clue, I was in and out of that farm in about thirty seconds flat.'

The policeman smiled, 'That's the sergeant's early warning system in action.'

'How d'you mean?' Jim asked.

'Well when the Dees are on the prowl, the sergeant gives the farm a ring, so they never find anything.'

'What are the Dees?'

'It's not what it's who, they're detectives, anyway let's have a look.' Jim climbed out the car and opened the boot. Boxes upon boxes of eggs were stacked inside the car on the back seat and on the floor there were boxes of bacon.

'You know,' said John, 'I can't understand why you run around in a car when a van would be more convenient.'

'Harry says vans get pulled over by your lot but cars don't.'

John started to laugh, 'So what's happening now?'

'No I think Harry means by proper police.'

John continued to chuckle, 'Right then what goods do I take?'

'Take your pick John,' Jim replied.

'OK I'll have some have some of each, otherwise when I tell the sarge that there was bacon and eggs, if I take just eggs I'll be wrong or just bacon, I'll be wrong, you just can't win with him.'

'Don't you like him then?'

'Can't stand the sight of him, to be honest, I would have nicked you the first time we met, but he made it very clear that life for me would be so uncomfortable that I would be out of the force, and I always wanted to be a

111

copper and not a bent one at that.'

'Believe it or not,' said Jim, ' I'm not really a villain, it's just sort of happened and now I'm in so deep I can't get away, if I tried I'd be at the bottom of the Severn with the rest.'

'What you know of more than one?'

'More than one, I don't know how many, but if anybody gets in the way of Harry James, it's curtains for them.'

'Right then, I'd better put this lot in the car and get you on your way.' Together they carried the boxes to the police car between them. 'See you next time then Jim.'

'I was thinking, no forget it.'

'No go on, Jim what were you going to say?'

'Well I was thinking that perhaps we could have a drink sometime, but I don't suppose you are allowed to rub shoulders with the criminal classes are you?'

'I rub shoulders with the sergeant, don't I?' they both started laughing. 'Tell you what Jim I'll think about it OK, thanks for the offer, cheerio. Look after yourself Jim.'

'And you too, cheerio John.'

Jim to be on the safe side did exactly what Weasel had done the week before and stopped before he got to the Charnbury, he gave John a cheery wave and waited until he was out of sight before he drove off to the pub; Jim walked around to the kitchen door, and gave it a tap. One of the ladies he had seen the previous week opened the door, 'Hello again, delivery?'

'Yes that's right,' Jim replied.

'I'll fetch the boss for you; you can start bringing it in,

if you like, stack it all up in the corner by the window.' Jim went back to the car, gathered up some of the boxes and returned to the kitchen waiting to run the gauntlet of the cackling women, he tentatively pushed the kitchen door open and was surprised and relieved to find the room empty.

He had unloaded everything and was sitting back in the car before the boss appeared, it was the same bald headed man that Weasel had been talking to the week before. 'Hello young man all done?' he smiled and asked pleasantly.

'Yes thank you sir,' replied Jim.

'No need to sir me young man, the knighthood hasn't come through yet, you can call me Harold.'

'Pleased to meet you Harold,' Jim said, 'I'm Jim.'

'Sorry I was so long I've been on the blower trying to get hold of Harry to see how much I owe him, but I can't seem to get any answer.'

'Harry had a bit of a heavy night last night,' said Jim.

'Harry has a heavy night ever night, that's nothing new, would you like to come in for a drink?'

'Thank you, but no I've got to get into town,' Jim was surprised at how affable the man was, as his appearance suggested he would be quite standoffish and stern, books and their covers thought Jim.

'I wasn't really expecting you yet awhile,' Harold said, looking at his pocket watch.

'Well unlike Weasel I like to be on time and there was a problem at the farm, so I was loaded up and gone in a couple of minutes,' Jim said.

'Not the Dees again?'

113

'Yes they were expecting a visit.'

'Haven't they got anything better to do? They should be out chasing bank robbers, murderers, proper crooks and the like.'

Jim said goodbye and headed off to the post office to see about the telephone for his Auntie Cath, as he left the post office he heard Audrey's voice, 'Jim.'

'Hello Audrey, what a nice surprise, fancy seeing you, no work today?'

'I do get a lunch hour you know.'

Jim looked at his watch. 'God is that the time, I seem to have been in the post office for ever. Come on I'll buy you a nice cup of tea.'

In the café Jim could see that Audrey was upset, 'What's up Audrey?' he asked.

'Jim I'm in terrible trouble at home.'

'Why, whatever's the matter?'

'It's the watch you bought me Jim, I was so pleased with it and so proud to wear it, but it's dad, I went in and showed mum and then dad and he hit the roof, he asked me if I had had to lay on my back to get the watch, he said I hardly know you and he said that chauffeurs don't earn twenty pounds a week, oh, and then he said that you aren't a real man because you don't smoke, oh Jim, I'm so unhappy,' Audrey began to sob and then the tears started to stream down her face.

Jim reached across the table and held her hand, he reached into his pocket and pulled out his handkerchief, 'Here,' he said sympathetically, 'take this, and please don't cry.'

'I don't think you had better come round anymore Jim, I'm sorry,' Audrey sobbed, and dabbed at her eyes with Jim's handkerchief.

'I shall come round, what time does your father get home from work?'

'No Jim, please, promise you won't come round, you'll only make things worse for me.'

Jim had already made his mind up that he was going to sort things out one way or another, but he said, 'All right, I promise, I won't come to your house.'

Jim noticed that Auntie Cath accepted the eggs and the bacon without any comments and he could see that she was pleased to get them. Jim, still seething from what Audrey had said, told Auntie Cath what her father had thought, 'What a damn cheek,' Cath said, 'go round there Jimmy and sort him out.'

'I've promised Audrey, I won't go to their house.'

'That's all right Jimmy, because I just happen to know where Mister Amos works.'

'How d'you know that then Auntie?'

'I told you me and Audrey had had a good chat.'

'More like twenty questions on the wireless, if I know you.'

Auntie Cath smiled and went on, 'He works at Hawkins.'

'What the pottery?'

'That's right.'

'I'll pay Mister Amos a visit a bit later on.'

Auntie Cath reached into her pinnie pocket, 'Here,' she said, pulling out her Woodbines, 'we can't have

115

Audrey's dad saying you're not a man because you don't smoke.' Half an hour later, and a lot of coughing and spluttering Jim decided that he would go through the motions but smoking definitely wasn't for him.

Tea break seemed like a good time to Jim, so he got to the pottery at three o'clock, where the girl in the office pointed him in the general direction of the canteen. George Amos was sitting at the far end of the canteen and Jim could feel a sea of eyes staring at him as he threaded his way through the tables. He approached and very politely said, 'Can I see you outside for a moment, please Mister Amos?'

Without answering George Amos folded up the newspaper he was reading, placed it on the table and stood up, 'We can settle this right now,' he snarled.

'Have it your way Mister Amos,' Jim, unlike George Amos spoke calmly. 'Firstly Mister Amos I haven't as much as kissed your daughter, secondly,' Jim reached into his pocket and pulled out a packet of cigarettes and lit one up, hoping above hope he wouldn't start coughing, 'and thirdly,' Jim produced a roll of bank notes from his pocket and spread them all across the table. Jim could hear gasps from the other workers, George Amos without a word sat down; Jim started to gather up all the notes.

'All right son,' he said eventually, 'you've made your point, no hard feelings eh?' George Amos held out his hand.

'No, no hard feelings Mister Amos,' Jim said.

'You can come around whenever you want.'

Money talks, Jim thought.

Jim thanked him and hurried home to tell Auntie Cath, and as per usual she had more questions than Jim had answers. When Jim got to the part where he had put the money on the table, he realised that he should have left that bit out, 'So where did you get all that money from then Jimmy?' Auntie Cath asked.

'It was Harry's,' he lied, 'he lent it to me when I told him about Mister Amos.'

'When did you see him then Jimmy, you didn't leave here until nearly three?'

'He was stuck in Warmley at the level crossing in his car waiting for the train to go by and I spotted him.'

'Why was he driving himself, I thought that you were his chauffeur?'

'He's got more than one car Auntie, and I can't drive two at once, now can I?' Jim said, he looked at his aunt and he could see that the explanation seemed to convince Auntie Cath and so Jim carried on with his story.

'Good for you Jimmy,' she said when Jim had finished, 'are you going to see Audrey tonight?'

'No Auntie I've got to go to work, maybe I'll see her tomorrow, that's the only trouble with this job, you just can't plan ahead.'

'Yes but you are earning good money, aren't you?' Jim felt that Auntie Cath seemed to be changing her tune about him working for Harry James, if only she knew what I really do, he thought.

Nine o'clock found Jim in the Charnbury Arms, Harry and the boys were for once not standing at the bar, instead they were gathered around a table in the corner,

117

whispering together conspiratorially.

Jim noticed an addition to the usual crew. Jim walked over to the bar, but was stopped in his tracks by Harry who called across, 'Here Jim come and meet Darky Dillon, Darky runs the Charlton Club for me.'

Darky was dark all right, his skin was the same colour as a highly polished brown leather shoe, and when he spoke Jim was surprised to hear that he had a strong Bristolian twang, 'So you're Jim, heard some good things about you,' Darky stood up and shook hands.

'Right then Jim,' Harry said, 'here's a quid, get the drinks in and we'll have a pow wow.' When Jim returned to the table Harry continued, 'I think I've come up with a plan to see to Newman, now we all know that he goes cottaging and that's the only time when he's on his own, although his boys, mind you are never far away, so this is the plan.'

Before he had time to continue, Jim said, 'Sorry Harry, but what's cottaging?' The whole gang roared with laughter, Jim could feel his colours rising.

'I can't believe that you've just done your time in the mob and don't know what cottaging is, tell him Anal,' Harry said.

'Cottaging means hanging about men's toilets looking for sex.'

'Oh gosh!' Jim exclaimed.

'Now where was I?' said Harry. 'Ah yes, and that's where you come in Jim, you're going cottaging as well.... don't look so horrified, I'll explain, all these homos all use the same toilets all of the time, they do a tour, until they get lucky,'

118

'You seem to know an awful lot about it Harry,' Anal interjected, and they all laughed

'Cheeky bugger,' Harry retorted. 'Now we know Mark Newman likes younger men, so Jim's the best choice, the only choice looking at you lot of geriatric misfits,' Harry chuckled. 'This is the plan, it's simple, it only needs two of you, Anal you drive, we'll use my old van, you'll go to the bogs on Bedminster bridge and just wait, you'll need a sign made up that says, "Toilet closed for repair," when Newman turns up, Jim you follow him inside, hang the sign on the iron grill and pull it shut behind you, then all you've got to do is shoot the bastard, cut his cock off, empty his pockets and get the hell out of there, simple.'

'You're a genius Harry,' said Weasel approvingly.

Harry just smiled, 'Any questions Jim?'

'Well it all seems a bit elaborate to me Harry, why don't we just shoot him from the car?'

'Because I told you his boys are never far away, and if they are watching all they'll see is one of his kind going in the gents, and also you can't cut his cock off sat in a car.'

'Why do you want his cock Harry?' And when are we going to do this?' Jim asked.

'I want his cock so that we can let them have it back, but we won't do it for a few days, we've got to get the toilets watched to see what sort of time he gets there, and anyway I've got other things for you to do.'

Business concluded Jim found himself sitting chatting to Anal, the others choosing to play a game of bagatelle 'So tell me Anal what happened on the ferry after I left? To be honest, between us I was glad to leave, I don't think I could have done it, I just didn't have the stomach for it.' Jim said.

'After you went Jim,' Anal said, ' it seemed that June wanted more and more sex, but I knew it was just her way of staying alive a bit longer, she knew the writing was on the wall, we had our orders and she knew it. Weasel was chomping at the bit to stripe her, and the poor cow was terrified and had had enough. I felt sorry for her, so I got up behind her, she must have thought I was going to give her one again, but I shot her straight through the back off the head, she never felt a thing.

'Then Weasel started shouting and bawling, "I wanted to stripe her," I told him, go on then, stripe her and he said, "it's not the same now she's dead, you wait till Harry hears about this." I said to him, you say anything to Harry about any of this and you'll have me to answer to and Ron said the same, then Ron caught hold of Weasel and gave him a good scragging; Weasel shit himself. So eventually when we saw Harry, Weasel went into all sorts of details about how he'd cut her up good and proper, and how she was screaming and struggling, to be honest Weasel overdone it a bit, mind you I know very well that he's shit scared of Ron.

'By the time we'd finished with her it was well gone three in the morning, it was freezing bloody cold and the concrete wouldn't go off, and by seven o'clock it was just as sloppy as when we put it in.'

'So what did you do Anal?' Jim asked.

'To be honest we didn't know what to do, we knew if we put her in the drink she'd float up and Harry would be none too pleased when she turned up again. Weasel just kept on moaning and groaning about the cold and wanted to go home, Ron just sat there staring into space, and I kept checking the concrete. Then about half past seven, a quarter to eight, it was just getting light, we heard a car coming, we thought it was old Jack Hemmings, he's the bloke who runs the ferry, then, this geezer walks in and it isn't him, and there's Harry's Missus stark bollock naked wearing concrete Wellington boots.'

'What a nightmare, I'm glad I wasn't there.'

'Nightmare's the word. Well to cut a long story short we ended up with two stiffs, not enough concrete for both of them and what we got won't go off, we're all freezing cold, we've got fuck all to drink between us, no fags and a bloody car to get rid of, it was all turning into a sodding fiasco.

'Then we heard another car pull up, this time it was Jack, moaning because his mate hadn't showed up for work, so we told him the score and he decided to take the ferry out into the middle of the river, Ron and Weasel went off to get rid of the bloke's car and get some more cement and stuff, and I sat in the ticket collector's office telling the punters that there would be no sailings as the ferry was broken down. Well Ron and Anal didn't get back until gone eleven, which started a row because we'd all been up all night and we were all tired and I hadn't had a smoke or a drink, I couldn't even scrounge a snout from the miserable bastards who were trying to get on the ferry. Anyway, Jack brought the ferry in, we put the cement on board and good old Jack said he would do the business, Ron bunged him a oner and we all went home.'

'Why didn't you put the car on the ferry and chuck it overboard?'

121

'Fuck me Jim, we never thought of that.

'Well I'm glad anyway that I wasn't there Anal.'

'No it wasn't the best night I've ever had, I can tell you.'

Jim looked at his watch, 'No, it's midnight it can't be,' he said.

'Oh it is all right Jim; Harold doesn't go much on the licensing laws.'

'Thanks for the chat Anal.'

'You're not going are you Jim?'

'No I want to have a word with Harry.'

Harry was sat talking quietly to Harold, 'Come on Jim sit yourself down it's nothing private.'

'I was rather hoping to have a chat Harry.'

Harold stood up, 'I'll go,' he said.

'No it's alright; in fact you might be able to help to advise me.'

Harold sat back down, 'What's the problem Jim?' Harry asked.

'Well as you know I've never had so much money in all my life.'

'And that's a problem,' both Harry and Harold began to chuckle.

'No it's what to do with it; I'm worried in case my aunt finds it.'

'You could always back horses,' Harold said with a smile.

'The boy's got more sense than that; remember the old saying, the day you see a bookmaker riding a push bike, start having a flutter,' said Harry.

'Very true,' Harold replied.

'Here Ron, come on over here a minute,' said Harry, 'tell young Jim what to do with all his new found wealth.'

'You're only asking me Harry because you know I take it all to the bookies; I heard what you were saying. Television, that's where to put your money Jim, anything to do with television, anything at all.'

'Bugger off Ron,' Harry said, 'you think people are going to sit at home in the dark and look at a square box sitting in the corner of the living room, when they can go up the pub, whatever is wrong with you Ron?

'Take no notice of him Jim, there's no future in television, no future at all, you can take that from me. There's a few things you can do with it,' Harry went on, ' for a start off, buy up some bomb sites that nobody wants, and as things get back to normal, all of a sudden you'll find that the value will go up and you can sell them on. Or the Workers Travel Association, they're taking holiday makers abroad now; you could invest some money in land for building abroad.'

'Don't listen to a word he says Jim, he's just as bad as Ron,' said Harold, 'I can tell you for sure, there is no future in bricks and mortar, none at all, especially in some fuck all shite country abroad. Look at all the houses Harry owns, nothing but trouble, always something needing doing and they're not worth any more now than when he bought them. Forget all that I've got a lot better way of making a few bob.'

'What's that then Harold?' Jim asked.

'Drugs my son, that's where the future lies. '

'What you mean open a chemist shop?'

Harry and Harold collapsed with laughter, Harry shouted over to Anal what had been said and the rest of the company and very soon the whole pub was filled with laughter.

'I don't understand,' said Jim, going red.

'I'm glad you don't,' said Harry. 'Now tip up son the night is young, and after all the criminal fraternity doesn't have to get up in the morning.'

The criminal fraternity, Jim thought, I'm one of the criminal fraternity. Jim couldn't remember leaving the pub, he couldn't remember getting home, but next day he found the car parked with three of its wheels on the pavement, he could vaguely remember Harry telling him to go to around to the Charnbury but he couldn't remember what time he had said, but he remembered that Harry wanted him to take him to see Red Ruth as one of the girls was playing up. He could vaguely remember everyone laughing at him, but he couldn't remember why. Jim took a chance and got to the pub at noon, Harry was already standing at the bar; Jim looked at Harry's face to see if he was in trouble.

'Here he is then,' Harry said, all smiles, 'smack on time as usual, how's your head this morning?'

'I'm a bit fragile to be honest Harry.'

'Here you are son, hair of the dog,' Harry had already ordered a large scotch and it was sitting on the bar waiting for Jim.

Jim picked it up, 'Cheers Harry,' he said and as he took a cautious sip he shuddered.

'Christ you are under the weather son, we'll soon cure

that.' He called over the bar to the barmaid. ' Give me a tomato juice please, with Worcestershire sauce, some pepper and three dashes of angostura bitters, get it down in one go Jim, it'll settle your stomach.'

Twenty minutes and another two scotches later Jim felt almost human. He was about to ask Harry what time he had to see Red Ruth when Harold appeared from the back room, 'Blower for you Harry, morning Jim.'

'Morning Harold.'

Harry went through the bar trap and into Harold's back room, within thirty seconds he was back, with a face like thunder, 'Tip up Jim, sorry Harold got to go, problems.'

'What's up Harry?' Harold asked.

'They've petrol bombed The Charlton, I'll tell you, if it's a fucking war they want they can have a fucking war.' Jim drove Harry to Lawrence Hill and as they came towards the railway bridges they could see a pall of black acrid smoke curling its way into the hazy blue sky in the distance.

As they approached Jim could see three fire engines and a couple of police cars. Jim parked up a little way away and sat inside the car watching, 'We'll stay here Jim, I don't want to see no coppers, and the Newmans might be around waiting to take pot shots.'

Jim could see that Darky Dillon was talking to one of the policemen, he looked at the front of the club, 'Bit of a mess isn't it Harry?'

'Yes son, Exodus twenty one, twenty three, and twenty four, an eye for a fucking eye. I've seen enough, Red Ruth'll have to wait, take me to Marshfield; we'll go and see the peter man.'

Jim was mystified, a peter man? But he could see Harry was in no mood for explanations. Jim had never been to Marshfield, but he more or less knew the way, Harry stayed silent throughout the whole three quarters of an hour journey, it was only when they arrived at the sign that read, "Marshfield" that he eventually spoke, 'Sorry I've been quiet Jim, I've been hatching a plan.'

'That's alright Harry.'

'If you just drive along the road quietly, I think I know which house is his.'

'What if he's not at home?'

'He's always home, well except in the dead of night, that is,' Harry gave a little chuckle.

Jim felt more disposed to asking Harry questions now, 'What's a peter man then Harry?'

'That's why he goes out at night; he blows safes, that's what a peter man does.'

'And what's the plan?'

'Pull over here I'll tell you later,' Jim pulled in and Harry went to the front door of   pretty little stone terraced cottage, with ivy around the front door, he knocked the knocker and disappeared inside. Jim was left with his thoughts. After ten minutes Harry emerged all smiles,' 'Look Jim you'll be back here tonight, clock which house it is.'

Heading back, Harry started to unfold his plan, 'I want you to pick up Ron at seven, come up here, and pick up the peter man, his name's Eric by the way, then you'll go straight to Wick quarry, there's only an old man there for a night watchman, Ron will take care of him, and Ron does a good Irish accent.'

'What does an Irish accent have to do with it Harry?'

'We're going to nick some explosives from the quarry and the IRA will get the blame, so the rozzers won't come looking in our direction, then go and pick up Weasel and Anal, we'll hit their club early tonight, they won't expect anything to happen so soon, they made a bit of a dent in the Charlton, Eric says all they will have left is a hole in the fucking ground.' Harry started to laugh. The laugh of a maniac, Jim thought.

With his usual punctuality Jim picked up Ron and was back in Marshfield at seven thirty, to pick up Eric. He sported white thinning straggly hair and wore wire framed thick pebbled glasses, perched right on the end of his long thin nose, he stood over six feet tall and weighed only about nine stones. Jim thought he looked like a retired postman, 'I know what you're thinking son,' he said, 'I'm seventy one next birthday and I'm still the best, that's why Harry uses me, and look I've still got all my fingers,' Ron chuckled away, he obviously knew Eric quite well and they started to natter away all the way to the quarry.

The night watchman at the quarry was a push over and looked even older than Eric, and Jim had to admit that Ron sounded every inch an Irishman. Jim was quite surprised that Ron asked the old boy, after he had tied him up to say if the rope was too tight and left him with a cigarette.

'That was nice of you back there Ron,' Jim said.

'How d'you mean?'

'Well giving him a fag and making sure he was

comfortable.'

'What d'you think I am Jim, I'll let you into a secret, if the old bugger had started to shout I wouldn't have had the heart to harm him,' he said.

As they drove through Bridgeyate towards Bristol, about two miles from the quarry, two police cars came towards them, bells ringing and lights flashing, 'Too late scuffers!' Ron laughed.

Jim picked up Anal and as usual they had to wait for Weasel. 'You're always late Weasel,' said Anal, when he eventually arrived.

'Yes and judging by the smell in here you're always shitting yourself.'

'One day Weasel, one day.'

'Have we got a plan?' Ron remarked to nobody in particular.

'No I suppose we'll just have to suss it out when we get there,' said Anal.

'At least it's nice and early, the club won't even be open yet,' said Ron.

'If we sit around and see how many turn up to open up, perhaps we could go in mob handed,' said Weasel.

'Let's just wait and see,' said Anal. Jim pulled up almost in the same place that he had the last time he had visited the club, looking in the mirror he didn't notice the same small boy that he had sent on the errand approach the car. "Bang bang" on the window went the boy's fist, Jim preoccupied, jumped off the seat, 'Jesus, that scared me to death,' he said and he wound down the window.

'Hello mister,' the boy grinned, 'got any errands for me tonight?'

128

'No not tonight Jimmy,' Jim replied. The little boy wandered off, hands thrust deep in his trouser pockets and sat down on the step outside the pub.

'What's that all about then Jim?' Anal asked. Jim told him about the shoe box, and Anal said. 'He might come in useful later on.'

'You can't expect a kid to plant a bomb Anal,' Jim said.

'It's perfectly safe it can't go off accidentally,' said Eric, 'I've nearly got it ready I'll put a two minute timer on it, that should be plenty of time.'

'Something's happening,' said Jim looking in his rear view mirror, 'there's one, hang on, I see three, no four, no another car's pulled up,' Jim paused, 'there's nine of them altogether.'

'That's suicide then,' said Weasel, 'send the kid in Jim.'

'Are you sure it's safe?' asked Jim, 'he's only just a kid.'

'I told you there's a two minute timer, nothing can go wrong, nothing, there it's ready,' said Eric.

'Jim give that kid a shout,' said Anal.

Jim called the boy over and gave him a shilling, 'Here take this box into the club where you went before and give it to the man at the desk inside.'

'A *shilling* mister,' the little boy couldn't believe his eyes; he took the box and skipped off down the road towards the club. Jim looked at the second hand on his watch.

'Plenty of time Jim, he's got plenty of time, don't worry,' said Anal. Jim looked at his watch a full minute had elapsed and there was no sign of the boy, Jim kept his eyes

129

on the rear view mirror, another thirty seconds, and still no sign.

Jim threw the car door open. 'Christ Jim, what are you doing?' Ron asked.

'I can't leave the kid,' Jim started to run down the road, the others all clambered out of the car and stood watching. Jim got to within twenty yards of the club when, the small boy, alone, emerged from the club doorway. '*Run*,' shouted Jim at the top of his voice, the boy broke into a trot, 'Run damn it, run.' The boy ran up to Jim, Jim scooped him up into his arms and ran hell for leather towards the car, Jim felt the blast before he heard the noise, it knocked him off his feet, still clutching the boy he scrambled up and ran back to the car. 'Why were you so long in the c lub?' he panted.

'There wasn't anybody at the desk Mister, so in the end I just left it.'

Jim fished in his pocket, 'Here,' and he thrust all his change into the boy's hand.

'Golly mister, thank you.'

'Do me a favour Weasel you drive,' said Jim, 'I'm all of a shake.'

'Sure thing Jim, anything's better than sitting in the back with stink ass.' They all scrambled into the car and Weasel quickly pulled away.

'Jesus Christ, how much explosive was in that bomb Eric? Half the bloody building's gone,' Anal said, looking out through the back window.

'I thought Harry would want the job done right, and I did tell him that all that would be left would be a hole in the ground,' Eric replied.

130

'Are you coming back to the Charnbury for one, Eric?'

'No I'll get young Jim to run me home if it's all the same to you, I can't be too long, the dog's got to have his walk and the cat's got to be fed.'

'What a nice man you are Eric, just killed nine men, and now sat there talking about walking the dog and feeding the bloody cat,' said Ron, 'you don't give a monkeys do you?'

'Yes that's me Ron, all heart, and as a matter of fact, I don't give two monkeys as it happens.'

'You seem to know Ron quite well,' said Jim to Eric after the others had been dropped off.

'Yes our paths have crossed a few times, mainly business mind. I first met Ron through Taff Davies, did you know him Jim?'

'No can't say as I know the name.'

'Well Taff came to Bristol during the depression looking for work like so many from South Wales. He was a dapper little man, always well turned out, always a trilby never a cap, everything about him was small, except one thing that is, so they say. The ladies used to love him dearly, I think they thought they could mother him, I don't think he even stood five feet tall. Men couldn't stand him, I hated the sight of him myself, and I didn't even really know him.

'He used to come in the pub; it was before I moved out to Marshfield, always seemed to have plenty of money and a different woman on his arm, and always a smart woman at that. Then one night just before

131

Christmas it was, he walks in the boozer with this big ugly piece. When I say big and ugly, I'm not exaggerating, no one could believe it, she towered over him, and she must have been twenty odd stone. He brought her in the pub for about two weeks, then one night he walks in through the door with her on his arm and somebody shouted out, "Here comes Taff with his shaving brush." Well she turns round, clocks Taff one straight in the face and knocks him right off his feet, then she burst into tears and ran out the pub. No one ever saw her again. A few days later he's back in the pub, only this time he's got a pretty little thing in tow.

'Then after about three months he comes in the boozer one night on his own and makes a beeline for me, he tells me he's setting up a job and was I interested. I couldn't believe he knew what I did, I mean it's not the sort of thing you broadcast, is it? Well I certainly didn't. Anyway it turns out the big piece he was going out with worked in the wages department of Douglas the motor bike makers and he only took her out to get the low-down on the set up at the firm.'

'So what was all that with the shaving brush about?' Jim asked.

'Well it seems that when they were at it, she used to rub his old man all round her chops like a shaving brush and he got somebody in the pub to shout it out, knowing what would happen.'

'The crafty devil.'

'Yes, anyway the plan was that Taff and another, it turned out to be Ron, would get into the offices, pinch the safe, it wasn't bolted down and stood about two foot high, pick me up and we'd go somewhere quiet and open it up. Taff said there'd be about twelve grand in the safe providing we did it on a Thursday, pay day being Friday. Big firm Douglas, lots of workers.

'I was all for it, a nice little retirement fund, I didn't have to even break in myself and all I had to do was what I was best at. The only problem as far as I could tell was that it was too near home, so I suggested that we took the peter a long way away and when they found it they would think it was a gang from out of town had done the business.

'First time I clapped my eyes on Ron was the night of the robbery, Thursday 14th April it was, 1938. We hit it off straight away, I told him what I thought about opening the safe a long way away and he agreed with me. Ron and Taff did the robbery, no trouble at all; the offices were a long way from the works and the night watchman only visited the offices once a night and as the safe was under the stairs he wouldn't even realise it was gone. Everything went smoothly and I got picked up about a half mile along the road. Ron was sweating like a pig; I'll always remember he greeted me with, "Fuck the heavy safes." We drove all the way to Minchinhampton Common near Stroud, and then with a pair of sack trucks we started out with the peter across the golf course. It was a full moon that night but there had been some rain and the going was hard. I tried to help Ron as much as I could but Taff didn't put much into it.

'It was nearly five in the morning by the time we decided we were far enough away from the road. We got the safe down in the bottom of a bunker and piled sand

133

all around it, by this time Ron and me were all in, I can tell you. Then I did my stuff. Say it myself it was the tidiest job I ever did, blew the door off clean as a whistle and we all rushed forward to see through the smoke.

'It was empty, not a sausage, nothing, we'd struggled our guts out for absolutely nothing. Ron and I both stared at Taff, and then he started to chuckle, then he laughed out loud. Ron asked him what was so funny, Taff said, "And what day is it today? I'll tell you what day it is, it's Good fucking Friday and we're a day late." Ron asked him whose fault that was and he carried on laughing. He should have shut up, there and then, that was his best bet. Ron looked evil, he strangled him with one hand, just one hand, I couldn't stop him, not that I tried.

'Ron said to blow him up, so that it would look like the safe cracker had come a cropper, so we stuffed a stick of dynamite in his mouth and left; the newspapers were full of it. The best of it was when we got back almost home Ron started pissing himself laughing, what's up I asked him, "Shame about Taff," he said, "I can see the funny side of it myself now."'

Jim dropped Eric off then made his way back to the Charnbury, a large scotch was already waiting on the bar, 'Come on Jim, said Harry, 'I hear you're something of a hero.'

'Bloody foolhardy, if you ask me,' said Weasel.

'But then nobody's asked you Weasel,' said Anal.

'Come on boys, no bickering, tonight we celebrate,'

said Harry. 'Raise your glasses and let us drink to our continued success and the downfall of the Newmans.'

The evening wore on and turned into night, Harry by now well-oiled put his arm around Jim's shoulder, 'Jim, back to business, rent collecting tomorrow, you pick Weasel up just for tomorrow, and then next week you'll be on your own, alright?'

'Yes that's fine Harry but tell Weasel if he's late tomorrow, he'll get left behind.'

'Well you can tell him that yourself, come on over here Weasel,' Harry said smiling.

'Why what's up Harry?'

'Jim was just saying, if you're late in the morning he'll leave you behind, isn't that so Jim?' Jim nodded his head in agreement; Weasel made no answer and made towards the bar. 'Hit a raw spot there Jim.'

'I can't stand unpunctuality Harry; I'd rather be half an hour early than one minute late.'

'Hear what Jim's saying Weasel,' said Harry, 'I'd be on time if I were you.'

And for the second night in succession Jim couldn't remember getting home.

CHAPTER SEVEN

Next morning Jim couldn't believe his eyes, Weasel was leaning on the front wall of his house reading the Daily Mirror when Jim pulled up, 'Morning Weasel,' said Jim, 'bright and early this morning then.'

'Don't think I dragged myself out of bed because of you Jim, you're fuck all, Harry read the riot act to me last night, that's all.'

'I didn't want to drop you in it Weasel, but work's work and play's play.'

Weasel folded his paper; put it in his pocket and shook his head, 'You're beginning to sound just like Harry.'

Jim had forgotten all about the shilling that the old boy had owed in rent from the week before and putting on his tough act for Weasel's benefit, he hammered on the front door and bellowed out, ' Rent.'

The old boy opened the door, 'Thanks for that last week,' he said, he thrust a pile of change into Jim's hand, 'it's all there son, it's not a penny short,' Jim turned and walked back to the car, he jumped in and gave Weasel the handful of change.

'There's a shilling too much here Jim.'

'He must have made a mistake,' Jim said.

Weasel stared at Jim, 'No Jim, I think that you're the one that's made a mistake.'

Jim could feel himself going red; Weasel was obviously a lot smarter than Jim had thought.

When they finally got to Passmore's house Weasel slipped his hand into his jacket pocket, 'Here take this,' he said.

'A gun,' Jim looked surprised, 'Passmore won't be any trouble after last week.'

'Take the shooter Jim, and stand well back from the front door when you knock, and keep the gun up. I'm telling you.' Jim walked up to Passmore's front door and gave the door knocker a hefty bang, Passmore was just behind the door and it opened almost immediately, Jim was glad that he had taken Weasel's advice, Passmore was brandishing a curved machete about eighteen inches long, Jim raised his arm and aimed the gun straight between Passmore's eyes, Passmore stopped in his tracks, and sunk to his knees, Weasel called out from the car, 'You just don't learn, do you? You stupid prick.'

The machete dropped to the floor with a clatter, Weasel was out of the car like a long dog, 'You'd better have another taste of Mister Sharp and Missus Sharper,' he said. From his waistcoat pockets he produced the mother of pearl handled cut throat razors.

'No Weasel,' said Jim, 'leave it.' Weasel looked at Jim and he knew that he meant it.

'Come on Jim, for Christ's sake, just one small stripe.'

'I said leave it. Jesus Weasel, just look at the state of his face from last week. Listen Passmore, any more trouble from you and you're history okay? Now give me the rent.'

Passmore still on his knees nodded his head.

'Come on Weasel you can buy me a drink.'

By two thirty Jim was in a sorry state and Weasel wasn't much better, the landlord of the Charnbury, although having scant regard for the licensing laws didn't extend his hospitality to afternoons, so Weasel and Jim found themselves standing on the pavement deliberating their next move.

'Miserable old bugger, I wanted another drink,' Jim said.

'He's always been the same, half past two and that's it, I expect he's already gone to sleep by now, that's why he's open all night, he's always sleeps every afternoon.'

'I need another drink,' said Jim.

'Me too,' said Weasel, 'I know where to go, there's a place up near the Suspension Bridge, I'll drive.' Weasel drove right to the very top of Blackboy Hill and parked up, 'Come on Jim, over here.' Weasel led the way to what appeared to be a boarded up shop, but closer examination showed that there was a door at the end of the shop window with a bell beside it. Weasel rang the bell and within two minutes Jim and Weasel were whiling away the afternoon inside.

By five o'clock Jim and Weasel, through a drunken haze were eating their way through spaghetti bolognaise in a little restaurant half way up Park Street, and by six they were sat in a corner of a bar just a little bit farther down the road, drinking yet more whisky, 'I think I'll finish this,' said Jim, 'and pay Audrey a visit, I'll take a cab, I'll see you later.'

'Don't forget to be in the Charnbury for nine Jim, pay night.'

Jim nodded, downed his drink, and lurched drunkenly out into the cold frosty evening air; perhaps it's not such a good idea to let her parents see me like this after all, he thought, maybe I'll just go home, Auntie Cath won't be any too pleased either, what to do? Jim walked to the taxi stand, he went to the first taxi on the rank, 'How much would you earn between now and nine o'clock?' he asked the driver.

'Difficult to say,' he replied.

'A quid?'

'No, nothing like.'

'Well if I give you a quid, will you let me kip in the back of your cab and you drop me at the Charnbury Arms at nine, will you do that?'

The cabbie scratched his head, 'Money up front and if you're sick it'll cost you a fiver.'

'Done,' said Jim, and a minute later he was fast asleep.

'Come on mate wake up, we're here.'

Jim stirred; his mouth was as dry as a bone and his bladder quite full, 'Thanks driver,' he mumbled, through parched lips.

Inside the pub Harry was propping up the bar and holding court, Weasel and Anal were there but of Ron there was no sign, 'Come on Jim, it's on the bar waiting for you.' Jim downed the scotch in one and immediately pushed the glass back across the bar for a refill. 'Weasel tells me you two had quite a session today Jim.'

'Yes, what I can remember of it.'

'Here you go son,' Harry handed Jim twenty pounds; 'you'll be getting a bigger pay day in a few days time.'

'Thanks, Harry, but what's on then?'

'In the next few days Jim, you will be seeing to the brown hatter and I know he's always loaded, he's a flash git who's always pulling out a roll of notes.' Bit like yourself, thought Jim.

'Come over here Jim, and we'll sit down and discuss the plan.'

'Where's Ron tonight, Harry?'

'He's south of the river seeing Sid Morgan, he works for the Newmans but he spies for us.'

'Yes,' said Weasel, 'and bloody expensive he is too.'

'Nothing to do with you Weasel, nothing whatsoever Weasel, keep your trap shut,' Harry said, 'he's worth every penny; you wouldn't be sat there now if it wasn't for Sid.'

'Why what happened,' Jim asked.

'The last time we had a little spat with the Newmans, Weasel here was going to be topped, Sid tipped me off, it was all arranged and they were waiting, just two of them, at The Crown knowing that Weasel would show up.'

'So what happened?'

'The bastard let me show up, that's what happened,' said Weasel.

Harry and Anal roared with laughter, 'I couldn't let Weasel know, now could I? He would have given the game away.'

'I might have been shot.'

'Bollocks, even the Newmans aren't stupid enough to pull guns out in a pub.'

'So what happened then Harry?'

'Weasel went to the bar of the Crown and bought a drink; the two of them walked in, came up and got each

140

side of Weasel, turned him around and one on each arm frog marched him out of the pub, his feet were hardly touching the ground,' Harry started to laugh again. 'You should have seen his face, we were watching him through the pub window, it was a bloody picture, and Weasel was shitting himself.'

'So would you have been Harry,' said Weasel irritably.

Harry carried on chortling away, 'Anyway as they came out of the pub doorway they had a nice surprise, Ron's stood there right in front of them with a sten gun. One of them said Ron wouldn't shoot as he might hit Weasel, they don't call him Mad Ron for nothing do they Weasel?'

'The bastard just let rip,' Weasel said, 'I couldn't believe it, there were bloody bullets going just about every bleedin' where.'

'I love that story Harry,' Anal put in, 'Mad Ron certainly lived up to his name that night,'

'Talk of the devil, here he comes now,' said Harry. 'Anyway the one who said that Ron wouldn't shoot was still standing and the other, well he was full of holes. We bundled the live one into the car and you definitely had a good night that night, didn't you Weasel? Just telling Jim here Ron, about the night when poor old Weasel got himself kidnapped.'

Ron pulled up a chair and eased his huge frame on to it, 'Weasel was lucky that night,' Ron said, 'I'd never used a sten before, they're a bit erratic. D'you know, I was reading somewhere that sten guns were called stens because the two people who designed them were Sheffield and Turpin and- '

141

'Shut up Ron you're full of bullshit, now down to business,' Harry said. 'Come on then Ron, what have you found out?'

'Well boss I've had a drink with Sid and I bunged him a drink. He's had his nephew keep an eye on Mark Newman; he goes to the same places nearly every day and more or less at the same time, creature of habit. His boys are never far away, and although they're not supposed to know what he gets up to, it's pretty much common knowledge. He usually gets to the gents on Bedminster bridge about half twelve, but if he's had success elsewhere he won't show up.'

'Who's this Cess he's been sucking then Ron?' Anal asked.

'What you on about Anal?'

'Never mind him Ron, get on with it,' Harry said.

'That's about it, oh, and there are always at least four of his boys in the car and it's an old pre-war Hudson, a left hooker.'

'What colour Ron?' Harry asked.

'Maroon,' he replied.

'Right then this is what you are to do,' said Harry. 'Take the old Ford van Jim, you might have to go there for a couple of days on the trot before he shows up, and listen if you see any sign of the maroon Hudson get out of there and we'll have to think of something else, but if he does show up you know what to do.'

'Why can't we just put the snatch on him Harry?' Weasel asked.

'I can read you like a book Weasel, that's because you want to stripe him, no it's too risky, it's risky anyway,

Weasel make sure you let Jim have your chiv, to cut his dick off, and make sure you're both well tooled up. Go on Monday morning, it will be too busy tomorrow, and on Sunday all you lot are coming to chapel.'

'Chapel!' exclaimed Ron and Weasel simultaneously.

'All of us, Harry,' said Anal gloomily.

'Yes all of you.'

'Turn it in Harry,' said Ron, 'the last time I was in a chapel was when I was a kid at Sunday school, before the war.'

'Yeah come on Harry, play the white man, I like a kip on Sunday afternoons, you know that,' Anal said.

'Jesus Christ, I'm surrounded by fucking heathens, it's time you lot saw the bleeding light, chapel it is on Sunday, and no fucking arguments.'

Jim woke up on Saturday morning feeling a little delicate but not too bad considering his intake the night before. He swung his long legs out of the bed and reached over to his coat which was neatly hanging over a chair, in the inside pocket was a half-bottle of scotch, just a little livener, he thought. He shuddered as the whisky slid down his dry throat; Jim rubbed his eyes and gradually focused them on his watch, ten to ten, he took another gulp and replaced the bottle top, five minutes later he was sitting in the kitchen drinking tea.

'Are you seeing Audrey today Jimmy?' Auntie Cath asked.

'No but I'm taking her to chapel tomorrow, Auntie,' Jim replied.

143

'Oh that's nice, how lovely, what a good boy you are Jim, tell me, have you popped the question yet?'

'Auntie I haven't even seen her.' Jim sounded exasperated.

'But you're going to aren't you?'

'Maybe.'

'I knew it I just knew it.'

'Oh Auntie!'

On Sunday, Jim arrived at Audrey's at two and he could tell her parents were delighted when he told them he was taking Audrey to chapel, Audrey he suspected was not so impressed.

When he sat her in the car he said, 'Audrey I don't think chapel is much of a date, but the truth is, the boss has decided that it's chapel and that's it.'

'Do you do everything he says Jim?' Audrey sounded a little peeved, 'I don't work for Harry James, please remember that.'

'Listen Audrey for the money he pays I'd jump through a flaming hoop if he said so.'

'Yes Jim, you might, but I don't have to.'

A motley crew was the way it looked to Jim as he surveyed the others in chapel, there were a couple of faces standing next to Mad Ron that he didn't recognise, but one look told him that they had been tarred with the same brush. The other chapel goers, he could see by the pointing and whispering didn't at all feel at ease in the presence of Harry's men. Harry on the other hand seemed non-plussed by the whole thing and oblivious to the whispering and pointing and he sang along heartily and loudly, if out of tune to all of the hymns. Now and again he would pointedly look around and check to see if all his men were singing and if not, raise his eyebrows at the offender. Jim felt increasingly embarrassed and totally out of place. Amazement filled him and he was taken aback when Harry stood up and with great sincerity and aplomb read the parable of the Good Samaritan. Jim's discomfort continued until at last, he was relieved to hear the final blessing, glancing sideways at Audrey he had the notion that she was of the same mind.

'Well that's your souls taken care of,' Harry said as they left the chapel, 'now let's get to the pub.'

'They won't be open yet Harry,' Jim ventured.

'They open for Harry James,' Harry replied with a smirk.

Sure enough one tap on the door of Harry's local in Rangeworthy, and the Rose and Crown was open for business.

Harry went straight to the bar and bought drinks for everybody, Jim noticed that the two strange faces he spotted in chapel didn't join the others, but chose to sit at the other end of the bar, he quietly asked Anal who they were, Anal surprised Jim by saying he'd never saw them before and Harry wasn't saying anything about them, other than they were acquaintances.

Harry beckoned to Audrey, 'Come and sit here by me Audrey,' Harry said and patted the seat beside him, 'and let's hear all about you, when can we expect for you and Jim to tie the knot then? When are you going to make an honest woman of her Jim?'

Audrey answered on Jim's behalf, 'I hardly know him Mister James.'

'Mister James, Mister James, call me Harry, what's to know about Jim, just look at him he's a fine catch, he's got a good job with me, our Jim here, he's going places, time you had a wedding ring on your finger.' He grabbed and lifted her hand. Audrey started to colour up.

'Leave her alone Harry can't you see you're embarrassing the girl,' Anal intervened.

'Nonsense, I want to see if her intentions are strictly honourable towards our Jim,' Harry said laughing.

'Yes I can assure you they are, Mister James,' Audrey said going even redder.

'Harry, I told you, call me Harry, you're going to have to fatten this one up Jim, if you know what I mean,' Harry gestured towards Audrey's stomach.

Jim could see Harry was in his element, suddenly crystal clearly, the realisation hit Jim, that Harry James despite his bluster was in reality a woman hater and that Harry was doing all he could to humiliate Audrey in front of everyone. Could he say anything? Did he dare? He should say, he should be brave, Jim glanced at his watch, but said instead, 'Is that really the time? Audrey, you are supposed to be having tea with your gran.'

'I forgot all about it.' Audrey replied quickly.

'Yes women tend to forget time when they get in my company,' Harry said arrogantly and looked around for approval. 'Go on then you two young lovers, shoot off, be a shame to keep gran waiting; don't I get a kiss before you go Audrey? After all you're almost part of the family now.'

Audrey leant over and brushed her lips briefly on Harry's cheek, Jim and Audrey said goodbye to all and sundry and went out to the car, 'Thank you for that Jim, I don't know how you can work for that man he's nothing more than a pig.'

'The money is all that keeps me there Audrey; I can't earn the sort of money that Harry James pays anywhere else.'

'There must be something else you can do Jim, I can always see about a job for you in the factory.'

Jim declined to reply and they drove on in silence. Suddenly Audrey started to laugh, 'What's so funny Audrey?' Jim asked.

'Well I was thinking, considering that I haven't got a gran she's come in pretty useful.'

CHAPTER EIGHT

'Jesus Christ Anal, that's disgusting.'

'Sorry Jim lad, it's got to be the nerves.'

'Nerves, nerves, I'm the one who's doing the business.'

'I don't think you'll be doing any business today son, it's twenty to one.'

'We'll give it another five minutes then we'll go to the pub, I'm dying for a wet.'

'Suits me Jim, we've been stuck here for three mornings on the trot now, we're starting to stick out like a sore thumb, I'm beginning to think that Harry's info is all wrong.'

'Hang on Anal, who's the bloke in the natty suit with the grey titfer walking towards us over the other side of the bridge?'

Anal pulled Harry's flat cap down over his eyes and slid down in his seat, 'You're in business my son, that's him.'

Anal and Jim watched as Mark Newman glanced furtively around him and disappeared into the gent's toilet. Jim's heart began to pound and he licked his now dry lips.

'Off you go my son, got everything?'

Jim patted his jacket pockets, 'Smith and Wesson and the chiv Weasel gave me.'

'Got the sign?' Jim nodded. 'Good luck son.'

Jim hopped out of Harry's old van and made his way

quickly along the pavement, he whipped the toilet closed for repair sign out from under his jacket, hung it on the sliding metal grill and pulled it to behind him. Stepping into the gents he could see that Mark Newman was standing by a cubicle door, he smiled at Jim and beckoned to him, is this how they do it? Jim wondered.

Without a word Jim went into the cubicle Mark Newman pulled the door together behind them, he reached down to Jim's crotch, 'Not bad,' he murmured, deftly he unbuttoned Jim's fly and reached inside, 'mmm,' he cooed. Quickly he sank down to his knees; much to Jim's embarrassment he had himself become almost instantaneously somewhat erect.

'Come on then,' Mark Newman said.

With shaking hands Jim fumbled at his buttons. 'First time eh! I can always tell, here I'll do it.' Mark Newman unbuttoned himself and thrust Jim's hand onto his stiff member. 'Come on you know what to do,' he said.

Mark Newman worked orally greedily away at Jim, Christ, I'm actually enjoying this, Jim thought. Before long Jim realised he was past the point of no return and tried to pull away, but Mark Newman was having none of it, Jim ejaculated and Mark Newman followed on close behind.

Jim stood, his knees shaking, his breath short and hurried. Now suddenly a devastating overwhelming guilt coursed like a lightning bolt through his mind. Shuddering and still breathless, he reached into his pocket and produced the Smith and Wesson, 'Pervert, dirty pervert,' he hissed through clenched teeth. Jim rapidly fired two shots, a halo of blood and brains splattered on the wall behind Mark Newman's head as he slid down into a crumpled heap on the cubicle floor. A surprised look on his face, his sightless eyes open and staring up at Jim.

Shaking uncontrollably, Jim took his handkerchief and wiped himself and his hands. He was filled with disgust to see that Mark Newman had ejaculated over his trousers, he quickly wiped away at them. Horrified now as some of Mark Newman's semen had ended up on Jim's fingers, he lurched over to the wash basin, turned on the taps, placed both hands on the edge of the basin and was violently sick, with tears running down his face he looked in the mirror above it, 'Jesus Christ, why me?' he screamed aloud.

Turning he went back into the cubicle, he reached inside Mark Newman's jacket and took out his wallet, Jim so preoccupied with his own thoughts and the enormity of what he had just done, failed to notice the wallet was stuffed full, he jammed it into his own pocket and looked down at the corpse, Mark Newman still had an erection, Jim kicked out at the corpse, looked away and quickly left.

'You took your time, everything alright?'

'Yeah, I couldn't come off, that's all,' Jim laughed nervously.

Anal laughed, 'Cut his dick off?'

'I couldn't do it.'

'Jim, Harry will go mad, you know what he's like. Here you'd better give me the chiv, I'll do it and you go and get me a paper.'

Almost in a trance Jim walked the short distance to the newsagents, I suppose I've always known it, he thought, ever since I was a teenager, I'm one of them,

Christ Almighty, why me? One of them, a homo, I'm a homo. Christ I could murder a drink.

Jim walked into the dingy newsagent's shop. A middle aged woman sat behind the counter, gypsyish looking in her features, her black lank greasy hair tinged with grey. It was obvious that an appointment with some soap and water wouldn't do her any harm, a cork tipped cigarette with a good inch of ash on it hung from her lips, the blue smoke drifting up lazily into her face and onwards to the cracked ceiling.

'Evening Post in yet, please?' Jim asked.

The woman glanced up at the bent minute hand of the grimy clock on the wall, and without removing the cigarette said, 'Another half hour yet,' barely giving Jim a glance, she continued, 'Evening World's over there if that will do?' she gesticulated drearily in the general direction of a shelf, the cigarette ash from her cigarette tumbled down the grimy front of her once white blouse. Jim picked up and paid for the paper, Jim noticed by her nails and hands he was right about the soap and water.

He walked back out onto the pavement, two men were peering into the van and further down the road he could see a maroon Hudson parked. As he took in the scene he saw Anal being bundled into the back of it by another three individuals. 'Shit!' Jim exclaimed, he hastily lifted the newspaper up in front of his face and stepped back quickly into the shop doorway. Jim scanned the headlines with unseeing eyes, he glanced over the newspaper, one of the two men who were looking into the van approached the Hudson, said something to the driver and returned to his colleague. A brief conversation

151

ensued and the two men crossed the road and stood by the wall opposite the van watching it.

Jim still pretending to be engrossed in the newspaper walked quickly away from the scene. 'Do something Jim,' he screamed to himself, he turned and watched, paper still up to his face, the Hudson was pulling away, the two men were still standing watching the van from across the road. Jim turned on his heel, tears welling up in his eyes, feelings of remorse over his sexuality and Anal both simultaneously coursing through his tortured mind. He walked quickly away up the street looking around for a cab, his heart pounding, his mouth dry and his breathing laboured. He lost all track of time and continued to hurry along the alien street aimlessly. Shoulders slumped and head down he rounded a corner and spotted a dingy little brown painted pub, this will do, he thought, his flight over.

'Large scotch please.' Jim asked.

'You got large scotch money?' The portly barman looked at Jim quizzically.

Jim pulled Mark Newman's wallet from his inside pocket, Jim gasped as he noticed for the first time just how fat it was.

'Large scotch it is sir.'

Strange how money talks, thought Jim, no not talks, shouts, shouts from the roof tops, suddenly I'm sir; ten seconds ago I was a piece of insignificant dog turd on his brogue. 'Tell you what,' said Jim, 'stick your whisky up your fat arse.' Jim wandered back out into the street, that was clever, he thought, gagging for a wet and I have to say that. Jim looked around, no sign of another pub, 'I don't even know where I am,' he said aloud. He wandered through the unfamiliar streets, thoughts still pounded through his brain, what will I tell Harry about Anal? What will I say when he asks did I cut Newman's dick off? Why am I a homosexual? What a mess, what a bloody, bloody mess.

Finally Jim spotted another pub, I'll need to be a bit more careful this time, he thought.

'Half of bitter, please,' he said to the man behind the bar who looked somewhat like the landlord of the Charnbury.

'You're not from round here, I know,' the man said.

'No, you're right; I've got a bit lost to be honest.'

'Lost? Where are you trying to get?'

'I need to get back into the centre of town.'

'There's a bus stop just along the road,' the man pointed.

'Is there a taxi stand anywhere handy?'

'Can't say as there is, I can phone Andy for you if you like, he runs people around.'

'Yes thank you, tell you what, forget the bitter, I'll have a large scotch and have one yourself,' careful not to let Mark Newman's fat wallet show, Jim produced a ten shilling note from his pocket.

'Well thank you young man, that's very kind of you, I'll just have a half of bitter, when would you like Andy to pick you up?'

'Not yet a while, I need a bit of a rest and I feel quite comfortable in here,' Jim said glancing around.

'That's good of you to say, you're from north of the river, am I right?'

'Spot on, but how do you know that?'

'Your accent, I can always tell. What's your local?'

153

'I drink either in the Sceptre or the Charnbury.'

'Well bugger me, the Charnbury, that's Harold's pub, he's my brother.'

'You know when first I saw you,' said Jim, 'I thought of him, quite a striking resemblance, except you're taller.'

'Yes and except he's the one with all the money,' tapping the side of his nose he went on, 'he's always doing this and that, wheeling and dealing, you know what I mean, if you know Harold?'

'Well why don't you get into something yourself?'

'Love to, but you need contacts for that sort of thing, here you're not a copper, are you?'

Jim laughed, 'Hardly,' then Jim didn't quite know why he said it but he blurted out. 'You're talking to the right man you know, if you want to do a bit of business.'

'What can you get?'

'What are you after?'

'Anything really, anything to make a few bob, you've only got to look around you, this pub hardly makes me a fat living, tell you what son let's go and sit in the corner and have another drink, I think perhaps me and you can do some business.' Jim sat in the back of Andy's taxi, mulling over what he and his new acquaintance had discussed. Would he be bold enough to cut Harry out of any deal he made? He knew Harry would skin him alive if he did the dirty on him, that was for sure, and then there was the problem with Anal, and then there was his other little problem, 'I don't even want to think about that,' he said aloud.

'What's that?' Andy said over his shoulder.

'Oh, nothing, it's just that I've got a lot on my mind

154

at the moment, that's all.'

'Got to be something to do with a woman, I reckon.'

'You couldn't be further from the truth,' Jim said, and started to laugh coldly.

'Here we are then that's just half a crown, please.'

Jim glanced at his watch, twenty past two, just in time he thought, he walked into the snug of the Charnbury, Harry James was at the far end, his face looked like thunder, ' And where the fucking hell do you think you've been?'

'Sorry Harry, they got Anal,' Jim said gravely.

Harry's face immediately softened, 'Harold, get the boy a large scotch, over here son, sit yourself down and tell me exactly what happened.'

Jim still even up to this point, didn't know what he was going to say, he slowly sipped his scotch and pulled up a chair, 'It was like this Harry,' he said, 'we were just about to call it a day when he showed up.'

'Go on, go on,' Harry said impatiently.

'Well I followed him into the toilet and did the business.'

'Then what happened?'

'I went back out to the van and Anal said he wanted a newspaper, so I told him I'd get him one, I went in the paper shop and when I came out I'm just in time to see Anal being bundled into the back the Hudson, they drove off and took the van as well. That's about it really, I couldn't do anything, there were at least six of them.'

'Christ, poor old Anal, did you get Newman's dick and his money?'

'Yes look,' Jim pulled out the fat wallet.

155

Harry barely gave it a glance, 'What about his cock, did you cut it off.'

'Of course I did.'

'So where is it?'

'I left it in the van with Weasel's knife before I went for the paper; I wasn't going to carry that thing around in my pocket.'

'All right son, now listen you can't go home, you're a marked man now until we nail the other two Newmans.'

'They don't know where I live Harry.'

'They will by now, get that girl of yours to go round and pick up a few things and tell her to be careful she isn't followed.'

'I don't think Anal will say anything Harry.'

'Listen son by the time they've finished with him he'd tell them where his own mother lives never mind about you. Now you shoot off and get yourself some digs and I'll see you back in here at nine tonight, got it?'

Jim determined rather than get Audrey to fetch his clothes he'd buy new and by the time he had shopped and found a room the afternoon was almost over. He looked around the room he had rented, clean enough, he thought, if a little drab. He sprawled across the bed and reached into his jacket pocket, the enormity of the Newman's wallet finally hit him. Quickly he sat up cross legged and pulled the wad from the leather, 'Jesus Christ,' he said aloud, his hands trembled as he started to lay the money out all over the bed without counting it, what am I doing here, he thought, with this lot, I could be staying in The Royal Hotel. Jim gathered the money up and started to count it into piles. Jim stared at the money all over the bedspread, I'd give all this, he thought, not to be the way I am, tears started to roll down his face, 'Why me? Oh God, why me?' he sobbed aloud through the tears.

Jim decided to meet Audrey from work, he didn't know how he was going to explain to her that he couldn't go home, I'll think of something, he thought.

Jim sat in his car outside the factory gate, drumming his fingers on the steering wheel, not through impatience, but unconsciously as he was trying to work out what he was going to say.

Audrey spotted Jim and hurried over to the car, 'This is a nice surprise Jim, finished work?'

'Yes until nine tonight anyway, listen up Audrey I need you to do something for me, it's very important.'

'What's up Jim, you look worried?'

'No I'm not worried, Audrey, but I can't go home and I need you to go and explain to my Auntie Cath.'

'Explain what Jim? What have I got to tell her?'

'Tell her not to worry and I'll be in touch.'

'But what's going on? Come on Jim I want to know.'

'Well you know that Harry does a bit of dodgy dealing, well the top and bottom of it is, he's upset some business associates of his and they know I work for him, and he's worried that they will grab me and make me tell them where he lives. They're not very nice people Audrey, they'll stop at nothing, it's better if I stay out of the way for the time being.'

'I knew it would be to do with Harry James Jim, I didn't like him when I met him after chapel, and I like him

157

even less now that he's put you in danger.'

'Will you go and see auntie for me Audrey?'

'Of course I will Jim, I'll go straight round after tea.'

'Thank you Audrey, thank you, and make sure you're not followed by anybody, anybody at all, and I'll see you at your house at seven, is that alright?'

'Yes, seven o'clock it is.'

Jim picked up Audrey a little before seven, 'How did you get on with Auntie Cath?' he asked.

'She's nobody's fool Jim; I think she was half expecting me. I had a good look around before I even knocked on her door, but there was nobody about, she invited me in and she told me that just after it got dark, she looked out of the window and saw a big American car pull up opposite. She told me that two men got out and went around the back lane and the others sat in the car, she put two and two together, she said she could tell they were up to no good. She said that after about half an hour there was a knock on the door, and when she answered it there were two men standing on the doorstep. They asked if a Jim lived there, and your auntie said that a Jim used to, but he had left that very morning owing her a weeks rent, she took them up to your room and showed them that all the drawers and wardrobe doors were open and they were empty. The men thanked your auntie and left.'

'But I don't understand, I haven't taken my clothes away.'

'I told you she was no fool; she took all your stuff and put it in her bedroom before they knocked on the door.'

Jim heaved a sigh of relief, 'good old Auntie Cath, I

can go back home now, it'll be quite safe, thank you for going to see her Audrey, I really do appreciate that.'

'Listen Jim, I want you to get another job.'

'Audrey I've explained I can't just pack in, it doesn't work like that;   I'm going to start up on my own but not just yet.'

'Oh Jim, what are you going to do?' Audrey asked excitedly.

'I'm still planning; I haven't got it quite worked out yet, but I don't intend to work for Harry James forever, that's for sure.'

'That's the best thing I've heard you say Jim,' Audrey threw her arms around Jim and kissed him on the cheek.

'Well keep it under your hat for the time being; now let's go for a drink.'

Jim was starting to think that telling Audrey he was going to start up on his own was a big mistake, sitting in the pub; Audrey bombarded him with a barrage of questions. 'Listen Audrey I've already told you nothing is decided yet, all I can tell you is I'm managing to save a fair old bit of money and as soon as the time is right I'll be off on my own.'

'You must have some idea what you are going to do Jim, surely?' she asked.

'All I know Audrey is that I'm not going to be with Harry James a moment longer than I need to be.'

'I'm so pleased Jim, I do worry about you, you know I think from what I've been told that that Harry James is nothing more than a crook, and I wouldn't want you to end up in trouble with the police.'

Jim laughed, 'Not much fear of that, Harry's got the

police in his back pocket.'

'I still worry though Jim.'

'There's no need to Audrey, honestly and I promise I'll leave Harry James as soon as I can.' Inwardly Jim wasn't so sure it would be that easy, but he smiled at Audrey reassuringly.

Audrey squeezed Jim's arm, 'I'm so glad, I do worry about you Jim, you know.'

'I've got a couple of irons in the fire Audrey, and as soon as the time is right I'll be away.' This seemed to placate Audrey and at last Audrey changed the subject. Jim his mind racing attempted conversation but eventually he looked at his watch, 'Sorry Audrey, I'll have to get you home, duty calls.'

Jim dropped Audrey off and drove to the Charnbury, Harry James was already propping up the bar, 'Anal's turned up Jim,' he said grimly.

'Is he alright Harry?'

'As alright as you'll ever be after having a red hot poker stuffed up your arse,' he replied.

'Christ that's what they did to-'

'Edward the second, just up the road in Berkley castle, They left Anal outside the Charlton, propped up against the door on the front steps, he had a sign hung around his neck saying that you're next Jim, and they'd stuffed Mark Newman's dick in Anal's mouth, I think they thought that Anal was a knob jockey.'

'Poor old Anal,' Jim said, secretly he was relieved that Anal had managed to relieve Mark Newman of his manhood, as he was now off the hook.

'Yes poor old Anal is right Jim, the bastards striped him, cut three of his fingers off, warmed the stumps up with a Zippo and smashed his toes on both feet, looks like they used a hammer on him. You'll have to be extra careful now Jim until this is all over.'

Jim explained to Harry how his aunt had covered for him and then asked, 'Where's Anal now Harry?'

'He's in the back room of the Charlton, it was Darky Dillon who found him out the front, and it's a strange thing but nobody saw him led there, just as well, we don't want the rozzers involved do we?

'I've sent Ron round to see Bill Grossman the undertaker, we're going to box Anal up and bury him in Rangeworthy, there's been too many questions being asked around the village about June's whereabouts, so I'm going to have to say she died suddenly and bury Anal instead.

'First thing tomorrow Jim I want you to go and see Doctor Kennedy up at Cockshot Hill, bung him two hundred quid and get the paper work for June. Don't leave it too late in the morning as he's always pissed as a fart by dinnertime. We always use him for digging out bullets and stitching wounds up, here cop hold of this.' Harry handed Jim two hundred pounds. 'Come on then son,' he said, 'let's have a good drink for poor old Anal's sake.'

By the time Ron turned up both Harry and Jim were the worst for wear, 'I've seen Anal boss, and he's not a pretty sight, they stuck a poker right up his arse,' he said.

'Yeah I know.'

161

'They did that to Edward the second in thirteen twenty seven. Did you know-?'

'Alright Ron just get on with it.'

'Grossman, the fat bastard wants a monkey to bury Anal.'

'Typical fucking undertaker,' Harry replied, 'no compassion, and no wonder he can afford to spend all his money in Sandra's knocking shop. Tell you what we'll get Anal dispatched then we'll let his missus know where he spends all his time.'

'Good idea Harry, I can't stand the sight of the fat git,' said Ron.

'You haven't had the pleasure yet have you Jim?' Harry asked.

'No I can't say as I've ever met the gentleman.'

Ron and Harry erupted into laughter, 'Gentleman,' said Harry, 'that's rich, oh yes, gentleman, I love it, when you go round to pay him Ron, take Jim with you, he can see the *gentleman* with his own eyes, he's got the right name Grossman,' Harry and Ron continued to chuckle. 'Tell Jim what they reckoned he did to that dead old girl that time, you know with the pig's trotter, and the wine glass.' Harry said.

When Ron had finished telling Jim the tale, Harry said, 'So there, he's in just the right job for a necrophiliac, the dirty slimy bastard, I've told all the boys he's not getting his fat greasy hands on me, I'll have a cheap and nasty Co-op funeral, I know your ass is falling out the bottom of the coffin within three weeks, and the shroud's probably second hand and been pissed on, but I'll take a chance on it.' Harry and Ron roared with laughter again,

Jim stayed quite silent. 'What's up with you then young Jim?' Harry asked.

'My mum and dad had a Co-op funeral,' Jim said softly.

Harry sank to his knees the tears streaming down his face, hanging on to the counter with one hand and dabbing away at his eyes with his handkerchief with the other. Ron collapsed onto a chair and he too reached for his hankie.

'I don't think that's very funny,' said Jim, he stood there with his fists clenched tightly by his sides, looking incensed, which just served to send Harry and Ron into more and more howls of laughter.

Jim stood facing Harry and Ron wanting to lash out at both of them, Harry collected himself, 'Nothing personal son, come on have another drink, just a joke that's all it was,' Harry put his arm around Jim's shoulder and gave him a squeeze. 'Large scotch over here, if you please landlord,' he said.

At that exact moment in time Jim realised that one way or another it was vital that his association with Harry James had to come to an end sooner rather than later.

CHAPTER NINE

Jim couldn't remember getting home again, he didn't know where the car was, but he knew he hadn't driven home, he remembered quite clearly what Harry had had to say about the Co-op, and he was beginning to feel that just leaving Harry's employment might not be quite enough.

Auntie Cath, with a face like thunder was in the kitchen when Jim came down stairs, 'Thank you for what you did Auntie,' he said.

'What's going on Jimmy, who are these men? I've been worried sick about you.'

'Harry James deals with some nasty characters Auntie, I'm going to get another job as soon as I can.'

Auntie Cath's face softened, 'Sooner the better Jimmy, the sooner the better, I told you what he was like, he's no good that one, you need to get another job and marry that nice girl Audrey, and start a family, you can bring her here when you get married, there's plenty of room.'

'Yes I could do a lot worse, the trouble is Auntie it might not be quite that easy leaving Harry's employment.'

'Don't be so stupid Jimmy just give him a week's notice to get somebody else, the same as anybody else would.'

'It's not that easy, Auntie, Harry doesn't take kindly to not getting his own way, I think to be honest the only way around it would be to move right away from here.'

'Jimmy you know it would break my heart for you to

move away, but I'd rather you did that than stay with that man.'

'You could come as well Auntie, the three of us, Audrey you and me.'

'No I couldn't leave here,' a hint of panic crept into her voice, 'I couldn't uproot at my time of life, but you've still got your whole life in front of you, you go Jimmy, and the quicker the better.'

Jim sat picking at his breakfast. Where to go? What to do? Money wasn't a problem; did he really want Audrey in tow? Perhaps she could straighten him out? What to do about Harry? What to do?

Jim glanced at the clock, 'Must go Auntie,' he said.

'Where are you off today, Jimmy?' Auntie Cath asked.

'I've got to see Doctor Kennedy to pick up some paper work for Harry.'

'God is he still alive, I would have thought that he'd drank himself to death long before now.'

Noticing his car was missing from outside Auntie Cath's Jim decided to walk to the doctors, but he had forgotten just how steep Cockshot Hill was, and by the time he reached the doctor's surgery he wished he had had the car. Funny, he thought, I never got this puffed out before; perhaps it's all the booze.

Doctor Kennedy turned out to be taller than Jim. Painfully thin, his bloated yellow face betrayed his addiction to the world and his runny bloodshot eyes were set close and too far back in his head, his talon like fingers extended out to Jim's, Jim could see that they were trembling, 'Harry sent you then, eh lad?' Jim could see the pound note signs glinting in Doctor Kennedy's eyes.

'Yes Doctor, Harry needs a death certificate.'

'Death certificates don't come cheap you know, let me see,' he stroked his chin and looked thoughtful, 'it'll cost a hundred.'

Jim watched as the doctor's eyes lit up as he handed over the money, 'Right then who is the deceased?'

Jim gave him the details and said, 'Tell me Doctor have you seen Harry lately?'

'I haven't seen Harry James in four or five years, he's too big a fish to bother with me these days, he always sends one of his men around if he wants anything, the only time I'll ever get to see Harry now is if somebody shoots or stabs him, and from what I know, there are plenty after his blood.'

I've just made a hundred quid, Jim thought. Jim watched as the doctor attempted to write, but his hand was so shaky in the end he said, 'Here lad, I'll tell you what to write and I'll sign.'

Jim walked out of the doctor's and along the road, yes Harry James, he thought, that's a hundred quid nearer to seeing the back of you.

Plenty of time before I've got to see Ron, thought Jim, and as if by magic a taxi appeared from around the corner, half an hour later and he was outside the pub he had found in Bedminster. Jim glanced at his watch, twenty past ten. He peered through the window of the pub and he could see the landlord walking around the bar carrying a beer crate, Jim knocked on the window, the landlord looked around spotted Jim and came to the door, 'Another ten minutes to opening yet,' he said, not recognising Jim.

'I'm here on business,' said Jim, 'don't you remember me?'

He peered at Jim, 'Ah yes, sorry, you're the one that Andy gave a lift to the other day, Jim isn't it?'

'Yes that's right, listen can I come in? I can get you some gear, remember we discussed it, but it's got to be just between us two, you mustn't even tell your brother.'

'No fear of that, I don't even see Harold at Christmas time anymore, come on in.' He gestured to a seat in the corner and bolted the front door behind them. 'Now, what's this gear you've got?'

'I won't know until I pick the stuff up but it's all stuff you can sell on at a profit, you know, stuff you can't get, eggs, cheese, tea, all sorts of stuff.'

'I don't know, I've been thinking, since you were in last, well I mean you could be a copper couldn't you? '

'Do I look like a policeman?' Jim asked smiling.

'To be honest, yes you do.'

Jim smiled again, 'Tell you what I'll bring you some samples, and if you want we'll have a deal and if you don't, well, there's plenty more pubs in Bedminster, and you'll never have as much money as Harold.'

'I'll think about it, I mean well I've got my licence to think about, I'd be out of here if the brewery found out, but yes I'll think about it.'

'Don't think too long; remember what I said, there are loads of pubs.'

'Alright, you bring me some samples and we'll see.'

Sitting in the back of Andy's taxi Jim was puzzling after what he had said to the landlord, just how he was going to supply him without Harry finding out, and then he didn't know if the farm would deal with him without telling Harry, he felt anyway that this was his first chance of a move away from him.

'Don't talk much, do you?' asked Andy, 'Myself, I like a chat in the cab, makes the day go round quicker.'

'Yes, I do like a chat,' Jim replied, 'but it's just I've got a lot on my mind at the moment.'

'Sorry I'll be quiet then.'

'No it's alright; it's nothing that won't wait.'

'You got a bit of business on with George then?'

'George, who's George, when he's at home?'

'Well George, in the White Cow, you've just been talking to him, the landlord.'

'Sorry I didn't know his name, well yes, I am trying to do a bit of business with him, as you put it.'

'He's alright is George, always done me a good turn, I could have done a bit of business with George myself, but I just didn't have the money, just when I was going to have a deal with this bloke I know, the clutch on the car went, and that was the end of that.'

'What exactly happened?'

'Well this bloke I know works for Wylds, in town, you know the wine and spirit merchants, they're the ones that supply all the Georges and Ushers pubs in the city, I had it all set up, he had a load of hooky booze and George was going to buy it. I went round and told him that the clutch was gone on the car, but he said cash up front or no deal,

168

I thought about taking a chance and leaving the car repair until after, I wish I had now.'

'This mate of yours, is he still in for a deal?' Jim asked.

'Funny you should say that, yes I saw him only last night, and he asked me if I had managed to come up with any money yet.'

'So the only thing stopping you is the funds?'

'Yeah.'

'How much stuff can this bloke get?'

'Any amount, the way he spoke.'

'How do you fancy working for me? What do you get out of the taxis?'

'On a good week I can make about twelve or fourteen quid.'

'Come and work for me part time to start with, you can still do your taxis and I'll pay you a fiver every week, how does that sound?'

'Sounds too good to be true, what have I got to do? A fiver part time that's a lot of money, nothing too dodgy, is it?'

'No a bit of collection and delivery work, that's all. First of all though I need to meet your mate who works for Wylds, can you fix it up?'

'I'll fix it up, and you got yourself a deal,' Andy turned in his seat and extended his hand; Jim took it and shook it warmly. 'What shall I do when I've fixed up a meeting, give you a ring?'

Jim didn't want to let on that he didn't have a phone, so he said, 'No, give me your number and I'll ring you in a couple of days' time.'

Jim was feeling rather pleased with himself, but the spectre of Harry James was never far from his thoughts, he knew Harry would never let go, and if he got wind what he was up to, well that wasn't even a thought that Jim wanted to entertain.

Mad Ron was already in the Charnbury waiting when Jim arrived, 'Sorry Ron am I running late?' Jim asked.

'No you're alright I'm early, fancy a wet before we push off?'

'Go on then Ron, scotch please, I see the car's outside, I must have walked home last night.'

Ron laughed, 'Walked home, I drove you home and put you to bed.'

'Never, Christ I can't remember a thing. Here Ron there's something that's been puzzling me.'

'What's that?'

'Well Harry owns the Charlton doesn't he?'

'Yes, that's right.'

'Why doesn't he ever go there or drink there?'

'Well it's like this, Harry used to run the Charlton with his brother, but he got stabbed to death just when he was locking up early one Sunday morning, right outside the entrance. He collapsed on the steps and died, right where they found Anal, Harry won't go there anymore; he says the whole place is too full of ghosts.'

'Newmans, was it?'

Ron nodded his head, there was a long pause and then Ron said forlornly, 'I've been sitting here thinking about Anal, I miss Anal, Jim,' Jim glanced at Ron, he looked troubled and close to tears, then Ron continued, trying to sound cheery. 'Come on Jim raise your glass and let's drink to absent friends.'

'Absent friends it is Ron,' Jim raised his glass and downed his drink in one. 'Go on then Ron one for the road.'

One for the road led to another and another and they eventually got to the undertakers parlour a little after one.

One look at Bill Grossman was enough for Jim, an extremely short man, only a little over five feet tall, bald headed, with a round red face, possessing several chins, bags under the bags under his eyes; he had a huge stomach and was wearing a greasy looking black suit with a waistcoat, the front of which was covered in cigarette ash and food. His black tie also betrayed what he had had for his lunch. His standard undertaker's shirt had a crumpled collar and was white a very long time ago. He continually dabbed at his sweaty brow with a grey crumpled handkerchief, and as Jim got close to him, he realised that the undertaker smelt not unlike his clients.

'Who's this then Ron?' he asked, peering at Jim.

'It's Jim, he replaced Lefty.'

'Delighted I'm sure,' Grossman's breath was short and laboured, he shook Jim's hand limply; Jim noticed his nicotine coated hand was as sweaty as his brow, but he managed to resist the urge to wipe his hand on the leg of his trousers. 'Got some money for me, have you Ron?' he panted.

Ron handed Grossman the paperwork from the doctor and a fat manila envelope, 'It's all there but you

171

can count it if you want.'

'No I trust Harry, many wouldn't,' he laughed and started spluttering and coughing. 'Come on through, I've got the deceased laid out in the back room, he's not a pretty sight mind.'

'No I've already seen him, thanks,' said Ron.

'I'd rather remember Anal the way he was, if you don't mind,' said Jim.

Grossman shrugged his shoulders, 'Please yourselves, tell Harry I'll phone him with the funeral arrangements, is that the time? You'll have to excuse me.'

When they got outside Ron mimicked Grossman's voice, 'Is that the time? You'll have to excuse me, but I'm off to shag Sandra.'

'I wonder he can manage it, the size of him,' Jim said.

'You see what I mean though Jim, don't you?'

'Yes I'd say Sandra certainly earns her money.'

'I can almost taste that horrible fat little bastard, I'd like to stick him in one of his own fucking boxes,' said Ron. 'Come on let's get the taste out of our mouths with a drink, while there's still time.'

Harry's Rolls Royce was parked in the car park of the Charnbury to the surprise of them both, 'I didn't notice Harry's car earlier Ron, perhaps he left it here last night,' ventured Jim.

'No never, not Harry,' said Ron, 'I've seen him drive when he couldn't stand up, but he's normally never around at this time of day.'

'One way to find out,' said Jim. Jim and Ron walked into the Charnbury; Harry was in his usual spot, accompanied by two of the men that were at chapel the previous Sunday, Harry was beaming, and he had obviously been drinking for some time judging by his demeanour.

'Come on in boys,' he said, 'we're celebrating, Eddie Simms sent his boys here round bearing goods news, Jack Newman had a terrible accident last night, seems the poor bugger ended up on the train line out at Westerleigh, and got hit by an express train Christ only knows how he got there,' Harry laughed. 'He's a memory, so that just leaves Lucky Luke, I tell you boys, he won't be so fucking lucky time we've finished with him.

'The word is from south of the river that his men are getting the shits up, so we're going to pay a couple of them a little visit, and put the shits up 'em some more, Sid Morgan is going to point out a couple of Luke's boys and by the time we've finished with them the rest will be ready to leave town. Jim I want you to go to see Sid; Luke's boys don't know you so you'll be safe enough, I'll arrange a time and a place, and we'll do the rest. '

Killing two birds with one stone, just the job, thought Jim, 'When do you want me to see him Harry?' Jim asked.

'Sooner the better, there's a collection from the farm this afternoon, and I've got a phone number for Sid, so try to see him this evening in the Black Dog in Bedminster.'

Even better, thought Jim.

Jim couldn't wait to get to the farm, he had hatched a plan, but he would have to be careful what he said to the farmer. Unusually the farm gate was propped wide open, so Jim drove straight into the farm yard.

'Hello Jim,' said the farmer, 'Harry said two o'clock and you're smack on time.'

'Yes,' replied Jim, 'I always try to be punctual, what is it today farmer?'

'Butter and bacon, my son, pull over to the barn there,' the farmer pointed. Jim drove the car to the entrance of the barn and the farmer showed Jim what had to be loaded.

'Farmer,' Jim said, 'I know this man who keeps a pub, and he knows who I work for, and he was asking me if I could catch hold of anything, you know like bacon or maybe tea or anything really, the thing is he doesn't get on with Harry, so he asked me to try to sort something out for him.'

The farmer smiled, 'Doesn't get on with Harry, not many do. Well I don't believe in putting all my eggs in one basket, so yes I can supply him, tell him to come and see me and we'll sort something out.'

Jim wasn't expecting that reply and for a moment was quite taken aback, 'I shall be seeing him myself later on, I don't suppose you could let me have some samples to show him, could you? I'll pay you of course, and then I'll ask him to get in touch.'

'What's his name this man in a pub?' Jim hesitated, the farmer went on, 'I'll bet his name's Jim same as you. I'll bet he's the same age and build as you as well. Listen son,' he said seriously, 'I never came down on the last raindrop, cross Harry James and you're a dead man, I'll sell you some butter, I'll sell you bacon and whatever else comes along, but you just watch out for yourself, understand?'

174

'You're no fool are you farmer?'

The farmer chuckled to himself but made no reply and started to sort through another box of butter, 'Here you are,' he said, 'take this lot for starters and see how you get on, I'll mark the price for you to charge on the side of the box and I'll charge you half of that. Happy?'

'Yes farmer, more than happy, thank you very much.'

Jim was delighted when the blue lights of the police car appeared in his rear view mirror, as he could see the driver was John and he was alone. 'Hello John,' he said, 'bacon and butter today.'

'Shouldn't that be either bacon and eggs or bread and butter?' he smiled.

'Yes I suppose it should be, anyway yours is on the back seat.'

'Listen Jim, I've been thinking, it's a bit dodgy for me to go out for a drink with you, I've got my career to think of. But if we did get seen together I could always get round it by saying you were an informer, you know, you could give me a snippet or two of information, something that doesn't really matter, so if you like we could arrange to meet somewhere out of the way, I'll take the chance.'

'Smashing, I know just the place south of the river, I've got some work to do down that way so, perhaps I could combine business and pleasure, what evenings are you free John?'

'I'm on early shift all this week, in fact I was supposed to finish at two, but the sergeant wanted his goodies, so any night really would suit.'

'Tonight about eight?'

'Fine where shall we meet up?'

'Meet me in Old Market Street by the Empire Theatre, I'll be in the White Hart next door and then we'll go on to this little pub I know in Bedminster, it's right out of the way.'

'Right, that's a date then. I see Jack Newman has been killed then Jim, anything to do with Harry James? Only it's just that the sergeant's been asking that's all.'

'No, nothing at all,' Jim decided that although he was getting along well with the John, he was still a policeman.

'Jack's cousin, how about him?'

'No, no good asking me John, I'm only a delivery boy.'

'Well how would a delivery boy know that Harry James had nothing to do with the murder of Jack Newman?'

'Things you hear. Listen John, can't you forget you're a policeman just for once and stop grilling me?'

'Sorry Jim, it's just the training, see you tonight.'

'Yes, cheerio John.'

As soon as Jim had delivered the butter and bacon, he drove to Bedminster, he could see as soon as he arrived that the pub was closed, Jim looked at his watch, ten past three, cautiously he tapped quietly on the pub window. No answer, Jim tapped a little harder, Jim heard a window above his head slide open, 'Who's there?' a voice called out.

Jim stepped back into the road. 'It's me Jim, sorry to disturb you, I've brought you some bits and pieces.'

'I'll be right down, hold on.'

Jim heard the bolts on the door slid back and he could

see that George the landlord was happy to see him. 'Come in, come in, I didn't expect you back so soon, what have you got?'

'If you're still interested I've got bacon and butter?'

George went straight to the cash register, 'What am I in your debt?'

'It's on the side of the box.'

George turned the box around, 'Very reasonable,' he said, 'that's very reasonable indeed. He counted out the money into Jim's hand, 'you'd better have a drink.'

'Andy told me your name was George, is it alright to call you by your Christian name?'

'Yes, course it is, Andy tells me you've given him a job, he's a good lad that one, he won't let you down.'

'In future I will be letting Andy do the deliveries to you, and I will just pop in now and again to collect the money, how does that sound?'

'Sounds just fine Jim, now come on let's have that drink.'

On the way back across town, Jim mulled over his new business venture in his mind, Andy could collect from the farm, that way even if Weasel or Ron came to the farm, they wouldn't see anything untoward, Jim could pay the farmer when he collected Harry's goods, perfect, he thought. All I need to do now is to see the Wylds man, of course there was still the problem of Harry James, what to do? Jim telephoned Andy, and he agreed to set up a meeting with the Wylds man at seven in the White Cow, just enough time to see him before meeting John. Yes, thought Jim, things were shaping up quite nicely, quite nicely indeed.

The Wylds man, whose name turned out to be Terry, was short, square and a cockney, in his mid-thirties. Jim took an immediate dislike to him. He had an angry looking scar which ran from high up on his forehead and arched around and down to the left hand side of his mouth. Acne had pitted his face and his hair was swept right over the top of his head in a futile attempt to hide his ever increasing baldness. His teeth and stumps, the small amount that he had, were yellow and black with decay. Jim noticed that he couldn't keep still and kept hopping from one leg to the other, and kept glancing furtively all around himself. 'Pleased to, meet you, I'm sure,' he said and offered Jim his limp right hand, Jim shook it reluctantly and briefly. 'Andy tells me you're in the market for some booze.'

'Yes, that's right, what can you get?'

Terry laughed, Jim again noticed his apology for teeth and the lack of them what an unsavoury looking character this one is, he thought.

'I can get any amount of anything at any time,' he said, 'I've got it sussed right out,' he tapped the side of his temple with his yellowy brown, heavily stained, nicotine coated, nail bitten index finger.

'Why aren't you offering to sale the stuff to the Newmans? You're south of the river.' Jim asked.

Terry ran his index finger down his scar, 'That's what the Newmans did to me; I've got no love for them bastards. I was in the Black Dog one night, I'd just come down from the smoke, so I didn't know nobody, or nothing, I ends up playing cards, three card brag it was, with these four geezers in a upstairs room after hours. I clean ran out of money and covered the pot, like you do, that's the rules of brag anywhere in the country, probably anywhere in the fucking world.

'Anyway one of them says, "What the fuck do you think you're doing?" Covering the pot I says. "Not in this game you don't, if you've ran out of money you can fuck off," he says, I told him he was out of order and he was taking the piss. Christ he was quick, he cut me, I didn't even see the blade come out of his pocket, the other two at the table grabbed me and threw me down the stairs, then they ran down after me and gave me a right good leathering. Christ I was bad for weeks, a few days later I was told that I had been introduced to the Newmans.'

'So you say you can get any amount at any time?'

'Yes I work in the packing department at Wylds, not that there's much packing, the warehouse boys make up the orders and bring them down, I check them and if there is a part case of wine or spirits I just tape it up and put it with the order.

'Going back just before last Christmas I noticed that when the orders went out either by van, carrier or post, they only counted the amount of cases, and checked them against the total number to be dispatched. Henry from the office comes down, sees that there are say thirty cases in the book to go to the carrier, and eight parcels in the post book, counts thirty eight and he's a happy man. He never looks at the addresses where they're going .

'So just as a try on in the lunch break I went up to the warehouse got meself a bottle of scotch, wrapped it up and put a label on it, and then I puts in the post book three parcels for an off licence in Bath, course two were for Bath and the other was addressed to me. Henry comes down looks at the post book, counts up how many parcels for the post, looks at the book for the carrier, checks the pile, he's happy, and I had a nice bottle of whisky.

'Now they've just done a stock check and they won't do another for a twelve month and by that time me and you will have made a tidy few quid and I'll be long gone back up to the smoke. Here want a fag?' Jim shook his head, 'All you need to do is to get yourself a warehouse, but not in Bristol, I don't want the firm's van delivering to you anywhere near here, get one in Bath or somewhere out in the sticks, that way the goods will go by carrier, I sell you the booze at a quarter retail, you sell it on for half or whatever and the landlord puts it out full price, what do you say?' Terry stuck out his hand.

'You got a deal,' Jim unwillingly took his hand, 'I'll be in touch through Andy, he's working for me now,' Jim looked at his watch, although he had plenty of time he didn't want to spend any more time in Terry's company. 'Sorry I've got to dash, can I leave you a drink?'

'Nah, I got things to do meself, cheers mate.'

My mate is the last thing you'll ever be, thought Jim.

Jim glanced at his watch, a bit early, he thought; he drove slowly to the Black Dog and pulled up in front of the pub on the large car park. He suddenly realised that he hadn't a clue what Sid Morgan looked like, but he had no need to worry as Sid Morgan knew who to expect. 'You must be Jim?' he said, as Jim got out of the car. Jim looked him up and down; this is the first gang member that looks quite ordinary, thought Jim, nice suit, no pencil thin moustache, looks like a family man. He must have read Jim's thoughts. 'What did you expect?' he said, 'someone with two heads carrying a machine gun.'

'Sorry, I didn't know what to think,' said Jim, extending his hand.

'I'm not a what, I'm a who,' he smiled, 'I can't shake hands with you, people might be watching, there's no need for you to come in the pub, just walk around the side with me.'

Jim did as he was told, 'See that door,' Sid pointed. 'Most nights there's a card school, through that door, up the steps and it's in the room facing the top of the stairs. They always keep the door bolted. I don't play cards myself but I do go up there now and again. The next time there's a card school I'll go up and offer to buy the drinks, I'll tell them I've had a tickle on the horses, I'll make sure they don't lock me out, then I'll come back down to get the drinks, tip you boys the wink, and Bob's your uncle.'

'Sounds simple,' said Jim, 'how many will there be in there?'

'Four maybe six, could be more, you never know, listen there's a phone box just outside Parson Street railway station, here's the number of it,' Sid passed Jim a piece of paper. 'You get Harry, Mad Ron, Weasel and the boys to wait there and when the games in progress I'll give you a tinkle, then it's up to you.'

'It will definitely be Luke's boys?' Jim asked.

'Definitely, no one else is allowed in.'

Jim remembered what had happened to Terry, 'Are

181

you sure?'

'Sure, I'm sure; they usually start playing around nine o'clock, about an hour before the pub closes, so you need to be at Parson's Street at about that time, go there tomorrow night, if I haven't rang by ten thirty you'll know there's no card school, and you'll just have to try the night after, just make sure you bring Harry along so that he can watch the fun, got any money on you?'

'Yes, of course I have, but why?'

'Pull out a fiver and give it to me, if anybody's watching out the pub window, and you can bet your life they are, they'll think I'm collecting a debt, and when I hit you in a minute don't try to hit me back, or you'll have the Newmans all over you like a rash, understand?'

Jim nodded his head and made a show of producing a fiver from his pocket, he handed it to Sid, 'Sorry Jim,' Sid said.

Later Jim told Harry that all the time he had been boxing he had never been hit so hard, Sid punched him just once in the stomach and despite Jim being young and fit, he was left on the ground gasping for breath. Retaliate, thought Jim, retaliate. Jim could hear loud prolonged cheering coming from inside the pub, Sid was right, they had been watching. Sid swaggered away and with his arm aloft waved the five pound note in the direction of the pub windows.

Eventually Jim dragged himself to his feet gagging and gasping for breath; he lent against the car with one hand, and then he bent forward and was violently sick all down the door and between his feet. Shakily he got in the car, wiped his mouth, started the engine and pulled away.

A few hundred yards from the pub he pulled into the side of the road and sat awhile recuperating from the blow.

He was still in pain as he pulled up in Careys Lane fifteen minutes later, he parked the car outside Hell's Kitchen and walked slowly up the road, around the corner and headed for the White Hart, next door to the Empire Theatre. Jim looked at his watch, how about that for timing, he thought, five to eight, he got himself a large scotch and took a window seat so he could watch out for John, by eight thirty and two more large scotches, he realised John wasn't putting in an appearance. Jim felt quite let down, he'd been looking forward to seeing John all day long, it must be his work, he told himself and John wouldn't let me down deliberately.

Just after nine Jim found himself in the Charnbury, Harry, Weasel and Mad Ron were already in attendance.

'Come on Jim,' Harry said, 'it's on the bar waiting for you, how did things go?'

Jim told the trio all that had gone on at the Black Dog, including him getting punched by Sid Morgan, he could see Weasel smirking as he related how he ended up on the ground.

'So we hit 'em tomorrow or the next day then?' Harry.

'I've been thinking about it ever since I left Bedminster Harry,' Jim said, 'it all seems too easy, too pat, I'm not convinced it's not some sort of a trap, Sid said twice to make sure that you are there Harry, there's something not right, and I mean there aren't many of us, are there Harry?'

Harry started to laugh, 'Jim you don't know just how many of us there are, do you think that my organisation runs to just the four of us here? No son you don't see the foot soldiers, go to the Charlton tonight and there will be thirty of forty of my boys in there, one phone call to Darky and all manner of things can be done. So listen up my son if you think it's a trap, then we'll just have to set a trap of our own, if you're right then Sid will suffer and if not no harm done.

'To think the money I pay him, the bastard. If you are right about this Jim, you'll be running the south side and Sid will be on the Aust fucking ferry.'

'One thing I don't understand Harry, if you've got all these foot soldiers as you call them, why did you need me to take over from Lefty? Why wouldn't one of them have done?'

'Bert said you needed a job, and I'm always happy to help one of our boys whose done his bit. Anyway it all turned out for the best, you're one of the boys now Jim, you're one of us.'

Jim knew very well that he didn't want to be, and it was a very troubled Jim that left the pub that night. Running the south side, he thought, I'm trying to get away from Harry and run my own firm, and what happened to John? Why didn't he turn up? What a nightmare.

CHAPTER TEN

Jim spent a fitful night, tossing and turning and the next morning he was no nearer finding a solution to his dilemma than when he went to bed.

'Hello stranger, I don't seem to see much or you these days.'

'Good morning Auntie Cath, I've been a bit busy, I've told you that I'm trying to get away from Harry and I've been busy working on it.'

'Good good, have you seen anything of Audrey, Jimmy?'

'I just don't seem to have much time at the moment Auntie.'

'Don't let her get away Jimmy, you'll regret it if you do.'

'I'll try to get to see her today Auntie, I promise.'

'That's a good boy Jimmy, that's a good boy.'

Jim saw Audrey at dinner time after he had collected the rents; he was greeted with hello stranger, the same as he had been earlier on by his aunt.

'Where have you been Jim? I've been worried sick about you,' she said.

'Anybody would think I was back fighting the war, it's only been a couple of days.'

'Jim I worry about you all the time that you're working for that Harry James.'

'It's not for ever Audrey, I've told you I'm working on it. Tell you what, take the afternoon off work and we'll go to Clevedon or somewhere, or even better let's go to Bath, I'm looking for some business premises there.'

'Business premises, Bath, why Bath? Won't Bristol do?'

'No it's got to be Bath, go back in work and tell them you're taking the afternoon off.'

'Oh yes, and what am I supposed to tell them? Oh, you're hopeless Jim, I just can't take time off just like that.'

'Come on Audrey let's just go, forget work for once.'

'I can't Jim I could lose my job.'

'When I've got my premises you can come and work for me.'

'Oh yes, and how am I supposed to get to Bath then Jim, ride a bicycle.'

'No taxi, I'll put you in a taxi.'

'You won't make any money that way Jim.'

'I'll teach you to drive and buy you a nice car.'

'Oh Jim you're hopeless, I'm going back into work, and I'll see you later.' Audrey reached up and pecked Jim on the cheek. 'Bye Jim,' she said.

'Cheerio Audrey.'

Jim, his mind made up, drove towards Bath. Along the Lower Bristol Road he noticed a line of railway arches on his right hand side, some were obviously in use and he could see that they were occupied by small businesses, I wonder, he thought, yes just the job, he slowed up and cruised by steadily. Then he spotted a sign, "FOR RENT", and a telephone number, he could see a small door which was to one side of the front of the otherwise bricked up arch and it appeared to be ajar.

Jim stopped the car and crossed the road, tentatively he pushed against the door, it swung creakily open, Jim was immediately aware of an ancient damp musty smell. He took a step inside; the smell worsened, perhaps not, he thought. Jim could hear the drip, drip, drip of water coming from somewhere in the darkness at the back of the arch. Gradually his eyes got used to the gloom, 'What a dump!' he exclaimed aloud.

'It's not much, is it?' said a cultured voice, behind him.

'Christ you made me jump,' Jim replied, looking around. Standing behind him was a tall slim middle aged man, well turned out in a long beige camel haired overcoat, a matching trilby hat, wearing black shiny shoes and carrying an ornate brass derby handled walking cane. 'Are you the owner?' Jim asked.

'Heavens above, no, The Great Western Railway own the arches, I'm their letting agent please let me introduce myself.' He handed Jim a business card, he took it and glanced at the name. 'I happened to see you pull up, that's all, I was on the way to my offices, are you interested in renting?'

'Yes and no, Mister Knowles, 'said Jim glancing at the card again.

'You won't find anything cheaper in Bath I can promise you, and with a bit of fixing up and electricity put in, and you're right on the main road. You need to snap one up; they don't stay empty for long.'

'Problem is, I don't know anybody in Bath, I don't know any builders; I wouldn't know where to start to get the place fixed up.'

187

'I can get you a builder, an electrician, a plumber, in fact I can get it all sorted out for you. I can have this place ship shape and Bristol fashion for you in two weeks, what do you say?'

'I say you're a good salesman, do I have to see you in your office?'

'Yes, you'd have to sign a lease and of course there's a deposit to pay, we're in Queens Square, it's on the card, it's not far. Tell you what, you follow me, in case you get lost, and I'll see you directly.'

Jim having signed on the dotted line and paid his deposit, drove back towards Bristol feeling rather smug, he was now the proud lessee of a somewhat shambolic railway arch, but at least it was a start. But at the back of his mind he had the niggling worry of Harry James and of course there was his other little problem.

The thought hit Jim like a lightning bolt. What if Harry James was no more? What would happen to his empire? Who would take over? Would anybody take over? By the time Jim was driving through Keynsham, he had formulated a rough plan, by the time he was in Willsbridge he was on to his second plan and realised that he had taken the wrong turning. His mind was racing nineteen to the dozen, 'That's it,' he said elatedly to himself, 'oh yes, that's it alright.'

Jim cornered Weasel in the Charnbury that evening, 'Weasel,' he said, 'have you ever thought what would happen if Lucky Luke topped Harry, before Harry topped Lucky Luke?'

'It won't happen.'

'But just for argument's sake, say it did.'

'I'm telling you it won't happen.' Weasel looked concerned.

'Well just say it does, how do you think it will that leave us?'

Weasel paused, Jim could see that Weasel considered Harry indestructible, 'God knows, I've never thought about it,' he replied.

'Well it could happen, and I mean Harry won't be around forever anyway, whatever happens, will he?'

'I'll ask Harry, when he gets here,' Weasel said, 'see what he says.'

'No don't do that, just have a think about what I just said, what would you do?'

'I don't know, I suppose perhaps Darky Dillon might give me a job.'

'You'd be a marked man if Luke got Harry wouldn't you Weasel?'

'Christ Jim; if you're trying to put the shits up me you're doing a good job? I'd have to leave town, that's what I'd have to do. I've got people I know in Bournemouth; I'd have to move down there. Yes that's what I'd have to do, now change the subject eh, and get the drinks in.'

'Where is Harry?' Jim asked.

'Gone to suss out whether Sid Morgan still packs a punch,' Weasel started laughing.

Jim smiled wryly, 'What you mean to see if I'm right about it being a trap?'

'Yes he's taken a few of Darky's boys; he said he

wouldn't risk any of us.'

'He's a bit late though isn't he? I hope he's alright,' Jim said, although he was hoping and praying that Harry wouldn't be. Jim kept glancing at his watch, nine forty five and no sign of him.

Just as Jim had convinced himself that something had happened to Harry, the door swung open and in he swaggered, munching on a fat cigar. 'Quite right Jim, you were quite right,' he called from across the bar, 'I picked the biggest of Darky's boys, because he looks like Ron from a distance, one that looked a bit like you, one like Weasel and I made one of them put my hat and coat on, then I sent them to the phone box, the rest of us stayed well away, right up the road, the poor bastards didn't even make it inside,' he shook his head.

'My bloody overcoat is probably ruined, cost me an arm and a leg that coat, get me a drink, will you, Weasel? Whatever did Sid think was going to happen, we were all going to turn up like lambs to the slaughter, I don't fucking understand him, I don't understand him at all, I trusted him, he was going to run the south side for me,' Harry shook his head again and chewed on his cigar. 'Cheers Weasel,' Harry took a gulp of his drink. 'What's the world coming to, you can't trust anybody anymore, I'm really very disappointed, really fucking disappointed.' Jim could feel his colours rising.

'So what now Harry?' Weasel asked.

'It's all done and dusted; Sid's a memory and so is Christ knows how many more of them, as soon as we saw

190

what happened at the phone box we went back to the Black Dog and waited until they turned up, surprising what a half a dozen men and a couple of hand grenades can do,' he chuckled. 'Now we go after Luke. I've got a monkey bet on with Eddie Simms that our boys get him before he does,' Harry started to chuckle again, his chuckle turned to raucous laughter, Harry looked around, and everyone, right on cue joined in.

That night for the first time in a long time, Jim went home almost stone cold sober, he had gone through the motions of downing several drinks, but wanting to stay sharp, surreptitiously he had discarded them throughout the evening. His mind was totally engrossed in formulating his plan with regards to Harry, thinking about his business plans, and as unexpectedly he would be doing a farm run the next day Saturday, pleasurable thoughts of John came to mind.

In the event the farm run proved quite uneventful. He arranged for Andy to call at the farm that afternoon and collect some sugar and tea, the farmer was quite genial and seemed quite pleased to be doing extra business with Jim, Jim for his part could feel the restraints of working for Harry easing. Driving away from the farm, Jim continually watched his rear view mirror but there was no sign of John or the sergeant. Disappointedly he pulled into the pub yard, and started to unload the car, he decided to leave the sergeant's share of the booty in the car, just in case.

The killings south of the river featured on radio and in

all the newspapers and it came to Jim as he read the various accounts of the carnage that he lacked any feelings one way or another about what had happened. What's happening to me? he thought, I was never like this, surely not, was I?

At tea time, at Auntie Cath's, Jim could tell as soon as he walked through the door by his auntie's face that he was in trouble, 'Everything alright Auntie?' he ventured.

'A policeman has been here looking for you Jimmy, I knew that you working for Harry James would end in tears, oh Jimmy what have you been up to?'

'What did he say Auntie?' Jim sounded anxious.

'He said they wanted to talk to you, that's all, what have you been up to Jimmy?'

'Nothing Auntie, honest, I don't know what the police want,' Jim's mind was racing. 'This policeman Auntie, did he give you his name?'

'No he just said he'd be back later.'

'Was he about my height and my build and about my age?'

'Well yes, he was, yes that's right.'

Jim breathed easier, 'That's John, you were talking to John.'

'You know him then Jimmy?'

'Yes, no need to worry Auntie,' Jim said confidently, 'he's one of Mister Harris's colleagues, you know the policeman I work with, did he say when he would be coming back?'

'He just said later, that's all.'

Jim alternated glancing at the clock on the mantle

and the watch on his wrist, then at five to seven, there was a knock on the front door, 'I'll go Auntie,' Jim said. Sure enough John was standing at the front door, 'Come in John, come in, please come through into the front parlour.'

'I can't stop long Jim, this is business and pleasure, first of all I'm sorry about the other night, I had to work unexpectedly, I was really disappointed that we couldn't have that drink together, but you know how my job is.

'Listen Jim,' John grabbed at Jim's arm, 'you've got to get away from Harry James, we know what's going on with the Newmans, we know it was Harry's lot that did the Black Dog over, the nets closing fast Jim, and you'll go down with the ship, I can't save you, I like you Jim I like you a lot and I'm risking my career coming here and telling you this, but listen you must get away now get away now while you still can.'

'I'm working on it John, I'm starting up on my own, I do appreciate you telling me, but I just can't up and leave like that, you know what would happen to me.'

'Get out Jim while you still can. Look meet me in the Bear and Rugged Staff in town tomorrow night about eight thirty, what do you say?'

'Yes alright I'll be there.'

'I can't stop I'll see you then, then, don't forget what I've said.' John turned on his heel and was gone. Jim closed the front door and with a heavy sigh walked back into the living room.

'Whatever's the matter Jimmy, you look like you've got the whole world on your shoulders, what did the policeman have to say?'

193

'That's John, Auntie, he's a friend of mine, and he was warning me that's all, about Harry James.'

'There you are, I've been right all the time, I told you no good would come of all this, get away from him Jimmy, get away now.'

'That's exactly what John said, the police are after Harry and John's worried in case I get caught up in all of it.'

'All of what Jimmy, what's been going on? What have you been up to?' Auntie Cath was close to tears.

'Nothing Auntie, honestly I've done nothing, I just drive the car, you know that.'

'I don't know anything anymore Jimmy, what's happening to you? You're not the same Jimmy Britton that left the army, that's for sure.' Auntie Cath began to sob.

Jim walked over to his auntie and put his arm around her shoulder, 'Don't cry Auntie Cath,' he said, 'please don't upset yourself, everything will just be fine, I promise everything will be just fine.' Jim only wished he believed it himself.

As soon as it was practical Jim said goodbye to his aunt, using the excuse that he had to go to work, he headed for south of the river and the White Cow, George the publican was standing behind the bar, there were a handful of customers standing at the bar, and sitting in the corner four elderly men all wearing flat caps were playing cribbage. 'Good evening Jim,' George was all smiles, 'I was just thinking about you, come in for a settle up?'

'I'm in no rush, I just had to get out of the house,

family problems, you know how it is. Give me a large scotch please George.'

'No, pay and be paid that's my motto,' George pushed a piece of paper and a pen across the counter. 'Just write the damage on there.' Jim did as he was asked and meanwhile George got him his drink. 'On the house my boy,' he said, 'I'll just slip out the back,' he took the paper from Jim's hand and went through the door at the back of the bar. Jim glanced about, this place needs a lick of paint, he thought, he was still looking around when George returned.

'I know what you're thinking Jim, you're quite right, I don't seem to have the energy or the inclination to bother since I lost the wife.' He gave Jim the manila envelope that he was holding. 'It's all there. You know Jim since we've decided to have these little deals, I feel that at long last I can make a few bob.'

'I didn't realise you've been widowed George, I'm sorry.'

'That's all right lad, it's almost two years now. She drank herself to death Jim, cirrhosis. She was a happy drunk, everybody loved her, but she was still a drunk nevertheless. Her family won't have anything at all to do with me now; they blamed me for her drinking. You see, they say she'd still be alive if she hadn't met me. It was all different when I met her first, oh yes, they thought I had plenty of money and she'd landed on her feet, they thought the sun shone out my arse, Then she started to drink and it was only after she died that her family found out about her drinking. One of them saw cirrhosis of the liver on the death certificate then of course it was all my

195

fault. I never held a gun to her head Jim; she drank because she liked it. They said that they thought that I was responsible; they won't have anything to do with me now. But putting it bluntly Jim I really don't give a toss what they think or thought anyway.'

'Well,' said Jim, 'I'm sorry to hear about your wife, anyway come on George, cheer up, another for me and have one yourself.

'Oh and I should be getting some spirits soon George, I'll get Andy to take an order from you the next time he comes back from the farm, if that's alright?'

'Sooner the better Jim, like I said, I think I could well be on the up now.'

'Me as well George, me as well.'

By the time Jim arrived at the Charnbury, he was feeling quite tipsy and he was starting to think that the only way he could be in Harry's company for any length of time these days was to fortify himself beforehand.

Harry as usual was in his customary spot sucking on an oversized Havana and talking loudly and incessantly. Jim thought, God how I've become to despise this man, instead he said pleasantly, 'Good evening Harry, evening boys.'

'Good news Jim, the bastard's gone to ground,' Harry said, 'nobody's seen him for a couple of days. He knows his days are numbered. Now it's just a case of flushing him out, and then it's a nice little one way trip on the ferry,' Harry laughed. 'Here get yourself a drink,' Harry threw a ten shilling note on the counter. 'Remember boys put it around, there's a grand in it for whoever tracks Luke down.'

'Harry,' Jim said, 'I've still got the sergeant's stuff in the car.'

'Don't worry about it son, take it home, the good sergeant is keeping his head down, he says there's a rumour going around that Scotland Yard's taking an interest down here. Must be all those terrible goings on south of the river, must be an awful fucking place to live,' Harry chuckled. 'So he won't be having anything for a while.'

'How about John?' Jim asked.

'John who?'

'John the young policeman.'

'Who cares?' Harry waved his hand dismissingly, 'I want you to get yourself over to the Black Dog tomorrow Jim, they're supposed to be reopening, if anybody recognises you, it will only be from when Sid Morgan gave you a smack, so you've got nothing to worry about. Keep your ear to the ground, and see if you can get any info, you know anything at all. You might as well get used to it over there, that's where you'll be working soon.'

'Working there soon?'

'Yes I told you you'll be over there looking after my business interests, as soon as Luke's a goner, you, Ron and a few of Eddie Simms boys will move in on their territory, crack a few heads, show them who's the boss, and Bob's your uncle.'

'I'll go over tomorrow then Harry, see what I can see.' Jim was pleased, it would give him the chance to talk to Andy and drum up some trade in the pubs south of the river, and if he could find out where Luke Newman was hiding, well it would be a grand in his pocket and a day nearer parting company with Harry.

Jim took his drink and sat quietly in the corner on his own, 'Jim,' Harry boomed across the bar, 'over here with us.'

'Yes Harry,' Jim reluctantly moved back to the company.

'Oh, boys, I almost forgot all about it,' Harry said, ' Grossman phoned, the funeral's the day after tomorrow, all meet at ten, we'll get Anal planted and be in the pub in Rangeworthy by one.'

Almost forgotten, thought Jim sadly, Anal, he's almost forgotten already.

On the basis that taxi drivers seemed to be well informed about most things, Jim had arranged to meet Andy the very next morning in the White Cow at opening time, his intention was to sound Andy out about the whereabouts of Luke Newman.

Andy was smack on time which pleased Jim. They were both warmly greeted by George and took their drinks to a quiet corner away from the bar, 'Right then Andy before we get down to business,' said Jim, 'some people I know north of the river are interested in the whereabouts of a character called Luke Newman, ever heard of him?'

'Who hasn't?'

'There's a good drink in it, and I mean a good drink, enough to buy a real tidy car if they can find out where he is.'

'A car,' Andy said, 'Christ, and he was in my taxi only

last week.'

'When was that? Where did you take him?'

'It was during last week, sometime; problem is every day's the same when you drive a taxi,' Andy scratched his head mystified, 'I think it was last Tuesday, or it might have been Wednesday, no hang on a minute, or was it Thursday, anyway I picked him and a couple of his boys up from the Hen and Chicken in North Street at closing time, one night in the week.'

Jim interrupted, 'Where did you take them Andy?'

'Oh, I can remember where I took them all right, best fare I've had for a long long time, you know the sweaty gave me three quid, I couldn't believe my luck.'

'The sweaty?'

'Yeah, sweaty sock, jock, Scotsman, great big bloke, a face like a road map, horrible looking, Glaswegian I think, had a job to understand a word he said.'

'So where did you take them?'

'Pensford.'

'Pensford?'

'Yes out through Whichurch, south of the city, you know the little village.'

'So whereabouts in Pensford did you drop them off?'

'Luke said to forget I saw them.'

'Remember, there's a new car riding on this Andy.'

'The pub on the main road, well I take it that's where they went, the George and Dragon, they got out there and went off around the back of the pub.'

'Did you pick them up again? Did you wait for them, or anything? Think this is important Andy.'

'No, I just drove off.'

'Did they say anything? Anything at all.'

'No, I don't think so.'

'How do you know they went around the back? If you dropped them and just drove away.'

'I saw them, well I saw them walk around the side of the boozer, I was out of the car, trying to shut the boot, I think it needs oiling.'

'Did they have bags then Andy?' Jim was beginning to think it was like drawing teeth.

'Yes they had two suitcases and a large Gladstone bag.'

'How long would it take you to drive me to Pensford?'

'What if they saw me, I'd be a goner, no, can't be done, sorry Jim, get on the train Jim, please, it's quicker than by car anyway, I'll take you to the station and wait until you get back.'

'It's Sunday Andy, there won't be many trains. You're scared of them aren't you? That's what the problem is, isn't it?'

'Shit scared's the word Jim, I'm absolutely shit fucking scared.'

'Alright Andy I'll take the train, come on drink up, we can discuss our other business in the taxi on the way to the station, I'll leave my car here.'

By the time Jim had settled down in his seat on the train, he had managed to encourage Andy to use the time while he was in Pensford to call on a few pubs in Bedminster to try to sale some wines and spirits.

The journey to Pensford didn't take very long; Jim

was quite surprised, but the train station turned out to be quite a hike from the George and Dragon. Jim kept looking at his watch, with pubs closing at two he knew he was cutting it fine.

As soon as Jim set foot inside the George and Dragon he knew he had made a mistake, he looked distinctly out of place with his smart suit, shiny shoes and trilby hat. The few men that were in the bar all stopped talking as Jim entered and stared at him. Jim felt that he had wandered into a Wild West saloon. There should be a piano going silent he thought. Jim walked to the bar, and the middle aged lady behind it gave Jim the once over as he approached.' Good afternoon,' she said, 'what can I get you?'

A decidedly uneasy Jim mumbled, 'Half a bitter please, I'll have half a bitter.'

The plump barmaid drew the bitter, still with one eye on Jim, 'Not from around here are you?'

'No I'm from Bristol,' Jim replied, 'I'm here on business.'

'What on a Sunday, you won't find much business in Pensford, not on a Sunday, definitely not on a Sunday, unless it's at the colliery? Perhaps it's the colliery.'

Jim said the first thing that came into his head, 'No actually I work for a solicitor; I'm here to see a client.'

'On a Sunday, who's that then? I know everybody in Pensford.'

Jim was wishing he hadn't set foot in the pub, 'Can't say, I'm afraid it's a confidential matter.' Jim tapped the side of his nose.

'I bet I know who it is anyway, it's alright I won't say

201

anything, he's the only one in Pensford that would need a solicitor.'

Jim refrained from asking who, instead he said, 'I'm here just for the day today, but next time I come down here I'll need lodgings, do you know of anywhere handy?'

'You'd be better off just getting the train every day from Bristol, there's nowhere to stay around here.'

'What about here, the pub?'

'No we don't do B and B.'

'Oh, I thought you did.'

The barmaid shook her head, Jim took his drink and sat down away from the bar, he noticed he was the only person to be drinking beer, everyone else was drinking cider. Jim lifted the glass to his lips, the glass smelt and tasted of cider, it had been tainted by cider after years of use, pushing the glass to one side, he looked across and he could see that a couple of the customers were eating, Jim got up and walked to the bar, 'Excuse me,' he said, 'I don't suppose you sell food do you?'

The woman laughed, 'Well we don't give it away, but I can do you some bread and cheese with some pickled onions, if you like.'

'Yes that would be fine, thank you.'

'I'll just get my husband to look after the bar and I'll go and get some for you.'

'Thank you,' said Jim and he returned to his seat.

After a minute or so the landlord appeared and judging by his glowing ruddy complexion, Jim suspected that he was partial to a drop of cider himself, he greeted his customers cordially and looked across to Jim, 'I hear you're down here on confidential business,' he called as loud as he could across the bar, 'on a Sunday too, must be pretty important business to turn up here on a Sunday, I suppose.'

'Yes,' Jim replied quietly.

'Bristol solicitors, isn't it?'

'Yes that's right,' said Jim, he decided to return back to the bar.

'Who's that then?' the landlord asked, still in his booming voice. 'What's the name of your firm?'

Oh dear, Jim thought, 'I don't expect you've ever heard of them,' he replied still very softly, 'you see we don't advertise.'

'Try me,' the landlord said, 'I used to work in the centre of town before I had the pub.'

'Well it's not in the centre of Bristol; our offices are out at Chipping Sodbury actually, that's why I was looking for lodgings down here.'

'You won't get anything here, I'm afraid.'

'No your wife told me that.'

'I suppose this is all on expenses, do you want a receipt?'

'Yes if you don't mind.'

'I'll put a bit on the top for you, after all he'll be paying and he isn't short of a bob or two.'

'Sorry,' said Jim, 'you've lost me.'

'It's alright, me and the wife worked out who you're down here to see, don't worry, we won't say anything,' the landlord winked.

'Look I really can't say.'

'Some say he's no ordinary business man, he only

comes down here now and again to see *her*. Don't know exactly what he does but he's not short of a bob or two. From your neck of the woods apparently, Bristol that is. They do say that he's already got a wife and kids, and this one's just his bit of fluff on the side.'

Jim was beginning to put two and two together, and hoping it wasn't going to make five, 'I didn't know about the girl friend,' he ventured.

'There I was right, I knew it,' the landlord said triumphantly, 'and so you are down here to see him.'

'Does he ever come in here?' Jim asked.

'Not very often, very rarely, she does, all the time, always got plenty of money to splash around, thinks she's alright she does, she's as common as muck really, must be at least twenty years younger than him. They do say when he's not around she entertains, if you take my meaning.'

Sounds like June, thought Jim. 'Is he around at the moment?' Jim asked.

'Well you should know it's you that's got the appointment to see him.'

'No I meant is he likely to come in now, I wouldn't want him thinking I was in here drinking.' Jim realised he had almost put his foot in it.

The door behind the landlord opened, and his wife carrying a tray with Jim's bread and cheese came into the bar, 'Here you are,' she said. 'The finest in Somerset, you won't get bread or cheese like this in Bristol, I can tell you.'

'I was just saying about the girlfriend, to our young friend here,' said the landlord.

'Oh Esme,' said his wife, 'she a one, that one, I think Mister Cotterell would be better off without her

204

personally.'

'Cotterell,' said Jim, 'did you say Cotterell?'

'Well yes, that's who you're here to see, isn't it?'

Jim started to chuckle and shook his head, 'No it definitely isn't anybody called Cotterell.' Jim took his bread and cheese and feeling rather dejected sat back down in front of his almost untouched drink. He could see that the landlord and his wife were whispering conspiratorially together. A waste of time, a total waste of time, Jim thought, just as I thought I was getting somewhere, ah what the hell, 'Can I have a large scotch, please?' he called across to the bar.

The landlord poured and set the scotch down on the bar, 'Here you are, sir,' he said. Jim smiled to himself as he approached the bar, suddenly a large scotch had bestowed him with a knighthood again, 'Anything in it, sir?' he asked.

'Just your best wishes, thank you,' replied Jim.

'You know, I don't think you work for a solicitor at all,' said the landlord.

'You don't, what do you think I do then?' Jim asked.

'I think you're a policeman,' his wife nodded vigorously in agreement.

'What makes you think that, then?'

'For a start off,' he pointed, ' you haven't got a brief case, and it's Sunday, and another thing is your eyes are everywhere, all round the pub, you don't look like you miss a trick, and your clothes don't look like they've ever seen the inside of a solicitors office,' he pointed, 'the elbows aren't worn.

'I don't think you're just an ordinary policeman

205

either, I think you're a detective, at least a sergeant with that new lot they've set up, the fraud squad, I was reading about them in the paper, and I think you might be here not to see Cotterell himself, but his visitors, am I right?'

Jim's heart jumped, *visitors*, he could be on the right track after all, 'You know you should be a detective yourself,' he said.

'There, I knew I was right,' the landlord said triumphantly, he banged the counter with his hand and looked at his wife for her approval.

Jim leant forward right over the bar and lowered his voice to a whisper, 'Right then, tell me about these visitors, quietly.'

The landlord leant forward and lowered his voice, 'Well last week, Thursday after closing,' the landlord began.

'Hang on love, start at the beginning, and tell him about Esme's car.'

'Oh, yes, sorry dear, Esme turned up here on her own just before closing, she only had just the one drink and that's not like her I can tell you, then she went and sat in her car, well it wasn't her car, she was driving the Bentley, that's his car, Cotterell's. When I went out to lock the front door, she was still just sitting there staring up the road, I went out and tapped on the window, you alright Esme I said, she smiled and said she was fine. I came back in and told you didn't I love?'

The landlord's wife nodded her head, 'So you decided to go upstairs and watch her through the window didn't' you?' she said.

'Yes, to be honest I thought she was meeting a

boyfriend on the q.t. Anyway after quite a long time, I'd nearly gave it up as a bad job, this taxi pulled up, and she ducked down under the steering wheel out of sight, three men got out of the taxi and then the driver, then the driver went to the boot of the taxi and got out some bags, then the three of them walked off around the side of the pub. I thought that's funny I wonder where there're off? There's nothing around there you see. Then as soon as the taxi pulled away Esme sat up and the three men reappeared from around the corner, got into the Bentley and off they went.'

'Did you hear any conversation at all?' Jim asked.

'No, not really, nothing to speak of, one was from Scotland by his accent, it was only hellos and stuff like that.'

'Did you hear any names?'

'No can't say as I did.'

'Look you've been most helpful, I'll be glad if you keep our little chat to ourselves, I don't want to warn-'

The landlord interrupted, 'We won't have to go to court, will we?'

'I sincerely hope not,' Jim replied smiling. 'Just one other thing, where do you suppose the Bentley went?'

'Well back to Cottrell's place of course, that's obvious.'

'And where might that be?'

'I thought you knew, he lives in the cottage next to that big Georgian house over at Hunstrete, it's only about three miles, you can't miss it, it's the one with all the cars in the drive.'

'In Hunstrete, you say, what's the name of it?'

'You don't need a name it's the only one there, just along the road from Hunstrete House, this side.'

Jim now wished that he had driven to Pensford himself, so that he could go on to Hunstrete, wherever that might be. Still he had enough information to claim the thousand pounds from Harry and with some luck it would be the perfect opportunity to kill two birds with one stone.

Andy was dutifully waiting for Jim when he got back to the station, 'Any luck Jim?' he enquired.

'You might well be on the way to that new car,' Jim said with a broad grin.

'They're staying at the George and Dragon then Jim, are they?'

'No they are holed up in a place called Hunstrete, ever heard of it?'

'Hang on Jim, I've got a map here, I've got a feeling that it's quite near where you've been.' Andy produced a map from the glove compartment and briefly poured over it, 'Ah,' said Andy poking a finger, 'Here you are, Hunstrete.'

'Yes,' said Jim, 'and look here, Hunstrete House is actually marked on the map and the cottage they're holed up in is just along the road from it, so the landlord said. Come on Andy start driving remember there's a new car riding on this. '

'Tell you what Jim I'll drive but let's take your car, the taxi sticks out like a sore thumb.'

'Suits me fine,' said Jim.

In the car Jim realised just how close to Bristol

Pensford was, but like a different world, quiet and tranquil, I could be very happy in a place like this, he thought. They passed by the George and Dragon,   'I don't see any signs for Hunstrete,' said Jim.

'I don't expect they've got round to replacing them since the war finished,' said Andy,

'I never thought of that, we'll just have to keep our eyes peeled.'

'Here we are,' said Andy, 'we've got to turn towards Marksbury.'

'Are you sure?'

'Positive.'

Seeing the cottage proved to be a bit of an anti-climax although Jim didn't know what to expect, but all there was to be seen from the road was a driveway with several cars parked on it, and at the furthest end a ramshackle, wheel less old caravan. 'Not much of a love nest,' Jim said. Wispy grey smoke, curled upwards from the lop sided chimney and they could just see a couple of the upstairs windows. 'Looks like there's someone in, by the smoke, I've got a good mind to bang on the door.'

'What, you must be crackers. Sorry boss, come on we've seen enough, let's go.'

Jim looked around at Andy, his face had turned grey, his breathing was laboured and Jim could see he was shaking, 'Christ Andy, calm down, we're quite safe sitting here.'

'Let's go please Jim.'

'Alright, I've seen enough for now, let's go.' Andy rammed the car into gear and accelerated along the narrow lane; Jim could see the relief on his face and the sweat on his brow. 'Andy, have you ever had any personal dealings with the Newmans?' he asked, 'apart from the taxi ride last week that is.'

'No and I don't want to, I've heard enough about the Newmans to last me a lifetime.'

Jim wriggled down in the seat and closed his eyes; I wonder what tonight will bring? He thought.

CHAPTER ELEVEN

Jim picked up his drink from the counter in the bar of the Bear and Rugged Staff and glanced around, there were only a few people in evidence, but because the bar was so small it looked quite busy and crowded, Jim kept glancing at the door hoping and wondering if John would show up.

At a quarter to nine Jim was on his second drink and there was no sign of John, he kept glancing at his watch, knowing that Harry would have something to say if he was in the Charnbury much after nine. Jim had just swallowed the last drop of his scotch when the door opened and John walked in the pub, 'What can I get you John?' Jim asked.

'Just a half, I know what you're going to say, but I can't stop long, work again.'

'Don't you just do ordinary shifts then John?'

'Normally, but there's so much, more or less compulsory overtime at the moment, and you know the sergeant, he won't take a no for an answer.' Jim handed him his drink and they opted to sit at a table in the far corner of the bar. 'Still with Harry, are you Jim?'

'Not for much longer, a couple of days tops.'

'Listen Jim I don't want to sound like a gramophone record, but get out while you can, please,' as if to emphasise the point John lent forwards and firmly gripped Jim's forearm.

In that instant Jim knew that John had the same feelings for him as he had for John.

Jim placed his hand over John's arm and squeezed,

211

'So you're one as well then?'

'That's a funny way of going about it, but yes I am, the first time I saw you Jim you sent shivers up my spine, a queer policeman, what do you think of that?'

'I'm glad you are, the first time I saw you I had, um, you know, feelings.'

'Listen Jim, we'll have to be careful, what with my job and especially you with Harry James.'

'Yes, Harry can't stand homosexuals.'

'Yes I know.' John said.

'You know?'

'We know a lot about Harry James, we know a lot about the rest of you, that's why it's important for you to get away as soon as possible, Jim look at me, leave town, do something, anything, before it's too late.'

'A couple of days John, that's all it's going to take, just a couple of days more.'

'Have you thought what you're going to do?'

'More or less, I've got an idea, but I haven't ironed out the details yet.'

'Want to tell me all about it?'

Jim glanced at his watch, 'I've got to go John, Harry will be expecting me in the Charnbury, it won't do to keep him waiting, and can I give you a lift?'

'Yes thanks, just as far as the St. George nick will be fine.'

Jim drove out of Bristol through Lawrence Hill, Redfield and towards St. George, 'When can I see you again John?' he asked.

'The day after tomorrow, I've got to go up to London for the day tomorrow.

212

'What's that for?'

'Nothing exciting, just Police stuff, boring really. Here Jim, turn left here and park up behind the park.'

Jim drove around the back of St. George's Park and pulled up, John leant over and kissed Jim tenderly on the lips; Jim hesitated then kissed him back. John slid his arms around Jim and drew him to him, Jim's breathing shortened, he gave himself totally to the moment, and they kissed avidly with a passion Jim had never experienced, Jim knew he would never be able to kiss a woman in that way. But as quickly as it had started, it was all over, John pulled away, 'I've.....I've got to go,' he stammered, 'Bear and Rugged Staff eight o'clock, day after tomorrow.'

Jim nodded his head.

'Well I was just wondering about you then, Jim.' Harry didn't sound any too happy.

'Yes sorry Harry, evening boys, I've been busy.'

'Busy, busy, cheeky bastard,' Harry's eyes flashed and his voice hardened instantly. 'What sort of fucking busy keeps Harry James waiting?'

Jim felt quite cocky, 'The sort of busy that tracks Luke Newman down,' he replied.

'You'd better be serious Jim, are you serious Jim?' Harry sounded eager, although his face was still grim.

'I've never been more serious in my life, Harry.'

'Come on then give, where is he?' Harry started to smile.

'Hunstrete.'

'Hunstrete, never fucking heard of it, where is

Hunstrete?'

'It's near Pensford,' Ron interrupted, 'I was reading somewhere that-'

'Shut up Ron, go on Jim.'

'It's near Pensford; he's staying in a cottage that belongs to a Mr Cotterell.'

'Cotterell, never heard of him, who is he?'

'He's supposed to be a business man, that's all I know, but that's where he's staying alright.'

'Wonderful, that's wonderful,' Harry turned to the bar. 'Break out that crate of champagne I got you Harold, tonight we celebrate and after the funeral tomorrow, Hunstrete.'

Strong rays of sunlight flooded through Jim's bedroom window, Jim in that twilight world between sleep and consciousness was savouring John's kiss again, and as full consciousness came to the fore, he was aware of his erection, I'll need to do something about that before I get up, he thought.

Somehow he didn't feel guilty about John, like he had in the past, when he had seen males he admired. Yes, he had tried to go along with his friends at school and in the army when they made smutty jokes about women. He gawked with them at pictures in the Health and Efficiency magazine. He'd joined in conversations about what they would do with certain girls and what they said they had done, he'd boasted and bragged with his chums, said all the right things, made all the right noises, but now he didn't to have to pretend anymore and then of course

214

there was Audrey. What to do about Audrey? He didn't want to hurt her, didn't want to let her down. Then of course there was Harry. Jim smiled, his erection had deserted him.

'You're bright and early Jim,' Auntie Cath said.

'Yes Auntie I've got a busy day today, I've got to drive the boss to a meeting,' he lied.

'Yes, well I'm not interested in Harry James and his meeting, sit down and I'll get you a nice cup of tea, it's only just made.'

Jim arrived at Harry's, as arranged at ten, and this time to Jim's surprise he was waved straight through the gates. Harry was standing, cigar in mouth, talking to Grossman the undertaker as Jim drove up.

'Morning Jim, nice day for it,' Harry said.

'Morning Harry, good morning Mister Grossman.'

'I'm glad to see you've remembered a black tie Jim, I don't expect any of the rest will have, here put these in your pocket and get yourself on over to the chapel,' Harry handed Jim a handful of black ties, 'and tell them I'll expect them to put more into the singing today than when we were in chapel last.' Harry abruptly turned his back on Jim, nothing really changes, thought Jim, I've been dismissed.

At the chapel Jim he could see that there was no sign of Weasel, Ron was leaning on the chapel wall puffing away on a cigarette, with his head in the racing page of the newspaper and a pencil in his hand, 'Morning Ron,' Jim said, 'here's a black tie for you from Harry, where's Weasel?'

'You know Weasel, I got round there waited nearly ten minutes for him and he didn't come out so I fucked off.'

'Harry will go mad,' Jim said.

'Yes you're right, he most probably will,' he smiled.

'I wouldn't want to be in Weasel's shoes. You don't like Weasel very much, do you Ron?' Jim asked.

'Can't stand the sight of the little bastard.'

'Anal didn't like him either, did he?'

'Nobody likes him, not even Harry, especially Harry.'

'So why's he still around?'

'Well it's like this, Harry was devoted to his mother, he worshipped the very ground she walked on, he never knew his old man, well at least he always says he didn't, but that's another story. His mother lived with her sister, Weasel's mother; her old man had left years before so Harry, Harry's brother and Weasel were being brought up by the two women. Anyway Weasel's mother died of TB and so then Harry's mother had the three of them, eventually she went the same way as her sister, and on her death bed made Harry, because he was the eldest, promise that he'd always look after his brother and Weasel. Like I said Harry worshipped the ground his mother walked on, and what she said went, he'd never break a promise he made to her.

'Did you know that Harry still keeps all his mother's clothes in a room at his place, all stashed away neat and tidy, he goes in there now and again, gets them all out, lays them on the bed and talks to them. Then he pats the side of his face with the sleeve of one of her dresses, he reckons for hours at a time sometimes. He told me that one night when he was pissed right up, bit weird that, don't you think Jim?'

Jim nodded, 'So Weasel's untouchable, even by Harry, then?'

'You got it in one Jim. Harry's bought a pig farm,' said Ron out of the blue.

'What's that to do with Weasel?' Jim asked.

'I read somewhere that pigs will eat everything you give them,' Ron drew on his cigarette, 'everything.'

'I'm not with you.'

'Harry's decided that the Aust ferry is too much of a bother, then there's the expense, so he thought two birds with one stone, sell some bacon and get rid of our little problems.'

'I didn't know any of this,' Jim said.

'Well you know Harry; his right hand doesn't know what the left is doing most of the time.'

'So what's it all to do with Weasel being late?'

'I know that Harry is itching to see if it's true that pigs will eat everything, so Weasel might be the first client, with a bit of luck.'

'Christ Ron, you don't think Harry will kill Weasel if he doesn't turn up this morning?'

'If we make enough fuss about it he might.' Ron started laughing.

'You're getting me going, aren't you Ron?'

Ron carried on laughing, 'Am I?'

The hearse when it arrived was an impressive affair, drawn by four black horses, immaculately turned out, with black plumes attached to their head collars. The casket inside was of solid oak and was covered in ornate carvings, with sumptuous brass fittings Along the side of the roof was an ostentatious wreath, some four feet long bearing the inscription " June." Jim was amazed that apart from the flowers, which turned out to be Harry's idea, the seedy looking undertaker had more than surpassed himself.

Following on behind the hearse was a solitary gleaming black limousine; Jim could see Harry sitting in the back accompanied by a female that he didn't know. As she alighted, Jim noticed that she bore, more than a passing resemblance to June, but was obviously a few years older.

Harry looked quickly around and one look at his face told Jim that he was expecting more of a turn out.

Once inside the chapel however, Harry's face brightened up. Instead of following the coffin into the chapel most of Harry's men and the villagers were already seated. Jim noticed an absence of black ties and hoped Harry wouldn't notice, but he remembered that Harry didn't miss a trick. There was still no sign of Weasel and Jim thought that if he didn't show up, with a bit of luck, Harry would vent his anger on him and forget all about the ties.

Three quarters of the way through the service Jim glanced around and could see Weasel standing just inside the front door of the now jam-packed chapel; Jim nudged

Ron, and glanced over in Weasel's direction.

'Bollocks,' whispered Ron.

A very sombre Harry led the way to the pub and once inside called to Jim, 'Come on over here Jim and meet May, Jim this is May, June's sister.'

Jim recognised her as the other occupant of the limousine, he took her hand and said, 'How do you do.'

'I was just saying to May,' said Harry, 'how unexpectedly we lost June. The doctor said her heart attack was so sudden she wouldn't have known anything about it at all, such a blessing.'

Quite right there Harry, Jim thought, Anal said she wouldn't have known anything about it.

'You know May, I worshipped the very ground your sister walked on.... I've lost a saint, a veritable saint,' Harry's voice trembled with emotion, 'sorry...you'll have to excuse me...' his voice petered out, Jim looked on in amazement as he started to sob and floods of tears started to roll down his face. Harry turned away dabbing at his eyes with his hankie and made a bee line for Weasel, Jim was left stranded with May.

'Did you know my sister very well Jim?' she asked.

Jim noticed her North Country accent was far stronger and less cultured than that of her sister's. 'Not really,' he answered, 'you see I've only been with Harry for a very short time, I've just been demobbed from the army.'

'So tell me, what do you actually do for Harry then Jim?'

'I'm his chauffeur.'

'You mean like the chauffeur before you.'

'Well I drive, Harry and I used to drive June, I mean Missus James around, if that's what you mean.'

'You know very well what I mean Jim,' May caught hold of Jim's arm tightly and pulled him close; Jim suspected that May knew what had been going on with her sister and Lefty. May lowered her voice, 'This heart attack Harry said she had, was she with you at the time? If you take my drift?'

'I don't know what you want me to say.'

'Oh come on Jim, do I have to spell it out to you? Harry's an old man; my sister was young, vibrant and so full of life, although we lived apart we were very close, she told me *everything*,' she paused and then pointedly repeated, 'everything. I knew all about her and Lefty, did she die happy? Was she with you at the time of her heart attack? That's what I'm asking.'

Jim nodded his head, 'She died doing what she liked best.'

'Splendid, thank you Jim, that's all I wanted to know, you know I just had a horrible feeling that Harry had had her done away with, I know that they didn't get along, I can't tell you how relieved I am; now that I've spoken to you.'

About two o'clock May bid farewell; Jim was thankful to see that she had her own transport, and that his services wouldn't be required.

'So what did you make of May then Jim?' Harry asked, as soon as she was out of the way.

'She's not stupid,' Jim said and proceeded to relate

to Harry their earlier conversation, Harry roared with laughter at the suggestion that he had had June killed, 'I'm surprised she didn't want to see June's body,' Jim said.

'She did, I knew she would,' said Harry, 'so I made sure the body only turned up as we were ready to leave for the chapel,' Harry's tone changed. 'Didn't do very well with the black ties back there, did you Jim?'

'Sorry Harry, I didn't realise that most of the people were already waiting inside the chapel.'

Harry glanced across the bar to where Weasel was sitting, 'That little toe rag was late, it won't be forgotten.'

Suddenly Jim remembered the conversation he had with Ron about the pig farm, 'Ron tells me you've bought a pig farm Harry.'

'Yes, a couple of weeks ago now, pigs eat everything and anything, well that's what I've been told, with a bit of luck Jim they'll be eating Lucky Luke before long.' Harry smiled at Jim. 'Tell you what, pick me up tonight about seven and then Ron and we'll go and have a look at, what was that place called?'

'Hunstrete.'

'Yes that's it Hunstrete.'

'What about Weasel, do I pick him up as well?'

'No, fuck him; I've seen enough of that little shit for one day.'

'Christ,' said Harry, 'I've lived in Bristol all my life, but I've never been this way before.'

'It's a good hideaway Harry,' Jim said, 'and just a few miles out of town, but nobody has heard of it.'

221

'Not so Jim, not such a good hideout, you've found the bastard in no time flat,' Harry said. 'Anyway, you haven't told us, how did you suss out where he was?'

'Simple really, I was in the right place at the right time and I talked to the right people,' Jim thought he had better not mention Andy.

'So how much further is it?' asked Ron, 'there's not enough room to swing a cat around in this motor. I can't get comfortable, I can't stretch my legs.'

'Stop moaning Ron, for Christ's sake,' Harry said.

'Well I usually get to sit in the front.'

'Well you don't today, now fucking shut up, is it much farther Jim?'

'No we're nearly into Pensford, and then it's only a couple of miles.'

'Pensford,' Ron said, 'that's where John Wesley preached in 1763, you know Harry, the Methodist preacher.'

'Jesus Christ Ron, course I know who John Wesley was, I'm just fucking amazed that you do. How d'you know it was 1763? I think you've just made that up.'

'Honest Harry, it's true, I read it somewhere, he preached in Pensford at eight in the morning then went on to Shepton Mallet for dinner time.'

'You're full of crap Ron,' said Harry. 'Look, there's a pub, stop Jim pull over, and let's have a wet.'

'Can't go in there Harry, I told the governor I was a rozzer.'

'You little rascal, so that's how you found out about Luke.'

As before, the cottage could hardly be seen from the road, and now, as it was dark   it was even more hidden, all that could be seen from the roadside was a dim light shining out from one of the upstairs rooms. 'He's in there,' Harry said, 'yes he's in there alright, I just know it; I can smell him, the bastard's in there, go and have a look Ron.'

'Piss off, I'm not committing suicide.'

'I'll go,' said Jim.

'Here take this Jim,' Ron produced a hand grenade from his pocket.

'Jesus Christ Ron, put that away, I'm going to go in there and tell them I need some water because the car's overheating.'

'Rolls Royce's don't overheat, think of something else Jim,' Harry said.

'They won't know it's a Rolls Royce.'

'What if they come out?' Ron said.

'Chuck the hand grenade, but stand well back Jim,' Harry was laughing.

'Look Harry, I know,' Jim said, ' if you get out of the car and go up the road out of sight and they do come out they won't see you.'

Jim walked cautiously along the long path towards the front door, I hope they haven't got a dog, he thought. They didn't need a dog; Jim hadn't got within fifteen yards of the front door, when the racket of a flock of geese broke the silence. Almost immediately the front door opened and a light flashed on blinding him, 'Who's out there?' called a male voice.

Jim could see nothing for the light, and then he was

aware of another torch light shining directly in his face. 'I'm sorry to bother you;' he ventured his hand shielding his eyes, 'my car's overheating, and I need some water.'

Another voice joined the first, 'Who is it?'

'Just somebody who's broken down, that's all.'

'Tell him we don't know anything about cars.'

Jim approached the voices, 'I'm sorry to bother you, I need some water that's all.'

'You got something to put water in?'

'No I haven't got anything.'

'Bit stupid, going out without anything.'

'You don't expect a Rolls Royce to break down,' Jim said.

The light was lowered out of Jim's eyes, 'Rolls Royce, you're too young to own a roller where did you get it from, nick it did you?'

Jim's eyes were gradually becoming accustomed to the light and he could see past the two men in front of him. The front door opened up straight into a living room and Jim could see one man sprawled in an easy chair in front of a log fire, and the legs of another, but the front door was obscuring the rest of him. 'I'm a chauffeur, it's not stolen.'

'Pity, I'm in the market for luxury motors, wait there, I'll get you some water.'

The man disappeared inside the house, Jim slowly moved over to one side, trying to see past the door, all too soon the man was back carrying an old watering can, 'Here, don't bother to bring it back in, just leave it out by the front gates.'

'Thank you very much, sorry to have troubled you.'

Jim took the watering can and made his way back up the pathway, the geese, which had quietened down started again. Jim poured the water away and left the can by the gates, he could just make out Harry and Ron standing against the tall hedge further up the road. Jim jumped in the Rolls and drove up to meet them.

'Christ it's freezing out there, turn the heater up Jim, and let's find a pub,' Harry said.

'Not going to be easy to creep up on that lot, Harry,' Jim said.

'Dogs?'

'No worse, geese, you can't get near the place before they start.'

'So that was the row we heard,' said Harry.

'Did you know Jim,' said Ron, 'that in 365BC the Romans used geese to save them from a surprise attack by the Gauls.'

'You're full of bullshit Ron,' Harry said.

'I'm telling you Harry, it's true.'

'Bugger off.'

They continued their journey in silence until, 'Come on Jim, and find a pub for Christ's sake.'

'I don't know the lay of the land down here Harry, let's head back to Bristol, it won't take that long.'

'Tell you what, Jim boy, the Sceptre, we haven't been in the Sceptre for Christ knows how long, it should be safe enough now and I owe Bert a drink for the other day.'

Bert was genuinely pleased to see Harry, Ron and Jim, 'Hello strangers,' he said genially, 'the drinks are on me.'

'Here you are Bert,' Harry said, 'stick that in your arse pocket, and thanks for keeping your trap shut the other day.'

'Cheers Harry I won't say no, things have been a bit quiet lately, where's Weasel tonight?' he asked.

'Don't talk to me about fucking Weasel, he almost missed Anal's funeral.'

'Yeah, that was very sad about Anal; very sad indeed, good man was Anal.'

'You'll have to excuse us Bert, but we're going to sit in the corner and do a bit of scheming.'

'Well that is something you've always been good at Harry, scheming,' Bert laughed.

'Right then Jim,' said Harry when they were seated, 'now that I've thawed out a bit, how many of them did you say were there in that cottage?'

'I saw four; there might have been more but I didn't see them, and there should have been a girl, but I didn't see her either.'

'What girl?' Harry asked.

'She's the girlfriend of this bloke Cotterell, but that's all she is.'

'Why don't we just go down there with a team and shoot the lot?' Ron asked.

'That would be the easy way, I know that Ron, but I want the bastard alive, I want to know as much about his business as he does. Then I want to inflict as much pain and damage as I can before he dies. I want to see him beg for his fucking life, not that he'll get it. No, we take him alive, any ideas Jim? You were in there.'

'Well one of them said he was in the market for

luxury motors, I can't think of anything else.'

'What if you turned up again offering to sell a motor, it would get one out of the house, and we could take care of him, then that would leave three.'

'What then?' Ron asked.

'They would just think that their chum was coming back in, and they wouldn't take any notice, shoot them and Bob's your uncle.'

'What if they don't go for the bait?' Ron asked.

'Everybody likes a good deal; Look at Peter Newman he couldn't help himself, yes they'll go for it alright, are you up to it Jim? You've got a grand to come for finding Luke Newman, and there's another grand going if we take him alive, what do you say?'

'I say when do we do it?'

'That's what I like to hear,' Harry called across to the bar, 'Bert, this is a real gem you found for me, a real gem.' Harry stood up and clasped Jim's cheeks with both hands and squeezed. 'Right,' said Harry, 'this is what we are going to do, we hit them in daylight, they won't be on their guard so much in daylight. Can't make it too early mind, and we need a motor to flog them.'

Ron interrupted, 'Leave that to me boss, how do you fancy a nice Jag Jim?' he rubbed his hands together.

'I don't mind Ron, but I remember he said he was only interested in flash motors.'

'Ron used to nick cars for a living, didn't you Ron? That's before I set him on the straight and narrow.' Harry and Ron smiled at each other. 'I'll get Darky Dillon to send down some of his top boys and Lucky Luke will be history. If you can come up with a motor Ron, we'll do it tomorrow.'

'Go and get the drinks in then Jim,' Harry ordered.

Bert smiled at Jim as he approached the bar, 'Hello again young Jim and how are you getting on working for Harry?'

'I know I shouldn't say it Bert, 'Jim lowered his voice, 'but I wish I had taken a job in the boot factory, but I'm in far too deep now...' Jim's voice tailed away.

'Yes son, and it's all my fault, I thought I was doing you a favour, but I can tell by your face that I wasn't and I'm truly sorry.'

'Don't blame yourself Bert, you did what you did for the best, I could have said no, after all said and done I'm over twenty one, here stick another in there, put up one for Harry and Ron and have one yourself.'

CHAPTER TWELVE

Jim spent a fitful and restless night, not that he was in fear of what the new day would bring, but it was just that there were too many confusing thoughts bombarding his senses. He was up way before Auntie Cath and she was astonished to see him already sitting pensively at the kitchen table sipping tea, 'What's this then Jimmy peed the bed again this morning?'

'No I've got another busy day, Auntie; I've got to drive a car that Harry's selling down to Somerset.'

'I expect it's stolen,' she replied disparagingly.

'Don't be such an old cynic Auntie.'

'I expect it is. Haven't heard much about Audrey lately, have you two had a fall out?'

'Auntie I just haven't had the time.'

'Well you should make time Jimmy, make time. You don't want to lose her now do you?'

Ron was leaning on his front wall reading the newspaper and smoking a cigarette when Jim arrived, 'Got anything then Ron?' he asked.

'Come on round the back lane,' Ron discarded his cigarette, folded his newspaper up and put it in his jacket pocket. Jim followed on as Ron led the way. 'Feast your eyes on this, my son,' he said.

'You don't mess about, do you Ron?'

'A beauty isn't it?'

'It looks like it's brand new.'

'Can't be more than a couple of months old, I still haven't lost my old touch.'

'That's unusual for a Buick Ron; it's a right hand drive.'

'Yeah the owner would still have it if it was a left hooker, could never get used to them, the last time I drove one, it was a left hand drive Merc.

'I was out with Weasel, there we were tootling along the road and then we came to this hump back bridge. Well suddenly this motor came towards us, to be honest, I was too far out in the road, and bang,' Ron started to chuckle. 'Anyway, this geezer got out of his car, went straight to Weasel's side of the car, thinking he was the driver, leant in through the window and smacked Weasel straight in the chops. Then the bloke looked and could see that there was no steering wheel in front of Weasel, well that stopped him in his tracks, he started to come round to my side, so I got out a bit quick, he took one look at the size of me, jumped back in his car, and he buggered off.' Ron started laughing at the memory. 'What do you think Weasel said, Jim?'

'I don't know.'

'I bet you do, true to form, he was shouting through his fingers, which were dripping with blood-.'

'I know,' Jim interrupted, 'he wanted you to catch him up so he could stripe him.'

'You got it in one, Jim boy.'

'Anyway Ron, we had better make a move, Harry won't want to be kept waiting.'

'That's for sure.'

A convoy of four cars drove towards Hunstrete, Harry accompanied by Weasel in front although he didn't really know the way, followed on by Jim, then Ron and finally Darky's boys in a pre- war Ford V8.

After Pensford Jim took the lead and they all pulled up about half a mile away from the cottage.

'Right,' said Harry, 'you know what to do Jim, no weapons mind Jim, just in case, and coax him out, Ron you take care of him and then we'll take things from there.'

Jim drove the Buick to almost the front of the cottage and Ron pulled in just behind. Apprehensively, Jim looked back at Ron, as he went in through the front gate; Ron smiled and gave him the thumbs up. Jim's heart started to thud, into the lion's den, he thought.

He had barely set foot on the drive when the cacophony began, the front door of the cottage opened and half a face appeared around it. Not feeling as confident as he tried to appear, Jim walked forwards, 'What do you want?' the face was still half hidden by the door.

'Sorry to bother you, I was here last night and the man I was talking to said he was interested in buying tidy cars.'

'He's not here.'

'But I've come all the way from Bristol and I can't take the car back, if you know what I mean?'

'What sort of car is it?'

'Buick, but it's a right hand drive.'

'Well like I said he's not here.' The man started to close the door.

Jim walked right up to it, 'How long will he be?'

The man opened the door back up, Jim could see that he appeared to be alone, 'Well they've gone into Pensford for some fags and newspapers, and they shouldn't be too long, unless they go in the pub that is.' The man glanced at his watch; Jim noticed by the gold strap it was obviously very expensive. The man continued. 'Probably too early for the pub, you shouldn't have too long to wait,' and he began to close the door again.

Jim noticed he said they, 'Would you, like to see the car?' Jim asked quickly as the door was closing.

'Yeah, alright,' the man started to open the door again. 'Why not, it'll pass the time.'

Jim sauntered slowly back up the garden path his hands thrust deep in his trouser pockets, trying to give the impression of being casual, the man followed on behind, the geese started up once more. As they got to the roadway, the man stopped suddenly in his tracks. 'Hang on a minute,' he pointed, 'what's that other car doing there?'

'Got to get home, haven't I? If we have a deal.' Jim replied as casually as he could.

'Who's that in the car?'

'It's only my buddy.'

For such a large individual Ron was out of his car in an instant, he bounded over to the man, ran straight into him and knocked him off his feet, Jim was flabbergasted, ' Quick Jim,' he said as he sat on him, 'look in his pockets, is he tooled up?'

Jim searched, the man struggled, screaming

obscenities, but he was no match for Ron, 'Nothing Ron, he's clean.'

'We've only got ourselves first prize, Jim boy, meet Lucky Luke,' Ron pulled his revolver from his pocket and discharged it into the air. Almost immediately Darky's boys came running up the road hell for leather, all brandishing weapons, closely followed by Weasel and finally Harry. 'Look what we've got Harry,' Ron cried out triumphantly.

'Well well, fucking well,' Harry said, 'get him in the car Ron, and let's get going while the going's good.'

'There's no rush Harry, they're all gone to Pensford shopping,' Jim said.

'Right, well get in the cottage then Weasel, and turn it over, then put a match to it. You other boys cover Weasel's arse and we'll all meet up at the pig farm.'

Ron bundled Luke Newman into the back seat of Harry's car, with his revolver cocked and held an inch from his nose, Jim slid into the driving seat, and Harry sat on the other side of Ron, he too produced a revolver, ' Well Luke,' he said, 'you haven't got much to say for yourself, have you?'

'How the fucking hell did you find me?'

'That's better, thought you'd lost your tongue. Actually, you might later on,' Harry giggled. 'It's all thanks to young Jim here,' Harry leant forward and patted Jim on the shoulder. 'A little bit of detective work and before you know where you are, you aren't.' Harry started to chuckle, then laugh and Ron joined in. 'You're not laughing Jim,' Harry said, 'didn't you get it?'

'Sorry Harry, I was concentrating on the road.'

233

Harry's pig farm turned out to be on the outskirts of the village of Siston, eight miles east of Bristol. Jim with his driving window down smelt the farm long before he saw it. A short drive leading to a walkway between some pens led to a ramshackle building. The Welsh slate roof on one side had collapsed and the aged stonework was going the same way. The stench got worse as they got out of the car; Ron pushed Luke in front of them and they made their way between the pens. It was the first time Jim had been so close to pigs, he was amazed at the sheer size of them and he was glad to see there were thick coils of barbed wire strung along the top of their pens. The pigs reacted to the convoy of human beings by snorting, squealing and running back and forth excitedly along their small enclosures.

'Where's Ned?' Harry asked nobody in particular. No one answered, 'I'll kill him if he's gone to the pub.'

Luke Newman was frog marched in through the ramshackle galvanised door of what appeared to be less than salubrious living quarters, 'Told you,' Harry said, 'the bastard's gone out, he'll regret this, Jim go and have a good look around, will you? And see if he's anywhere about.'

Jim wandered back out into the open and started calling out, 'Ned, Ned,' but all he could hear was the sound of the pigs grunting and snorting, of Ned there was no sign.

By the time Jim had looked around and came back, Harry and Ron had Luke Newman trussed up like a turkey, and sitting on a chair similar to the one on the ferry, 'Any sign?' Harry asked.

'No, nobody, nothing,' Jim replied.

'You know anything about pigs, Jim?' Harry asked.

Jim shook his head, 'How about you Ron?' Harry looked enquiringly at Ron.

'I know they used to farm pigs in Roman times I read it somewhere.'

'Probably in the Sporting fucking Life, you're full of bollocks Ron, where's the nearest pub?'

'Miles away I expect, 'Ron answered.

'You two stay here and keep Luke company, while I'm gone. Luke you're going to tell Ron and Jim all your business dealings and I mean all. We know most of it anyway, from your mate Sid Morgan, and it might be a surprise to you Luke but he was on my pay roll, well for a time anyway.'

Luke Newman remained silent; Harry turned away and left the room.

'Let me go and I can put you on to some real money,' Luke said, his voice quavering with fear.

'Real money, how much?' Ron asked.

'More than you'll earn in your lifetime.'

'How much? I want to know how much you think your life is worth,' Ron said.

'Fifty grand.'

'Hear that Jim, he's only worth fifty grand, I take it that's fifty for me and fifty for Jim?'

'A hundred then, I'll give you a hundred grand each.'

'Hear that Jim, his life's worth two hundred grand. You've got a couple of hundred grand and you're staying

235

in a shit hole in the back of fucking beyond, pull the other one.'

'I was only staying there until next week, and then it was to be South America, Rio de Janeiro '

'You got more chance of going to the moon now, Luke my cock,' Ron said. 'There you are Jim boy, now we know how much Luke's willing to pay us we'd better tap Harry up for a rise,' Ron started laughing.

'I'm serious; you'll never get a hundred grand from Harry.'

'Say we took you up on this offer,' Ron said, 'how would we get the money?'

'I've got it stashed; I'm the only one who knows where it is, you take me there, I'll give you the money and then you let me go.'

'Hear that Jim, he's the only one, alright then Luke this is the plan, you give Harry what he wants to know about your business dealings, that'll keep him sweet, then we'll talk about this hundred grand.' Jim was flabbergasted, he couldn't believe that Ron would sell out, but when Ron turned away from Luke and gave Jim a broad grin and a wink, he knew Ron hadn't changed his allegiances. 'Right Jim, Luke's going to tell us all about his businesses, and without any violence, you know Luke I felt sure that we'd have to beat the crap out of you. Find some paper to write on Jim and a pen.'

'Hang on, what if Harry comes back before you get me out of here?'

'Once Harry finds the pub he'll be gone for hours, right come on then Luke, give,' said Ron, 'we want everything, we want names, addresses, any girls that you run and anything else, understand?'

Luke started talking and Jim started writing, he was amazed just how far the Newmans' business empire stretched, ten minutes or so went by when they heard a car pull up, 'Is that Harry?' Luke asked.

'Doubt it, I expect it's Weasel, never you mind Luke I'll get shot of him,' said Ron.

Weasel walked in the room, closely followed by Darky's men, 'Here he is then,' said Weasel, Weasel walked across to where Luke was sitting, he delved into his waistcoat pockets and started to produce his cut throat razors.

'No you fucking don't,' said Ron, 'you cut him and I'll cut you.' Weasel hastily put the razors back from where they had come. 'Go and find a pub for an hour Weasel, and take them with you,' he pointed at Darky's men.

'What's going on Ron? Where's Harry?' Weasel asked, 'I've got something to show him,'

'We're sorting things out, now bugger off.' Weasel knew Ron of old and he knew it would do no good to argue. Weasel and Darky's men sloped off through the door, Ron cocked an ear and waited until he heard the car engine start, then he said. 'Right now where were we?'

Luke continued and after a few more revelations said, 'That's it.'

'Now you're sure you've left nothing out Luke?' Ron said menacingly.

'That's everything, honest everything, now about you letting me go.'

'Letting you go, what d'you mean?'

'A hundred grand, a hundred grand each,

remember?'

Ron reached into his jacket pocket, 'Know what these are Jim?' he asked, holding up what he was holding.

'Looks like a pair of pinchers to me, Ron,' Jim replied.

'Yeah, they look like pinchers, I'll grant you that, but they're not, they used to belong to Anal. If you look at them Jim, you'll notice that the handles are longer than pinchers, broader, a lot broader, more comfortable in your hand, you can get more purchase, and they are a lot sharper, a lot sharper altogether. Anal used to use them, they were his, when he was an iron fighter; they're called nips, well end nippers if you want to be precise about it, they make them in America, we can't get anything like them over here. Strange that really considering our steel industry, don't you think that's odd Jim?' Jim looked bemused. 'All the stuff we produce, ships, airplanes, motor cars, heavy machinery, all of it made here in Great Britain and it all goes all over the world and we can't make a decent pair of fucking nips.

'Remember Anal, Luke?' Luke shook his head. 'Don't sit there shaking your fucking head, you prick,' Ron's voice began to rise. 'You know who Anal was alright. You'll tell us where the two hundred grand is and I might just spare you Anal's nips.'

Luke shook his head again; his voice trembled, 'Honest, I don't know who you're on about.'

'I don't believe you, you prick,' Ron stood over him and holding the nips an inch away from the end of Luke's nose opened the jaws. 'Who killed Anal, was it you?'

'No, please don't hurt me,' he sobbed, 'it was Angus.'

'The Jock?'

Luke nodded his head, 'I wasn't even there, I didn't know anything about it until after.'

'Alright now where's the fucking dosh?'

'There is money but it's not that much, I'll let you have it, just let me go, please, I'm begging you.' Luke said, his voice quavering.

'Did Anal beg you, when you were stuffing the red hot poker up his ass, you *cunt*.'

Luke began to twist and turn against his restraints, the tears started to roll down his face, 'I told you I didn't do it...please, please, don't hurt me...please,' he sobbed, 'I'll tell you where the money is.'

'Oh, you'll fucking tell us alright, you little cunt,' Ron stepped forward and with his left hand clamped Luke's hand firmly to the arm of the chair, opened the nips wide with his right hand and slid the jaws over the end joint of Luke's little finger. Ron roared, Luke screamed as Ron squeezed the handles of the nips together. 'Where's the fucking money?' Ron shouted.

Luke slumped in the chair with his head down, he whimpered, 'It's at the cottage.'

'There you are, that was easy, wasn't it Luke?' Ron said more quietly, 'now how much is there and where do we find it?'

'I'll tell you, please don't hurt me again, there's seventy grand.'

'Only seventy, you said two hundred. Right you fucker, come on then, where is it?' Ron stuck the nips back under Luke's nose.

Luke snivelled, 'It's in a Gladstone bag, it's on top of the wardrobe in the first bedroom on the right at the top of the stairs, just promise you won't hurt me.'

'I promise,' said Ron, he grabbed Luke's hand again and scrunched the handles of the nips together, this time the top joint of Luke's index finger dropped to the filthy floor. 'There,' he said smiling, 'that didn't fucking hurt, did it?'

Jim stared with horror, although he had witnessed the atrocities of the war, and although Luke Newman was probably responsible for Anal's death, he didn't have the stomach to stand and watch as Ron coldly and pleasurably cut pieces from Luke's body. 'Ron,' he said, 'I don't think Harry will be too pleased if he's a goner when he gets back.'

'Fuck me Jim; just as I was starting to enjoy myself, here put something over his hand, he's bleeding like a pig.' Ron wiped Anal's nips on Luke's suit front and put them back in his pocket, ' I've only just started with you,' he said, and just for good measure he cuffed Luke across the face with the back of his hand.

Jim took out his handkerchief, and attempted to wrap it around Luke's fingers, the blood oozed through the material, 'I can't stop it with this, Ron, go and see if there's a towel or something.'

Ron strolled off to what appeared to be the kitchen and returned with a grey crumpled tea towel he tossed it to Jim, 'Here try that,' he said.

Jim wrapped Luke's fingers in the filthy tea towel, 'That should do it,' he said.

'Any chance of a fag?' Luke whispered.

'I don't smoke,' Jim replied, 'Ron, he wants a

cigarette.'

'I don't know if he deserves one.' Ron said callously.

'Come on Ron, he's told us what we want to know.'

Ron pulled his cigarettes from his pocket, stuck two in his mouth and lit them both, 'Here,' he said, 'puff on this, it's the last you'll get, because that sounds like Harry's car now.'

Luke was sucking greedily away on his cigarette when Harry came in, closely followed by Weasel, Darky's boys and a seedy looking, thin, scruffy individual. 'Everything alright, is it boys?' Harry asked. 'Look what I found, pissed up in the pub, this time of the day as well, disgusting,' he pointed at his scruffy companion. 'Give him a fucking good smack Ron.' Ron stepped forward. 'No, not in here take him outside; I want to talk to Luke.' Ron dragged the man effortlessly through the doorway; before Harry had even spoken again they could hear the man's muted screams of pain.

'That'll teach him,' Harry said, 'pay him good money and that's the way I get repaid, now then Luke my son, my boys, they've been looking after you have they? See you've given him a smoke, does he deserve it Jim?'

Jim showed Harry the list of Luke's businesses, 'Took a bit of persuading then Jim, looking at his hand.'

Jim chose not to answer, 'You got anything to tell me Jim?' Harry asked.

'How do you mean Harry?' Jim asked.

'Did he tell you anything else?'

'He tried to bribe us with seventy grand he says he's got to let him go free.'

241

'Where's this seventy grand?'

'He says it's back at the cottage in a Gladstone bag, Harry.'

'Good lad Jim, Weasel's found the money already. See that Luke, loyalty, that's what you call loyalty. Harry James' boys don't hold out on Harry.

'There's a good drink at the end of this for my team, and for you and your crew nothing but fucking misery. You boys,' Harry looked at Darky's men, 'you can get back to town now, and tell Darky I'll be in touch.

'Weasel you go out to the motor, bring the bag in and a couple of bottles, and hurry Ron up while you're out there.' Jim noticed that Weasel hadn't opened his mouth once since he had come back with Harry, he assumed he still wasn't in Harry's good books, although turning up with Luke's money, he thought should have made a big difference.

Harry lit up one of his large cigars, took a long puff on it and turned his attention to Luke, facing him he said, 'Did you kill Anal?'

'Not me Harry, no.'

'Mister fucking James to you, were you there when he was killed?'

Luke bowed his head, 'No, Mister James,' he murmured.

'We've already asked him Harry,' Jim chipped in.

'Well now I'm asking him. Who killed Anal?'

'Angus the Jock did it.'

'What did *you* do Luke?'

'Nothing, nothing at all, I didn't touch him, I swear.'

'No you didn't touch him. You said, don't do that

Jock, don't hurt Anal, don't stuff that red hot poker up his ass, didn't you?'

Luke hung his head, 'I wasn't even there, it's the truth,' he whispered softly.

'I'm fucking talking to you,' Harry screamed, his face inches from Luke's.

'I didn't do anything,' he answered despairingly.

'Where's the Jock now?'

'I don't know.'

'Wrong fucking answer,' Harry pulled the tea towel from Luke's hand. 'Fuck me Luke,' he said, 'you really will have to s stop biting your finger nails.' Harry puffed on his cigar, took it from his mouth and held it against the severed end of Luke's little finger. Luke tried to pull away and screamed out in agony. 'Where's Jock?' Harry said again, replacing his cigar in his mouth.

'On my life I don't know.'

'Oh, it is on your fucking life alright.' Harry grabbed Luke's hair with one hand, pulled his head up and back and taking the cigar back out of his mouth, bit Luke on the nose. Luke screamed out with pain, trying to pull his head away, Harry kept biting.

Ron and Weasel came back through the door carrying bottles and glasses, 'What's up Harry?' said Ron, 'feeling a bit peckish?'

Harry turned away from Luke, and spat a sizable lump of Luke's nose on the floor; from his blood splattered lips there came howls of wild laughter, Ron joined in followed by Weasel, who laughed loudest of all. Jim felt three pairs of eyes staring at him and belatedly he joined in the laughter. 'What's up with you Jim?' Harry asked, wiping his mouth with his handkerchief, 'no stomach for it.'

'No, not really Harry, if I'm honest,' Jim replied.

'Remember what that cunt did to Anal, bite his fucking ear off Jim,' Jim didn't move. 'Bite his fucking ear off, I said,' Harry shouted insanely, 'bite it off you fucker!'

Ron came to Jim's rescue, 'I expect he's already had something to eat, Harry,' he said, and they all started to laugh again, 'I'll take Jim's share, if it's alright?' Ron moved in on Luke and clamped his mouth onto Luke's left ear, Weasel not to be outdone and in an attempt get back into Harry's good books, went to Luke's other ear and followed suit. Luke screamed and struggled, but to no avail, both Rom and Weasel turned away from Luke, their mouths bloodied. Ron spat a sizable chunk of Luke's ear to the dirty floor.

Luke cried out, 'For God's sake just shoot me, please.'

'Shoot you, fucking shoot you,' said Harry, 'we haven't even fucking started on you yet, this is for Anal, you'll going to take fucking days to die my son, days and fucking days.'

Days, thought Jim, days.

'Where's that toe rag Ned, Ron?' Harry asked.

'He was still unconscious when I came in Harry,' Ron replied.

'Chris Ron, you haven't killed him have you, we'll be fucked without somebody who knows about pigs, get on out there and bring him round.' Ron ambled off outside, 'Jim pick those bits of finger up, I want to see if pigs really will eat anything.'

244

Jim picked up Luke's fingers in his already bloodied handkerchief and walked outside, Ron was crouched down by the side of Ned patting his cheek with the flat of his hand and telling him to wake up, 'Here Jim, see if you can get him to stir.'

'Cop hold of this then Ron,' Jim said, and handed Ron his handkerchief.

'What is it?' Ron asked.

'Luke's fingers, cop hold of them a minute,' Jim got down by the side of Ned, felt for a pulse in his neck and his wrist. 'Ron, sorry but you're right in the shit, he's dead,' he said.

'What's that, what's going on?' Harry and Weasel appeared in the doorway.

'I've croaked him boss,' Ron said pointing.

'Charming, that's fucking charming, well done Ron, well fucking done, you stupid bugger,' Harry was livid, Weasel looked pleased, 'I've got a pig farm with no farmer, nobody knows fuck all about pigs, you've fucked up good and proper this time Ron, any bright ideas?'

Ron shook his head, 'Sorry Harry,' he said.

'Sorry Harry,' Harry mimicked.

'We could always catch it all on fire, Harry,' Weasel said.

'I'll catch you on fire, you little prick,' Harry started to stamp his feet childishly.

'Can I make a suggestion Harry?' Jim spoke up.

'It'll better be sensible, well go on then.'

'How about the farmer at Hambrook, he'll know all about pigs.'

Harry started to calm down, 'I don't know, black

market's one thing, murder's something else. Might work, I don't know,' Harry walked around, head bowed, rubbing the scar on his cheek, 'I'll have to go and see, right then, Weasel, you stay here,' Harry pointed at Ned's corpse on the ground. 'Chop this lump of shit up and feed him to the pigs, and Ron, don't you dare touch Luke, you hear, you've done enough fucking damage for one day.' Harry puffing away on his cigar strutted off towards his car.

'Here Jim, chuck his fingers in the sty, let's see what happens,' Ron said.

Jim walked over to the nearest sty followed by Ron and Weasel, and shook his handkerchief out over the barbed wire; one of the pigs came straight over, sniffed at the fingers and walked away. 'Not hungry, by the looks of it,' said Ron.

'Just been fed, I expect,' said Weasel.

'Bit pointless cutting him up really,' said Ron pointing at Ned.

'We'll be in the shit, if we don't,' said Weasel.

'You already are,' said Ron, 'here take this, Jim,' Ron handled Jim his pistol, 'go and keep your eye on Luke, me and Weasel will sort something out, out here.'

Jim took Ron's gun and walked back inside, Luke was sat, shoulders slumped and head down, and as Jim came in he looked up. Jim could see the look of dread, desperation and foreboding in Luke's eyes, he looked down and could see that Luke had wet himself, 'I'm going to tell you something Luke,' Jim said very softly, 'and then

I'm going to do you a favour.'

'You're going to let me go?'

'Not exactly, no,' said Jim, 'I just wanted you to know, that I'm going to...' he lowered his voice even more, walked around behind Luke and said even quieter in his ear, 'I'm going to kill Harry,' Jim took a step back, raised the pistol and quite calmly shot Luke through the back of the head.

Ron closely followed by Weasel came running in, 'Jesus Christ Jim, what's going on?' Ron shouted.

'I've shot him Ron,' Jim handed Ron the pistol.

'What the fuck did you do that for?'

'I couldn't watch him suffer anymore.'

'What after the way Anal suffered? You prick.'

'Sorry I just couldn't.'

'You're right in the shit now Jim,' Weasel said, he looked relieved and pleased at the prospect.

'Don't just stand there gloating Weasel,' Ron said, 'let's get our thinking caps on.'

'What d'you mean?' Weasel said.

'I mean we've got to sort something out, Harry is going to go crazy when he finds out Luke's dead....I know, we'll say he tried to escape.'

'Oh yeah, Harry's sure to believe that,' Weasel said.

'Well can you think of a better idea?' Ron looked at Weasel, Weasel shook his head. 'How about you Jim?'

'Quite honestly Ron,' Jim said quietly, 'I'm gone beyond caring what Harry James thinks anymore.'

'Christ Jim, have you lost your marbles? Get a grip of yourself; Harry will have me shooting you, talking like that. Come on help me untie him and we'll get him out in the yard.' Weasel stood motionless smiling. 'I'll wipe that grin right off your chops, in a minute Weasel,' Ron said, 'now come on and help.'

Between them they untied Luke's lifeless body and carried it outside into the yard, Jim could see that in the short time he was inside the farmhouse Ron had already severed both of Ned's arms. A large woodman's axe lay on the ground where Ron had dropped it.

'Right,' said Ron, 'the pigs are going to get fed whether they want it or not, I'll chop, you two dish it up.'

'No chance Ron, I'm doing nothing,' Weasel turned away, reached into his pocket, produced his cigarettes and lit one up. 'You're next Weasel,' Ron shook the axe in Weasel's direction, 'and that's a promise.'

'Fucking hell, Ron,' Weasel said, and threw his cigarette away.

Between them they made short work of the unpleasant task, and then all three leaning on the wire surrounding the pig sties watched and waited. 'They're still not hungry,' said Ron, 'come on let's go inside and have a drink.'

'What shall we tell Harry, Ron?' Jim asked.

'I told you, say he tried to escape.'

'D'you think he'll swallow it?'

'He hasn't got much choice, and you Weasel, you keep your mouth shut, understand?' Weasel declined to answer, 'I'm telling you Weasel, you keep your mouth shut or else. In fact Weasel, I've got a brilliant idea, you can tell Harry that it was you that shot him.'

'Why me?'

'Because I've fucking said so, that's why.' For over an hour they kept listening for Harry's car, Jim kept going out to check on the pigs, and by the time they eventually heard the soft clunk of the door of Harry's car shutting, the trio were well into the second bottle of scotch. Ron glanced at Weasel with a look that said everything, Harry entered the room and looked around, 'Well?' he said.

Ron glared at Weasel, 'Had a bit of bother, Harry,' Weasel said.

'Where is he?'

'He made a run for it.'

'Where is he?' Harry asked again.

'I had to shoot him Harry.' Weasel said.

'Where is he?'

'Pig food.'

'Pour me out a drink Jim, how did he get free Weasel?'

'Fuck knows, we'd just finished feeding Ned to the pigs, there we were leaning on the sty watching them and having a smoke, when I happened to look around and there was Luke legging it up past the sties.'

'So you just shot him.'

'I tried to wing him Harry honest, but I got him in the head instead.'

'Oh well, at least he's dead,' Harry paused and took a sip on his drink, ' I've sold the farm boys, farmer will be here late the day after tomorrow, with a bit of luck there'll be fuck all left of those two by then. If there is, the bits will just have to go for a swim.' Harry took another sip on his drink and lit up another Havana, Luke Newman was forgotten. 'Come on boys; let's have another drink and we'll divvy up.'

Jim sat on his bed late that afternoon, looking at all the money he had amassed in the short time since he had left the army, just to think three weeks ago that I was in Woolwich and the week before that Hamburg, he thought, now I'm a rich murderer, a gangster with a girlfriend I don't even know if I want, I'm an extortionist, I'm turning into an alcoholic, I've become an accomplished liar, oh yes, and I'm homosexual.

CHAPTER THIRTEEN

'When are you seeing Audrey again Jimmy?' asked Auntie Cath dishing up Jim's tea.

'I thought I might see her tomorrow Auntie.'

'Can't you see her tonight Jimmy? I don't hear anything at all about her these days; you don't want her to get away, now do you?'

'Auntie the way you go on, you'd think that I've neglected her for weeks on end, it's only been a short while, I'll see her tomorrow, promise, I've got the whole day off tomorrow.'

'A day off on a Wednesday, well I never did.'

Jim impatiently waited until the clock said seven; he knew he was still an hour early before his date with John, but just like a child he felt he couldn't wait, 'I'm off now then Auntie,' he said.

'Where are you going at seven o'clock then Jimmy?'

'That's why I can't see Audrey tonight Auntie, and that's why I've got tomorrow off, I've got to drive Harry to a meeting and wait for him.'

'What sort of a meeting?'

'Freemasons, I think Auntie.'

'Don't make me laugh Jimmy, Harry James wouldn't be allowed to join the devil worshippers let alone the Freemasons.'

Jim arrived at the Bear and Rugged Staff twenty minutes early, he ordered his drink and took it from the

251

counter with a shaking hand, Christ I'm nervous he thought. He sat in a corner and watched the door and the clock on the wall, it was only when the clock said ten past eight and waves of disappointment were sweeping through Jim, that he realised that the pub clock was ten minutes fast.

Two minutes past eight by Jim's watch John and walked in, Jim jumped to his feet and made his way to the bar, 'Hello John,' he said, 'what are you having?'

John smiled, 'Hello Jim, gin and tonic, if that's alright?'

'Large gin and tonic please,' Jim said to the barmaid, 'and I think I'll try one of those myself.'

'Never tried gin then Jim?'

'Can't say as I have, first time for everything though,' he smiled at John, they took their drinks and sat down in the corner away from the bar, Jim sipped at his drink. 'Here this is a bit different,' he said, 'I could get used to this.'

'I always drink gin when there's nobody around,' said John.

'How d'you mean?'

'Well it's considered to be a bit of a woman's drink, or a Nancy boy's, it wouldn't do for you to ask for a gin and tonic when Harry James is around.'

'Yes, I see what you mean.'

'Tell me have you got to see Harry tonight?'

'Well, it's like this, there's no fixed arrangement but he expects that we all join him in the pub every night.'

'So did you plan on seeing him tonight?'

'If you haven't got to go, I'd rather stay here with you.'

John reached under the table and squeezed Jim's thigh, Jim could feel his heart start to pound, he reached under the table and caught hold of John's hand, and they both looked furtively around the bar. The barmaid was leaning on the counter with a cigarette dangling from her lips, studying her red fingernails, totally disinterested in her surroundings, and the only other three in the bar were sitting at a table engaged deep in conversation. 'Tell me Jim, how are your plans going with regards to leaving Harry?'

'It's just a question of picking the right time, and the opportunity hasn't come up yet.'

'You know what you're going to say to him then.'

'Oh yes, and I know what I'm going to do.' Jim realised he shouldn't have said anything.

'How do you mean? What you're going to do.'

'Well what I mean is what I'm going to do after I leave Harry.'

'Oh, I see, already made plans for the future then have you?'

'John you're sounding like a policeman again, twenty questions.'

John laughed, 'Yes unfortunately it's the schooling; let's talk about something else, how about football?'

'Football can't stand it.'

'Tell you what Jim; let's go to a pub where they won't bat an eyelid if we drink gin and tonic.'

'Where's that then, John.'

'Come on I'll show you, but not a word to Harry.'

'Why's that?'

'It's a poufs' pub, it's full of people just like us, come on drink up let's go.' Jim and John walked through the bomb site that used to be Wine Street, then High Street and into

253

St. Nicholas Street. 'Here we are Jim; this is it,' John said, 'The Radnor Arms.'

John led the way in through the pall of blue tobacco smoke. The pub was full to overflowing, they fought their way to the overcrowded bar, where they found that the barman was wearing heavy eye makeup, rouge and ruby red lipstick, ' Hello girls,' he said effeminately, ' what's it to be?'

'Two gin and tonics, please,' John asked.

'Coming up ladies, haven't seen you two in here before, London by your accent, isn't it?'

'Yes, just moved down.'

'Well I'm always here gorgeous and always available.'

They took their drinks and were lucky enough to find a couple of seats in the corner of the bar, 'What d'you think then Jim?'

'I didn't know this place existed, you've only been here two minutes, how did you find it?'

'I'm a policeman, remember?' They sat there in silence taking in the scene around them, there was a noisy row going on between two males along the bar, two more were in the corner fondling each other intimately. In another corner a middle aged male in a red flower-patterned dress and a badly fitting blond wig, wearing a string of pearls was pounding away on an out of tune piano, whilst his companion, a younger male dressed in an identical dress warbled away unsuccessfully.

'John,' Jim had to shout in John's ear to be heard, ' I don't know how to say this, I know what I am, but this pub, this place isn't right for me, it's the hubbub, it's too overpowering, can we go back to the Bear and Rugged

Staff please?'

'Yes,' he shouted back, 'it is a bit much, if you're not used to it, drink up and we'll go.' They walked back along Wine Street and resumed their place in the more tranquil and sedate atmosphere of the Bear and Rugged Staff.

'Look Jim I shouldn't be telling you this, but remember I said the net is closing, it's closing fast, there's an operation being planned to nail Harry James and the rest of you, and it's going to be sooner rather than later,'

'Harry's got connections John, he'll get warned.'

'Jim listen to me, Harry's connections won't save him, not this time they won't, I told you before, please Jim don't go down with the ship, you've a few short days that's all.'

They stayed in the Bear and Rugged Staff right until a quarter past ten when they noticed that the barmaid was giving them filthy looks, 'Sorry we didn't realise you were closing,' Jim said, 'thank you, good night.'

'Did you see her face Jim?' John asked as they walked to Jim's car.

'Yes she looked like she was chewing a wasp; do you want me to drop you off by the nick again?'

'I'm in no hurry.'

Jim pulled up outside his aunt's and he could see that all the lights were out, 'I thought she would be in bed by now,' he said, 'come on in John.'

They went quietly through the front door and through into the kitchen, Jim tipped the light on and turned, John

255

pulled Jim to him and kissed him full on the lips; Jim wrapped his arms around John's neck and tenderly kissed him back, John reached down to Jim's belt undid it and started to unbuckle his trousers. Jim continued to hold and kiss John as John undid Jim's fly buttons. John pulled Jim's trousers and pants down below his knees and ran his hands all over Jim's bare buttocks, Jim moaned with pleasure. John gradually ushered Jim backwards towards the kitchen sink, where he turned Jim around and nuzzling his neck bent him gently over the old Belfast sink. He took the bar of soap from the dish on one side, dropped his own trousers and lubricated himself.

Jim felt no pain as John entered him, only an intense and extreme pleasure; John reached around and masturbated Jim in time with his own thrusts, unhurriedly to start, then with more urgency. Jim moaned louder and louder. John's thrusts became quicker and deeper. Simultaneously they ejaculated. They stayed motionless, locked as one until, John pulled away breathlessly; he pulled out a chair from under the kitchen table and flopped down on it totally spent. Jim stayed where he was, both hands tightly clutching the edge of the sink, still slightly bent over. 'Christ,' he gasped.

CHAPTER FOURTEEN

'You promised to see Audrey today, Jimmy, remember?'

'Yes I haven't forgotten Auntie.'

'I think it's time you popped the question, you know.'

'Yes I do as well Auntie.'

'Oh Jimmy, am I hearing right?' do you really mean it?'

'Yes, I've done a lot of thinking Auntie, and I think you're right, it would be for the best.'

'I'm glad to see you've seen sense at long last Jimmy,' and she looked up at the clock, 'so when are you going to see her then Jimmy, tonight?'

'No time like the present,' he replied, and put his knife and fork down.

'But she's in work now, it's just gone one.'

'I'll soon sort that out.'

Jim arrived at the boot factory and going into the reception area; he asked to see Audrey on an extremely important family matter. A young girl was dispatched and a breathless Audrey appeared, 'What ever's the matter Jim? Is it Mum or Dad?'

'Sorry Audrey, I'm afraid it's bad news, it's your gran,' he said grimly. Before she could say a word Jim grabbed her arm and frog marched her outside.

'Jim, you know that I haven't got a gran.'

'Yes but they don't,' said Jim with a mischievous grin, 'we're off to Weston-super-Mare.'

'But Jim I'll lose my wages,' Audrey protested.

257

'I'll make them up, your mum and dad won't be any the wiser and if I get you home by the same time that you normally get home from work, everything will be fine.'

'You've thought of everything, haven't you?'

'Just about.'

'You know Jim, that's the second time my non-existent gran has come in useful.' Audrey smiled.

They drove to Weston where the tide was out, there was fine drizzle in the chill grey air and the wind was gusting, blowing the sand in spirals along the prom. 'Well this is Weston for you,' said Jim, 'just look at it, I don't think I've ever seen the tide in.'

'Me neither,' said Audrey, 'and it looks to me like everything is shut.'

'Look,' said Jim, the pier's open, come on Audrey, let's pretend we're kids again.' Jim and Audrey indulged their whim with the amusements and the penny slot machines, and then like young lovers do, they left the pier hand in hand and headed off to the Winter Gardens, where they settled in the cosy chic tea room and ordered a cream tea.

Eventually after several cups of tea and cakes Jim plucked up courage, 'You know Audrey, I really have enjoyed myself this afternoon, the time has just flown by, you and I, well we seem to belong together....Audrey there's something I want to ask you.'

'Please don't ask me that Jim.'

'But you don't know what I'm going to say.'

'I think I do.'

'Audrey, I think we should get married, will you marry me Audrey?'

'Oh, Jim, I wished you hadn't asked me that, we were

getting on so well, now it's all spoilt.'

'Don't you like me then Audrey?'

'Jim I love you, but like a sister loves a brother, I'm sorry I can't explain.'

'Perhaps there's someone at work you fancy, is there Audrey?'

'No that's not it Jim.'

'Look Audrey, we could still get married and if another man came along well...'

'Jim, oh Jim. I just don't know how to put it.'

'I don't understand.'

'It wouldn't matter if Errol Flynn, Clark Gable, David Niven or any man came along Jim, any man at all.'

'What d'you mean Audrey, what are you saying?'

'Oh Jim...' she hesitated, 'I prefer girls...women. There I've said it.'

Jim sat looking at Audrey for a few moments, and then he smiled, then grinned, then chuckled and then started to laugh. Audrey burst into tears, jumped up from her seat and ran hastily from the restaurant. Jim quickly pulled a bank note from his pocket, threw it on the table and ran out of the restaurant after her. A little way through the gardens he managed to catch up with her and grabbed her arm, she desperately tried to shake him off; 'Leave me alone,' she cried through the tears, 'leave me alone.'

Jim caught hold of her more firmly with both hands and forced her to sit on a bench, 'Listen Audrey I wasn't laughing at you, honestly, I was laughing at the situation.' Jim took his handkerchief and handed it to Audrey. 'Here dry your eyes and I'll explain.'

'I don't understand you Jim,' she said still sobbing,

'how can you find my situation something to laugh about?'

'No it's not your situation, it's *our* situation,' Jim paused, and then looking directly into her eyes, said seriously, 'you see Audrey, I like men.' Audrey sat gazing into space, Jim's words gradually sinking in. 'It's true Audrey, truthfully, ever since I was a boy, I've preferred males, I'm homosexual.'

Audrey sat quietly for a few moments then she asked, 'So then why did you ask me out in the first place Jim?'

'Pressure, Audrey, pressure from my auntie, pressure from all around, you know, the right thing to do, find a nice girl, get married, settle down, have a family. But I really do have feelings for you Audrey; I really do, but not like that, if you know what I mean, not... not those sort of feelings. So tell me, why then did you agree to come out with me?'

'Exactly the same reason as you, I just got fed up with mum and dad keeping on and on at me, telling me I'd be left on the shelf, telling me they wanted grandchildren, telling me I'd end up an old maid, trying to get me to look more feminine, and then when I saw you Jim, I knew I liked you straight away, I suppose I was hoping that perhaps you could make me feel like... that, you know what I mean. But I'm sorry Jim there's no man alive that could. So you see I couldn't marry you.'

'But don't you see Audrey, it's just perfect, it's an ideal situation. We could get married that would keep everyone happy, your family and mine. We can buy a place in Bath say, a big place, a little bit away from the families, and we can have separate bedrooms rooms. We'd be like brother and sister, it would be near my new business; you could come and work for me. Audrey it's perfect. Come on

Audrey, what d'you say?'

'I don't know Jim; I just don't know what to say.'

'Just say yes Audrey, in Bath we'd be far enough away to carry on and live our own lifestyles, but we would still be together, I can look after you, take care of you, say yes Audrey, please, just say yes.'

'Can I ask you something, Jim?'

'Yes Audrey, of course you can.'

'Jim, are you seeing anybody? You know, have you got a friend?'

'Well yes, we've only just met and it's my first time.'

'You don't mind me asking do you?'

'No I don't mind, it's nice to be able to share my secret with someone, how about you, is there anyone?'

'There was someone just after I left school. Sally, that was her name; I really loved her Jim...' Audrey paused. 'My first love Jim, my only love, she's gone now; she got killed in the blitz.'

'I'm sorry Audrey, that's just how my parents went.'

'Yes I know your auntie Cath told me.'

'So what's it to be then Audrey, shall we get married?'

'I'm not saying no and I'm not saying yes Jim, I'm not like you, I need time to mull things over, you realise you'll have to ask dad don't you?'

'But you haven't said yes yet Audrey,' Jim started laughing.

'No I haven't, have I?' and Audrey joined in with the laughter.

'Come on Audrey we've got plenty of time let's go to Bath on the way home and I can show you my new warehouse.'

'You didn't tell me that you've actually got somewhere Jim.'

'No, well I've had a lot of other things on my mind, it needs some doing up, but, it's in the right spot and it'll be nice to go and see if the builders have started yet.'

By the time they got to Bath it was almost dark, but as they drew up they could see that there were lights on inside the railway arch. A large portly man wearing a flat cap, and navy blue bib and brace overalls, was busy cleaning off a shovel with a hand brush in a forty gallon water drum, he paused and looked up as Jim and Audrey got out of the car, 'Yes buddy, what can I do for you?' he asked.

'I was wondering if we could have a quick look,' Jim said pointing inside.

'Floors wet, just been screeded, I'm just going home,' the man said unhelpfully, leaning his shovel against the wall. 'Who are you anyway?'

'Me,' said Jim, 'I'm the one who's paying your wages.'

'You mean you're the client, help yourself sir, it's only a strip down the left hand side that's wet, all the rest is finished. Give me a shout if you want anything I'll be sat in my van.'

'Thank you,' said Jim, he ushered Audrey inside and walked towards the back of the railway arch. The damp smell was gone and right at the back there was a breeze block wall with a doorway in it. 'Look Audrey, this will be the office this is where you'll work.'

'Jim it's really smart, I'm impressed, when we pulled up outside a railway arch I thought, well.'

Jim and Audrey made their way back outside, and true to his word the man was sitting in his van, 'Everything to your liking, sir?' he enquired.

'Yes it's very impressive; you've worked very hard in a few days.'

'Yes I worked right through the weekend sir; you know how it is, with six kids to feed.'

Jim delved into his pocket, 'Well here you are, give them a feed on me.'

The man stood there speechless and stared at the two five pound notes in his palm. Eventually, as Jim was opening the passenger's door of the car for Audrey to get in he murmured, 'Thank you sir...thank you very much.'

Jim put the car in gear and pulled away, Audrey looked at him and shook her head, 'Jim, have you completely lost your mind, you just gave him more than a week's wages all in one go.'

'Spread a little happiness Audrey, I just couldn't get over the change in him when he found out I was the customer, what was it he called me?'

'The client Jim.'

'That's right, the client, I like that, the client. Come on then Audrey let's get you home.'

'I don't know about you Jim I really don't.'

'Auntie Cath, Auntie Cath, I'm home, I'm back.'

'You're looking rather pleased with yourself,' Auntie Cath said, wiping her hands on her pinnie as she emerged from the kitchen.

'I've asked Audrey to marry me, Auntie.'

'I'll have to get a new hat,' she replied.

263

'Hang on Auntie; you don't know what she said, whether she said yes or no.'

'Your face says it all Jimmy, come here and give me a cuddle, I'm so pleased, so when is it to be?'

'Well I've got to ask her father first, but soon.'

'Well when you're married there's plenty of room here, so you won't have to worry about finding yourself somewhere to live.'

Jim decided that it was not a good time to mention living in Bath, 'I won't be with Harry James for more than a couple more days Auntie, because I've found another job.'

'Good for you Jimmy, where is it? What's it doing? What did Harry James say when you told him? Yes and speaking of Harry James you're to pick him up at his house at seven thirty tonight.'

'Seven thirty tonight, how d'you know that Auntie?'

'A horrible little man, who said he works for him for him has been here, so what about this job Jimmy?'

'Well it's in a warehouse in Bath.'

'Bath, and how are you going to get to Bath?'

'I don't know yet Auntie.'

'What did Harry James have to say about you leaving?'

'I'll tell him tonight.'

CHAPTER FIFTEEN

Jim had already decided that the first time he got Harry alone he would shoot him, and the opportunity now looked like it was about to present itself. He sat on the edge of his bed and handled both guns in his possession one after the other. So with the thought, revolvers never jam, in his head, he slipped the Smith and Wesson, into his jacket pocket together with his knuckleduster. He put the other weapon back on top of the wardrobe with his stash of money. It's only a matter of time before Auntie Cath finds all this, he thought.

Quietly he slipped down the stairs and into the kitchen. Auntie Cath was sitting in the living room, with her back to the slightly ajar kitchen door, totally engrossed in the book she was reading. He silently and cautiously took a brown paper carrier bag from the drawer in the pine side dresser, and returned upstairs to his room. He filled the carrier with all the money and the pistol, and then slipping his battle dress tunic from its hanger, hung the handles of the carrier over the coat hanger and replaced the tunic on the hangar. He did the buttons up and hung it back in the wardrobe, he smoothed it down and stood back, yes, that looks perfect, he thought.

When Jim turned up a little before seven thirty, Harry James didn't seem his usual affable self; in fact his manner appeared quite to the contrary, Jim could sense hostility and aggression. As he was already waiting at the front gates talking to Tom, Jim realised at once that he would

265

have to bide his time to do the deed, 'We're paying Eddie Simms a visit, here pick that up,' Harry barked, Harry pointed to a large bright pink hat box. 'Go and park the car and bring the roller out here.'

Jim parked up, put the hat box in the boot of Harry's car and drove back up the drive to meet him, another look at Harry's face told him it would pay to keep quiet. Harry walked to the passenger's side of the car. 'You got any weapons?' he asked.

'Yes,' replied Jim.

'Give them here,' reluctantly Jim produced the Smith and Wesson and the knuckleduster from his pocket and handed them to Harry. 'Open the glove compartment,' he ordered. Harry placed the weapons in the glove compartment, he snapped his fingers, 'Keys,' he said. Jim handed him the keys and Harry locked the glove compartment. Jim was now thinking that when they got back later that night he could ask for his weapons back and that would be that, he could dispose of Harry and he would be free once and for all. Harry slammed the front passenger's door shut and climbed in the back of the Rolls Royce, Christ he is in a bad mood, Jim thought, he hardly ever sits in the back, I wonder if it's because I didn't turn up at the pub last night?

'Got the hat box?' Harry snapped.

'It's in the boot Harry.'

Jim decided to try and make a stab at conversation to see what was wrong with Harry, although he quite enjoyed the strained silence, 'I took Audrey to Weston today Harry, I've asked her to marry me.' he ventured.

It was as if Jim hadn't spoken, 'Drive straight to Eddie's

no stopping.'

Jim tried again, 'It's a bit early for Eddie's Harry, isn't it?'

'He's expecting us,' Harry terminated the conversation by opening his brief case and immersing himself in the papers he was carrying. The rest of the journey passed in total silence.

'Here we are Harry,' Jim said.

'I can see that,' Harry replied abruptly. Jim got out and made his way around to the boot. 'What are you doing now?' He asked snappily.

'Getting the hat box, Harry you do want it don't you?'

'Leave the fucking thing there for now.'

Harry marched on in front with Jim trailing on well behind. As they walked into the club proper Jim could see that they were so early that no one was in evidence, no gorillas and thankfully no Gloria. As soon as Harry spotted Eddie Simms his whole demeanour changed instantly, 'Hello Eddie my son,' he said all smiles and oozing charm, Harry clapped his hand on Eddie's shoulder and shook him warmly by the hand.

'Harry, good to see you, you old sod,' he looked at Jim, 'you clean son?' he asked.

Jim knew what he meant, 'Yes no weapons Mister Simms.'

'I believe you son, you're a good lad, go round behind the bar and get the three of us a drink, make mine a large brandy,' Jim did as he was told and poured the drinks. 'Thanks son you take a pew over there, Harry and me have got things to talk about up in the office.'

'Hang on a minute Eddie,' said Harry, 'how about the

monkey you owe me?'

'Well Harry the word on the street is you've taken care of Luke, but you know how it is, seeing is believing.'

'I knew you'd come out with that, you crafty old git, Jim go out and fetch that hat box.' Jim returned with the hat box held out in front of him. 'Give it here,' Harry ordered. Harry took the lid off the hat box and tipped the contents on the floor.

'Fucking hell Harry,' Eddie said, 'you're crazy.'

Harry reached down and picked up Luke's head by the hair and waved it in front of Eddie's face. 'Seeing is believing Eddie, cough up.'

'Yeah all right,' Eddie spluttered, 'just get that bloody thing out of here.'

Harry thrust Luke's head into Jim's hands, Jim could see that his bullet had passed right through his head and had exited via his left eye, and from its almost intact condition Jim could see that the pigs weren't partial to it. Jim placed the head back in the box and took it out to the car; he toyed with the ideal of retrieving his weapons there and then but decided against. When he returned he was just in time to see Eddie and Harry making their way up to Eddie's office, 'Help yourself to a drink,' Eddie called over his shoulder.

Jim settled himself into one of the booths that ran along the wall; facing the front doorway, he watched as Sid minus quite a large lump of his ear came in, Jim immediately stood up and eyed up the opposition. Sid came straight over and stuck his right hand out, 'No hard feelings buddy, I was being a prick.'

Jim shook hands, 'Can I get you a drink?' he asked.

'Bit early for me, but thanks anyway, Eddie said you were coming over, he's been taking the piss all day long.'

'I think him and Harry are tarred with the same brush,' said Jim.

'Yeah, I know what you mean.'

'You been working for Harry for long?'

'No I was in the mob.'

'I haven't been out long myself, what regiment were you in?'

'Royal Artillery, mind I was only a driver.'

'You'll never believe where I ended up, The Royal Army Pay Corp. me in the bloody pay corp.'

'Cushy though?'

'Yeah, but not a fiddle insight, Oh don't look know, here comes fucking glory hole.'

'Hello big boy, back again then, come on then Sid, get me a gin and orange.'

'Get your own Gloria, I'm on the door,' Sid turned and walked towards the front of the club.

'Miserable bugger,' she called after him, 'I'll get us a drink and we'll take it upstairs.' Gloria went behind the bar, helped herself to more than a generous amount of gin and just showed it to the orange squash bottle, 'Eddie can afford it,' she said airily, Jim settled back down in the booth. 'Don't get too comfortable there big boy, come on upstairs, I'm getting worked up just looking at you.'

Oh dear, thought Jim, it didn't look like Harry or anyone else was going to save him this time, ' I tell you what Gloria,' he said, 'can't we sit down and have a nice chat? I think it would be nice if I got to know you a little bit.'

269

'Oh, how romantic, course we can chat luvvie, squeeze up and I'll sit beside you.' Gloria plonked herself almost on top of Jim's lap, the smell of her breath was far worse than Jim had remembered it; she lit a cigarette which added to the objectionable stench. Jim attempted to make small talk for a good ten minutes, stalling for time, but he realised he was fighting a losing battle, Gloria just had nothing to say worth listening to and they had nothing in common and she had only one thing on her mind.

'Come on then talking's finished,' she ordered, 'upstairs with me.' Gloria took an unwilling hand and led him through the same door as Harry and Eddie had gone earlier. They climbed the steep flight of steps, went along the corridor and into a dimly lit room. Along one side of the room was a double bed and next to it a wooden kitchen chair, the room was otherwise empty apart from a long mirror on the wall opposite the bed. Gloria indicated for Jim to sit on the edge of the bed, reluctantly he did as he was bid. She went over to the mirror on the wall, stood in front of it and proceeded to unbutton her blouse, 'Watch me big boy,' she said seductively. Slowly and sensually she took off her blouse, she undid her brassiere and threw it on the kitchen chair, she cupped both breasts with her hands, lifted them and pointed them at the mirror, rubbing and squeezing her nipples with her index fingers and thumbs, then looking into the mirror at Jim's reflection she said. 'What d'you think then big boy?'

'Very... nice,' Jim stammered.

She turned, faced Jim and lifted her skirt high above her knees, 'So what d'you think of my legs? Are they turning you on?' Jim hung his head. 'Come on then big, boy,' Gloria said excitedly. She deftly removed her skirt and French knickers, then stood in front of him, legs wide apart, rubbing her crotch with both hands and moaning breathlessly. 'Come on let's do it, I'm nearly coming off already.'

'Gloria,' Jim said, 'there's something I've got to tell you.'

'Later, tell me later, come on do me now.' Gloria said eagerly.

'Listen Gloria, it's important, since I was here last, well I've got engaged to be married, she's an absolutely smashing girl Gloria, I do like you, I like you a lot ,honestly, but I just can't...I'm sorry.'

Gloria went straight to the chair, picked up her discarded garments and started to dress, 'What a lucky girl she is,' she said disappointedly, 'she's got one in a million in you big boy, I don't know any men that would turn it down, especially with *me*. When's the wedding?'

'It's soon,' Jim replied, 'we just haven't set a date yet.'

'I'd love to get married, planning on kids? Well course you are...what a stupid question, come on, let's go down and have a drink, and anytime, anytime, mind if you fall out with her, you can always come and pay me a visit, I won't turn you away, and you won't be disappointed.'

Three gin and oranges later and Harry reappeared, he glanced at Jim and indicated with his head that it was time to go, no improvement there then, Jim thought. Harry went out to the car and waited in silence while Jim unlocked it, Jim climbed in and Harry once again sat in the back. 'Sceptre Harry?' Jim asked.

'Pig farm,' Harry replied.

271

'I thought you said that you've you sold it.'

'I have, pig farm,' he repeated tersely.

Jim toyed with the idea of pulling over and choking the life out of Harry there and then. After all he was bigger and stronger than Harry, younger, fitter. Shoot him now perhaps, do the human race a favour, he thought. It would be easy to stop the car. But unlocking the glove compartment was another thing, was Harry armed? Jim decided it would be prudent to bide his time.

The pigs greeted Jim and Harry. Two strange cars were parked at the entrance, better not ask, Jim thought. Harry again swept off in front leaving Jim to tail along behind, as Harry went in through the front door Jim heard him say, 'Got the bastard then Ron.'

Jim followed Harry through the door; there inside was Ron, Weasel and a couple of Darky Dillon's boys that Jim remembered from the trip to Hunstrete. Tied to the same chair as Luke had been previously was a figure of a man, his head bowed and bloodied, 'Yeah we got him alright Harry, hello Jim,' said Ron.

'Hello Harry,' the others chorused.

'See who we've got here Jim?' Harry asked, Harry walked over and lifted the man's head by his hair, although the man's eyes were half closed, puffy and his face bloodied and swollen, Jim knew in an instant who it was.

'Jesus Christ!' He exclaimed.

'No, it's not Jesus Christ Jim, it's a rozzer; does it look like a rozzer to you boys? It looks like one to me,' Harry was regaining his normal composure. 'Was he any trouble Ron? Anybody see you?'

'No piece of cake, no trouble at all, we put the snatch on him and nobody's none the wiser, mind he did say we were all under arrest and anything we said would be taken down and given in evidence.'

'Don't take the piss Ron.'

'I'm telling you Harry, that's what he said.'

'Let me introduce you Jim,' Harry said, 'but then you two know each other don't you?' Jim remained silent, his mind in a turmoil. 'The good sergeant put us on to this toe rag,' Harry continued, 'he's not at all what he seems, are you?' Harry cuffed John across the face with the back of his hand.

'The good sergeant isn't as daft as he looks, he couldn't work out why a young policeman, straight out of training would come all the way down here to Bristol, out in the sticks as this git puts it, when his family were all in London. A few questions and he found out that he lived at home and got on like a house on fire with his mother and father, and all his mates were living up the smoke, so it seemed strange he was down here. So the sergeant made a phone call to Scotland Yard and asked to speak to Police Constable Crewe, and what d'you think, there was no Police Constable Crewe, but there was an Inspector Crewe, but he was away on a job.

'He told me he was a bit baffled, because look at him, he's a bit young to be an inspector, but he's not young at all, he just looks it, baby faced fucker. So the sergeant did some more ferreting around and found that he belongs to some specialist squad that investigates bent coppers. Well that would upset the fucking applecart wouldn't it? You see Inspector fucking Crewe, we got it all sorted out, us

273

carrot crunchers, out here in the sticks, you smart ass cockney bastard, and so you're history.'

'Christ Harry,' Jim spoke for the first time, 'we can't kill a copper, we'll all hang.'

'What d'you suggest we do with him then, pat him on the head and send him home with twenty Players and a bunch of flowers ? Got any bright ideas?' Jim didn't answer. 'Right then Ron,' Harry continued, 'found out where's he keeping all his paperwork?'

'He hasn't got any boss.'

'No paperwork, you sure?'

'Positive, he never has to write anything down, he's got a photographic memory.'

'What the fuck's that Ron?'

'You know like Leslie Welch the memory man, he remembers everything, he never forgets, I mean did you know for instance that Leslie Welch can recite Ruffs guide to the turf all the way through, page by page? And did you-'

'Yeah I got the general idea Ron, I know who Leslie Welch is, so although he hasn't written anything down, who has he told about what's going on down here?'

'Nobody Harry, not yet anyway.'

'You sure about that?'

'Yes positive boss, his bosses wanted to know the score, but he hasn't told them anything yet, he's been keeping it under his hat.'

'Good, that's good, right who wants the pleasure then, you Jim.' Harry stared at Jim. 'Well?'

Jim stood motionless his sweaty hands clenched down by his sides, 'Come on then Jim, kill me,' John said, 'or haven't you got the balls for it.'

Harry produced a revolver from his pocket; 'Here you are Jim,' he said, 'do it.'

Jim took the revolver from Harry and slowly walked around behind John, he cocked the revolver, and put it to the back of his head, 'Come on then,' said John, 'do it.'

Jim hesitated for a moment, and then he swiftly stepped in front of John, raised the gun, pointed it at Harry and pulled the trigger, Harry just stood there, Jim pulled the trigger, the gun rang out again and again, Harry shrieked with laughter, 'Blanks, Jim, just blanks.' he said, ' Ron.'

Ron ran at Jim and knocked him off his feet, much the same as he had with Luke Newman; Jim crashed against the wall and fell to the ground, all the wind and fight knocked out of him. Resignedly, he allowed himself to be bound and lifted onto a chair and placed at John's side.

'What we got here then boys,' Harry said, 'is a shirt lifter and a knob jockey. You were right Weasel, they were at it, you know you should have pulled the kitchen curtains together Jim.

'I thought I was disappointed with Sid, I didn't even know what fucking disappointment was,' his voice began to rise, 'I had big plans for you, big plans you little cunt, fucking try to shoot me would you.' Harry hit Jim full in the face; Jim felt his nose break and the tears and blood streamed down his face. 'When Weasel told me, you know I didn't believe him,' he turned to Weasel, 'I didn't believe you Weasel, I'm sorry,' he turned back to face Jim, 'There's a two way mirror in Eddie Simms's club. I watched you. Oh Gloria, I can't, I'm getting engaged,' he mimicked, 'you cunt,' he hit Jim again, this time full in the eye, Jim winced and lowered his head, Harry caught hold of Jim's head by the hair, and yanked his head up.' Keep your fucking head up,' he said. 'Then there was June, I didn't want her yesterday, I don't want her today Harry, no course you fucking didn't, you fucker, because you're a fucking queer.' Harry hit Jim again, this time, just on and below the nose, Jim felt his upper lip split. 'Well at least I've got one thing to thank you for, the copper was keeping what he knows to himself, to protect you no doubt.'

'He was keeping it to himself, because Jim told him he was leaving us boss,' Ron said, 'and then we'd all get nailed later, once Jim was safely out of the way.'

'Leaving, were you? You ungrateful fucker, after all I've done for you, you had fuck all, you didn't even have a pot to piss in and I gave you a good fucking job, paid you well, trusted you and treated you like a son. Come on then Weasel, do your stuff, I'll save you the fucking trouble of asking.'

'Can I do both of them Harry?' Weasel said eagerly as he was producing the razors, 'I've never done two at once.'

'Yeah, go ahead Weasel, be my guest.'

Jim closed his eyes and waited, Weasel brought both razors down across John and Jim's faces simultaneously, 'This is for the farm Jim, I haven't forgotten. You fairy, you fucking fucking fairy,' he screamed, he raised the tortoiseshell handled razors again and starting near their temples he slowly dug the blades into the waiting flesh and then even slower dragged them down to their respective chins, Jim cried out in pain and terror, John remained silent.

'Hark at him squawking like a fucking woman, give him a couple of extra, Weasel,' Harry ordered.

'My pleasure Harry,' Weasel said gleefully.

Jim screamed out again and again as the razor bit deeper and deeper again and again into his face, 'That'll do Weasel,' Harry said, 'I've got plenty more treats for the perverted little bastard.' Weasel stepped back and Harry caught hold of John's head by the hair and lifted it up. ' Right then scuffer, the way I look at it, is like this, you were only doing your job, so you're not quite as bad as this other piece of shit,' Harry pointed at Jim. 'But you're still a turd burglar, you depraved fucker, Ron what's that kettle on the hob like?'

'Not far off boiling Harry.'

'Poke some life into that fire, and push that kettle nearer the flames.'

Ron took his handkerchief from his pocket, wrapped it around the handle of the kettle and pushed it across the hob, 'Christ that's fucking hot Harry,' he said.

'Might as well put the poker in to warm as well,' Harry said.

Jim writhed and squirmed on his chair and tried to free himself, the poker that could only mean one thing, his face betrayed his thoughts. 'Yes you know what's fucking coming, you cunt,' Harry said, 'but not just yet, I'm going to make you fucking sweat first, I'm going to give you time to think about it. Bring that water over here Ron; it should be hot enough, pour some on the copper's bollocks for a start. Ron slowly poured the water over the front of John's trousers, and for a few seconds he sat motionless, then, as the scalding water seeped through his trousers he began to thrash about from side to side screaming out with the intense pain. 'Hope you've saved a drop for Jim, Ron.'

'Can't we just shoot the pair of them Harry?'

'What d'you mean Ron.'

'Well I mean they can't help being how they are, these homos. '

'What the fuck are you going on about? They can't help being how they are, what d'you mean? What's that supposed to mean?' Harry started to rave. 'They can't help it. Course they can fucking help it, it's not natural, it's against God's wishes, men don't fuck men, what the fuck's wrong with you?'

'Harry, I went to the library and read all about it, it's all about your genes-'

'Fucking library, fucking genes, give me that kettle, you cunt,' Harry emptied the rest of the contents of the kettle all over the front of Jim's trousers, Jim was screaming before the boiling water took its full effect. Harry was working himself up into a frenzy and panting heavily, he brought the now empty heavy kettle down over Jim's head time and time again, Jim slumped down in the chair, blood pouring from the wounds in his head, the screaming stopped immediately.

Harry walked across to the table, ripped off his overcoat, threw it across the room and shakily poured himself a generous amount of whisky; he flopped down on the remaining kitchen chair breathing heavily, and then he silently sipped away at his drink, staring wide eyed at the wall.

Ron watched as Harry gradually calmed himself down, 'Can I shoot them, now then boss?' Ron asked steadily.

'No you fucking can't,' Harry continued to sip his drink; an eerie silence only punctuated by Harry puffing loudly on his cigar and the crackling of the fire descended on the room. No one stirred, all watching Harry and waiting for his next move.

Suddenly Harry leapt to his feet, 'Ron, shoot that cunt,' Harry said, pointing to John, 'and stick the poker up Jim's ass, and we'll just about get to the Sceptre before closing time.'

Ron quickly walked over to John, producing his weapon as he went, he put the cold steel against John's temple and pulled the trigger, John jerked upwards and sideways once in his seat, slumped forwards and was dead. Jim in his semi unconscious state, heard the gunshot and instinctively realised what had happened, quietly he began to sob. Ron pointed the gun at Jim, and stood motionless looking at him, 'Harry,' he said, 'I'll shoot Jim, but that's it, nothing else, no fucking pokers, nothing else.'

'Am I hearing right?' Harry said his voice rising in fury again. 'Do I hear you right? That's mutiny Ron, that's fucking mutiny.'

'I'm not doing it, and that's that,' Ron pocketed his gun, turned away and started to walk out of the room.

'You know what happens to fucking mutineers Ron,' Harry screamed out, he pulled out another revolver from his jacket pocket, stood up and pointed it at Ron's back.

Ron turned and said quietly, 'You won't shoot me Harry,' and then he disappeared through the doorway.

'I'll do it my fucking self then. Weasel and you two get him down on the floor.'

Between them, Weasel and Darky Dillon's boys spread-eagled Jim face down on the filthy living room floor. 'Cut the trousers off him Weasel,' Harry ordered. Jim, now conscious thrashed around and screamed with terror as Weasel hacked away, at first Jim's trousers and then his underpants, with his cut throat razor, and by the time Weasel had completely exposed Jim's backside, it was criss crossed with lacerations and bleeding liberally.

Harry walked over to the fire and withdrew the poker, the tip was white hot and a cherry red glow extended three or four inches down the length of it, 'Hold him still, hold the bastard still I say. Weasel, spread his ass cheeks, I can't see fuck all.' Weasel crouched down beside Jim and grabbed at his buttocks, Jim continued to squirm and twist, 'Smack the fucker in the head with something Weasel.' Weasel grabbed the discarded kettle and hit Jim across the back of the head. 'Again Weasel, the fucker's still moving.' Weasel lifted the kettle once more with both hands and brought it down on Jim's head, Jim went limp in his captors' arms. 'Fuck it,' said Harry, 'he's out for the count.' Harry put the poker back in the fire, and waited. 'Keep a good grip you lot,' he ordered. Jim moaned, and as soon as he started to stir, Harry grabbed the poker from the fire and with a roar, threw himself down on the floor behind Jim and fished about with the poker for his rectum. As the poker touched Jim's flesh, smoke billowed up and the sweet stench of burning tissue filled the room, Jim let out a series of ear piercing screams and then mercifully as the poker entered him he passed out. Weasel relaxed his hold on Jim's buttocks and began to heave and retch at the smell, 'Keep a hold Weasel you fucker,' Harry ordered. Harry screaming obscenities, the sweat coursing down his face continued with both hands to push the poker for all he was worth and it gradually disappeared inside Jim's now still body. Clouds of evil smelling smoke billowed up into the room; Weasel at last finally succumbed to the sickly smell and heaved all over Jim's motionless body.

Harry's face was distorted, his crazed eyes wide open, he shouted out at the top of his voice, 'Thou shalt not lie with mankind, as with womankind, it is abomination, Leviticus eighteen, verse twenty two.' Harry staggered to his feet with his face running with sweat, he collapsed in a heap onto the kitchen chair; his breathing was laboured and his hands were trembling as he took his handkerchief from his pocket and with his unsteady hands wiped away at his face. Jim's body started to twitch and then as the life left him it stopped moving forever.

Harry unsteadily got up from his seat, picked up his overcoat from the floor, brushed it down with his hand and said, 'Come on Weasel let's fuck off to the pub and you two you can dispose of these two lumps of shit.'

CHAPTER SIXTEEN

Auntie Cath, carefully positioned her hat on her head, adjusted it and thrust a hat pin through the felt. She put on, buttoned and belted her gabardine coat, took her umbrella from its stand and with a final glance in the hallway mirror went out through the front door and pulled it quietly behind her. She started to walk the short distance to Audrey's parents' house. I don't know, she thought, it hasn't stopped raining since young Jimmy disappeared. She knocked the front door knocker and waited, Mrs Amos came to the door wiping her hands in her pinnie, 'I'm sorry to trouble you; I don't suppose Audrey is at home is she?'

'Yes come in, I'll tell her…'she hesitated.

'I'm Jimmy's aunt.'

'Yes I know, come in, come in, any news?'

'No nothing I'm afraid.'

'Come in; let me take your coat, would you like a cup of tea?'

'Thank you no…I really can't stop, I just wondered…' her voice petered out and she began to sob.

Mrs Amos put her arm around her and guided her into the living room; 'Sit there,' she said softly, 'I'll call Audrey.'

Audrey came into the room, Auntie Cath could see that she had been crying, 'I just felt I had to come to see you Audrey, it's been almost three weeks and no news.'

Audrey hugged Auntie Cath and sat facing her, 'I thought the police might have found something out by now.'

Auntie Cath shook her head, 'They're no nearer now to finding Jimmy or the policeman than they were three weeks ago, they say it's just like the pair of them have just disappeared from the face of the earth.'

'What do you suppose has happened?'

'There's only one thing that could have happened Audrey, only one thing.'

Auntie Cath, gently and lovingly ran her hand down the front of Jim's battledress tunic, she stood back, admired it and quietly shut the wardrobe door.

I suppose I knew really after the first day, she thought, but it's four weeks now. She switched off the bedroom light, softly closed the door of Jim's room behind her and went down over the stairs and into the living room. She stood in front of the mirror hanging over the mantelpiece and applied some fresh lipstick and powder to her face, she pulled her comb through her greying hair and fetched her old brown felt hat from the hall stand and carefully placed it on her head, inserting two hat pins, one along each side of her head. She looked up at the clock, ten past nine; turning off the living room light she walked into the hallway, put on her gabardine coat, buttoned and belted it, picked up her shopping bag and closing the front door behind her walked out into the stormy night.

Rounding the corner she paused and looked at the bomb site that was all there was of her sister and Jim's father's home. 'You're all together now,' she said sadly and quietly. She turned away and walked briskly on until she saw the illuminated sign for the Sceptre.

Auntie Cath peered in through the steamy windows of the public bar and then making her way around the side of the pub she looked in through the windows of the snug. Slowly she opened the door of the pub, and walked inside, Bert Tompkins glanced at her and seeing that she was quite alone looked at her disapprovingly. Harry James was in his usual position flanked by Weasel and Ron.

She approached the counter, 'Can I help you Madam?' Bert asked.

Auntie Cath completely ignored him, stared at Harry and said, 'Harry James isn't it?'

Harry flashed a smile, 'Yes Madam that's me, at your service, and to what do I owe the pleasure, a drink perhaps?'

'You don't change do you? All smarm, all charm.'

'Sorry madam, should I know you?' Harry stared at her quizzically rubbing the scar on his cheek.

'Yes, you knew me a long time ago, but you knew my sister better, a lot better.'

'Your sister?'

'Yes, it's long ago now Harry James, but you knew my sister alright, she was just seventeen when you met her, just seventeen, untouched and she worshipped the ground you walked on, you put her in the family way and then you discarded her, just like that, like you would a pair of old shoes, without so much as a second thought. She told me if it wasn't for the baby inside her she would have killed herself.

'She met a man when she was pregnant, an older man, a kind man, he took her in. She had the baby, a little boy and they got married, the little boy's name was Jimmy, her married name was Britton, does that mean anything Mister James?' Harry James took a gulp of his drink, 'Yes Harry James, Jimmy Britton was your son, and you know Harry James that I know you killed him or had him killed.

'You see, I watched him that night when he brought his friend home, I heard them in the kitchen, I know what they were doing, I saw that thing,' she pointed at Weasel, 'standing watching in the garden. The policeman's disappeared and so has my Jimmy. Don't ask me how I know, but I just know that you Harry James, you had him killed alright. I've got something for you here,' Auntie Cath reached inside her shopping bag and produced rolls of banknotes, and put them on the counter in front of Harry, then she put her hand in her coat pocket and tipped a handful of change onto the counter. 'Here, take it; take it all, I won't have dirty, tainted money in my house.

'Oh, and one other thing Harry James, you know that what's in the roots of a tree comes out in the branches,' Auntie Cath reached once more into her shopping bag, 'This is for my Jimmy,' she pulled out the gun that she had found in Jim's wardrobe, took one step forward, and pushed the gun against Harry's chest, without hesitating she pulled the trigger.

THE END

Bob pushed the mouse upwards and to the left,

clicked on save, closed Word and turned the computer off. He leant back in his battered leather office chair, stretched his arms high above him, stretched and yawned. Looking up at his wall clock he could see the time was ten past eleven, he got out of his chair, turned the light off and wearily wandered into the living room, his wife Fiona was stretched out on the settee watching TV, 'That's it,' Bob said, 'all finished just typed the end.'

'Pleased with it?' she asked, without looking away from the television.

'Yeah, on balance, should keep the wolf from the door, won't win the booker prize mind,' he smiled.

'Fancy a cuppa,' Fiona said, swinging her legs down off the settee.

'No you sit there, I'll get one in a minute, just let me draw breath,' Bob sat facing her on their other settee. ' You know Fiona, this time the characters in the book, they've really come alive for me, I can't explain it, I know they've come from my imagination, but somehow they're so real, it's very strange.'

'Well I've only read just a few pages of it so far,' Fiona said, 'so I'm no judge.'

'I'll be glad if you do hurry up and finish it you know I value your opinion.'

'You lying bugger,' Fiona said smiling, 'you only want me to proof read it.'

'Not so,' he chuckled back. 'Tell you what I'll get us that nightcap.'

Three o'clock that morning Bob stirred, he could hear his wife quietly snoring beside him, he squinted at the bedside clock, closed his eyes and snuggled back down in the bed, the strong aroma of cigar smoke came as a bolt from the blue, he opened his eyes again, quite wide this time and peered towards the end of the bed and around the room, nothing, but the smell was so strong, he flipped the bedside light switch on, grabbed at his spectacles and looked around again, nothing just the strong smell. Bob felt goose bumps appearing on his arms and the hair in the nape of his neck grow prickly. He took his glasses off and got back down in the bed, he was still sniffing and clock watching an hour later, but eventually drifted off into a sporadic fitful sleep.

CHAPTER SEVENTEEN

The warm sunlight percolated its way through the vertical blinds of Bob's bedroom window; Bob stirred and felt across the empty bed for Fiona, he pulled on his glasses, ten past ten, well I haven't got anything burning, he thought. He lay there for a few moments when he suddenly remembered the cigar smoke, must have been dreaming he thought.

'Good morning dear,' Fiona said, 'thought you'd have a lie in then.'

'Quite unintentional I assure you; I just didn't seem to have a very good night, that's all. Listen when I've had a cuppa I'll set the printer up, leave it running and print out the whole book, then you can get started.'

'I haven't got time to sit down reading books at this time of the day; I'll read it in my own good time.'

Bob knew it would be no good to argue, but he wanted Fiona's approval and the sooner the better. Bob went into his room set his computer to print his book and went for a leisurely bath armed with the morning paper.

He forgot all about the printer, and it was only when he realised that he couldn't hear it running, that he remembered. He went into his room and looked, the printer had stopped half way down page nine, and the message on the computer screen told him that the connection had been lost between the printer and the computer. Damn, he thought, that's happened before, I'll just have to shut it all down and start again. He closed down the computer, turned it all on again, set the printer to print from the top of page nine and waited, the printer stopped again half way down the same page, and the same message appeared on the screen. By the time the same thing had happened twice more and Bob not being noted for his patience decided that shouting at Fiona in the kitchen might help no end.

'Don't shout at me, you arsehole,' she said, 'I told you to have a new printer for Christmas but you wouldn't.'

'There's nothing wrong with the fucking printer,' Bob said angrily.

'It's not working though is it?' she retorted.

'Bollocks!' Bob went back to his room and decided to burn a copy of the book onto CD and take it to his friend Nick to print. Armed with some paper and the CD he went back to the kitchen.

'Got over your funny five minutes now have you?' she asked.

'It's my artistic temperament coming out that's all,' he replied.

'No you're always the same Bobby boy, impatient, where are you off now?'

'I'm going to see if Nick's home and use his printer.'

'What if he's gone out, why don't you phone first?'

'You know Nick, creature of habit, he'll be there.'

'Don't be late for lunch; I know what you're like when you two get together, and give Nick my love.'

Bob got back home at ten past one his face wreathed in smiles, 'There you are dear,' he said, putting a pile of paper on the kitchen table, 'mission accomplished.'

How's Nick?' Fiona asked.

'Oh, you know Nick, always in the depths of despair about something or other.'

'What is it this time?'

'Women trouble, same old thing,'

'Don't bother to tell me. That's it then,' Fiona said picking up the pile, 'four months' work, doesn't seem much for four months work, does it?'

'Blood, sweat, tears and lots of coffee, that's what's in that pile, now it's over to you.'

'I'll have a read later,' she said.

'That's my girl,' Bob smiled.

'So what d'you think so far?' Bob asked

'Give me chance I'm only on page ten,' Fiona peered over the top of her reading glasses.

'How can you be on page ten?' Bob asked, sounding frustrated, 'you read that four months ago when I started writing it first.'

'I wanted to refresh my memory and if you really want to know, anyway, I think that the Jewish tailor is too stereotyped.'

'Well that's because all Jewish tailors are like him.'

'So how many do you know then Bob?'

'Just read the book.' Bob went into his room and turned on his computer, checking his emails he found that he needed copies of three of them, he started his printer and proceeded to print them out, well look at that, he thought, no problem at all.

At half past ten Bob found himself yawning and decided that bed was the best bet, 'I'm going on to bed then Fiona,' he said.

'Yes dear, I'll be there shortly.'

Bob didn't hear Fiona come in as he was fast asleep within a couple of minutes of his head hitting the pillow. But at three o'clock he was woken up suddenly, for what seemed to be no apparent reason, he led there in the dark listening and looking, then through the gloom he could just make out smoke curling its way up to the ceiling and then the unmistakable aroma of a burning cigar.

Quickly he turned the bedside light on, 'Fiona, Fiona, wake up.'

'What, what's up?' she asked sleepily.

'Sniff, woman sniff, can you smell that?'

'Smell what, I can't smell anything, go back to sleep Bob, you're dreaming.'

'No, I'm not, sniff, and look cigar smoke,' he pointed.

'There's no smell and there's no smoke, now just go back to sleep.'

Bob was still awake as daylight started to lighten the bedroom; by the time it was fully light he was fast asleep again.

'Come on you wake up, here's a cup of tea, what was all that about in the night?'

'Dreaming I suppose, I don't know I could smell a cigar, so strong, the smell was so strong.'

'Drink your tea and I'll go and get you a nice bacon sandwich, that's better than the smell of cigars.'

Bob sipped his tea, but he couldn't get the smell of the cigar out of his mind, he swung his legs out of bed and sat on the edge, he put his glasses on and it was then that he spotted it on the windowsill.

He bent down until his nose was a few inches away and focused on the grey powder, 'Fiona,' he called, 'come in here and see this.' Fiona was busy in the kitchen, with the bacon sizzling and she didn't hear him calling. Bob appeared at the kitchen door, 'Fiona come and see I want you to take a look at something'

'I'm getting your bacon sandwich, it'll have to wait.'

'No come and see now.'

'Aren't you listening? I'm getting breakfast.'

'Please, it's important.'

'Oh come on then but be quick.'

Fiona followed Ian along the corridor and into the bedroom. Triumphantly Bob pointed at the windowsill, 'Look,' he said smugly.

'Look at what exactly.'

'Look, I was right about the cigar smoke, look cigar

ash, there,' Bob pointed.

Fiona brushed it away with her hand, 'Come on Bob stop messing about, the bacon will be burning.'

'But that was definitely cigar ash Fiona.'

'Oh for goodness sake Bob it was nothing, it was some dust, now come on.'

Bob approached bedtime that night with an uneasy trepidation, he settled down under the duvet and closed his eyes and as sleep eventually started to overtake him, the now familiar smell of cigar smoke shocked him back to awareness. I've had enough of this, he thought, he reached out for his glasses and sat bolt upright in bed. Standing at the foot of the bed puffing away on a large cigar was Harry James, 'I don't like your book,' he said, 'it requires some alteration.'

'You're not real; go away, I'm dreaming this.'

'You're not fucking listening, I said I don't like your book, it needs changing.'

'So what's wrong with it?'

'Everything and I get shot at the end.'

'No not necessarily, when Auntie Cath pulled the trigger it doesn't mean that the gun didn't jam, it wasn't a revolver.'

'Killing my own son, you know that really hurt me, even though he was a homo.'

'Well that's just the way it is, it's just a story.'

'Alter it.'

'I can't it's the way the story goes.'

'I'm telling you to alter it.'

'You can't do anything to me, you don't even exist.'

'What d'you mean don't exist, I'm fucking standing here aren't I, you'll alter it, just you see.'

'I know you don't exist because you just called it "a book"'.

'Listen you prick, of course it's a book, it's a book about me, about Harry James, alter it!'

Next morning Bob came to staring at the bedroom ceiling and thought to himself, it was just a dream, nothing more, just a dream; it must have been a dream. He got up, slipped on his slippers and dressing gown and went to find Fiona, 'Fiona,' he said, 'I had a weird dream last night, Harry James, you know the Harry James in my book was in our room, he says that he doesn't like the book.'

'Doesn't he dear, I hope the publishers do, oh and Bob I think you really ought to think about taking a holiday, a weird dream and then there was the non-existent cigar ash.'

'Yes perhaps you're right, but it was so real, ridiculous isn't it? I'll look on the internet and see what there is.' But nothing in the way of a holiday grabbed his interest, much to the disappointment of Fiona and he spent the rest of the day trying to blot the spectre of Harry James.

Bob wasn't looking forward to going to bed that

night, but he kept telling himself it was all a dream and nothing could happen, a figment of his imagination could hardly do him any harm. He fortified himself with a few large brandies before turning in and quite quickly was asleep

Harry appeared promptly at three o'clock, at the foot of Bob's bed, this time with Ron and Weasel in tow, 'Wake up, toe rag,' he said, 'you going to alter the book?'

'I've told you before no.'

'Hear that Ron, this is most upsetting, most upsetting indeed.'

'Look Harry,' Bob said, 'I've been thinking, Auntie Cath's gun must have jammed, because you're here, if it hadn't you couldn't be, could you?'

'It's Mister fucking James to you, so you'd better alter the book then so it jams then.'

'No the book stays the same; the readers' have got to draw their own conclusions, about what happens next, that's the whole point.'

'Let me stripe him Harry.'

'Shut up Weasel, I still haven't forgotten the funeral. Now I shan't ask you again, are you going to alter the fucking book or no?'

'No.'

'Last word?' Harry stroked his scar.

'Yes.'

'Ron, give him a smack.'

Fiona flicked her bedside light on; Bob was on the floor clutching the side of his head, blood oozing through his fingers, screaming with pain. 'Whatever have you done, no don't move, stay there, I'll get something,' Fiona ran to the bathroom and came back with a towel; Bob jammed it against the side of his head. 'What have you done to yourself Bob? There's blood everywhere, it's all down the wall.'

'I don't know but my ear feels like it's on fire.'

'Let me see,' cautiously she looked under the towel. 'You've caught your ear, must have been on the radiator, look it's covered in blood, you idiot you must have fallen out of bed, another bad dream I suppose?'

'Yes something like that, I suppose,' Bob replied.

Next morning Bob, nursing a very sore ear, called up his story on the computer screen and scrolled down to the last page, at the end of the last sentence, he wrote.

She pulled the trigger again, both bullets passed through Harry's ribcage and lodged deep in his heart, Harry's cigar fell from his mouth and with his eyes still wide open he slumped to the floor quite dead.

'There you are then,' Bob said aloud to himself, 'You've got your own way Harry James, I've altered the story for you, just for you, happy now? Rest in peace Harry.'

THE END